D·E·S·I·G·N
FOR
GREAT-DAY

D·E·S·I·G·N
FOR
GREAT-DAY

ALAN DEAN FOSTER
AND
ERIC FRANK RUSSELL

A TOM DOHERTY ASSOCIATES BOOK
NEW YORK

DESIGN FOR GREAT-DAY

Copyright © 1995 by Thranx, Inc.

This book is printed on acid-free paper.

A Tor Book
Published by Tom Doherty Associates, Inc.
175 Fifth Avenue
New York, N.Y. 10010

Tor ® is a registered trademark of Tom Doherty Associates, Inc.

ISBN 0-312-85501-X

First edition: February 1995

Printed in the United States of America

0 9 8 7 6 5 4 3 2 1

For EFR . . .
With whom I corresponded but never met
Who I understood but didn't know
The only writer of science fiction
Who could both make me laugh and cry
Here's to the futures he foresaw
And to true ecology
Wherein he was the wealthiest of men
Before it became common currency

i

The little ship, scarred and battered, sat on the plain and ignored the armed guard that had surrounded it at a safe distance. As an example of an extraplanetary vessel it was remarkably unimpressive. A featureless, flattened ovoid devoid of ports or visible doorways, no bigger than one of the lifeships or escape pods utilized by the dominant race of the world on which it had just arrived. It looked barely capable of transporting a few individuals between cities on the same continent, much less conveying them between worlds.

In fact, more than one of the newly emplaced guards wondered if it might not actually be some sort of lifeboat or emergency craft that had been cast off from a damaged mother ship locked in orbit high above. Though they had yet to receive any indication that this might indeed be the case, it seemed a plausible enough explanation. Possibly the parent vessel had been destroyed, or tumbled helplessly to burn up in the thick atmosphere. There were any number of rational possibilities that offered more plausible explanations.

Not only did the eccentric craft look too small to be capable of interplanetary travel, it did not give off a glow suggestive of rapid passage through the atmosphere, which meant that it either moved very slowly or exceptionally fast. The heavily armed soldiers who had hastily formed a defensive perimeter around the vessel's landing site were not prepared to speculate either way, but nothing could stop them from making offhand guesses. They were neither scientists nor engineers but ordinary troops.

In the average soldier speculation was a potentially dangerous quality, one devoutly to be avoided at all costs. Indulging in the process frequently brought down disapprobation and disaster and was only rarely rewarded. It was an activity best left to officers and non-military personnel. The heavily armed troopers were more than content to follow orders, aim weapons, and wait for someone to tell them what to do next.

It was impossible, however, not to wonder at the tiny vessel's composition or means of manufacture. Though without running appropriate scientific analysis it was impossible to tell for certain, it did not appear to be fashioned either of metal or the more familiar metaloceramic composites. There was some discussion among the more knowledgeable onlookers of nanocarbon tubes embedded in a bonding ceramic or glass matrix, but the dullish appearance of the intruder's matte epidermis provided little in the way of support or rebuttal for such theory.

In fact, depending on which way the early morning light happened to strike the ship's surface, it was not only difficult to guess what it might be fashioned of, but whether it possessed a solid skin at all. Light played tricks with the onlookers' eyes and with the ship's exterior. At times it seemed one could see halfway through the vessel, while when clouds scudded by overhead it appeared far more substantial.

In actuality, the little ship was possessed of a consistency that fell somewhere between an aerogel and the core of a neutron star. Its component atoms were arranged in such a way as to not only baffle an experienced observer but utterly defeat the best analytical instruments that could be brought to bear; so the urgently assembled troops could be excused their confusion.

A few voices suggested that the vessel itself might be nothing more than an illusion, a projection designed to deceive the eye and fool the mind. The War Department was known to be working on all manner of new projects. Perhaps the troops had been rushed out to check the efficacy of some new aspect of psychological warfare. Some suggested that if it were nothing more than a facile apparition it was an extremely clever one, because it had scorched the ground in its immediate vicinity and gave every indication from the earth that was depressed around its outer edge of having real mass and weight. It was no lustrous phantom, no incorporeal composition of smoke and carefully shaded floating films. It was real, and what it was made of might be quite prosaic, or contrastingly extraordinary. As the soldiers had been issued strict orders while outbound from the nearby city not to approach the craft too closely under any circumstances, they could not satisfy their curiosity even by simple touch.

Not that any of them particularly wanted to stroll up to the outlandish vessel and run a hand along its eerily indistinct flanks anyway, but it was natural to be curious about its makeup as well as its origins. There was always an air of mystery about the unknown, and this little ship trailed one behind it like an ethereal cape blowing in the wind. The hastily assembled squadron of guards could be ordered not to touch, but they could not be ordered not to think. Like ordinary soldiers anywhere, they had plenty of spare time in which to engage in that entertaining if not necessarily educational practice. Squatting on the open plain distant from the city, they availed themselves of the opportunity frequently and with inspired sarcasm.

However rapidly the intruder had penetrated the local atmosphere it gave off no heat from its passage. None, zero. Instruments confirmed what the soldiers suspected. It was most remarkable. All descending vessels gave off some residual heat, if not as a result of the passage through atmosphere, then from their engines and drives. Notwithstanding the singed soil that formed a blackened halo of modest dimensions around the base of the vessel, the temperature of the air in its immediate vicinity was no different from that elsewhere on the plain.

Some continued to argue that whether real or illusionary, it was nothing more than a clever training exercise, a trick of advanced dimensions designed to test their readiness and reactions to the unexpected and not immediately explicable. As time passed and nothing happened, this hypothesis gained credence among the assembled and increasingly bored ring of guards.

One suggested that a single shot would make myth of the vessel's reality. This headstrong individual was quickly restrained by his friends. Being friends, they had no interest in seeing their bold companion sentenced to an extended term in gaol. Besides which, he owed some of them money.

So they sat or stood, and guessed and guarded, the latter task in this particular instance turning out to be a very dull deal indeed.

A large, bluish sun burned overhead, illuminating their surroundings if not their thoughts. It lit the edges of flat, waferlike clouds in brilliant purple. While some might have found the scene starkly beautiful, few of the attending soldiers bothered to remark on what was to them a common occurrence. Regardless of species, soldiers on duty rarely had the time or inclination to ruminate on the aesthetics of their surroundings.

The strange sun was not alone in the sky. It was accompanied by two tiny moons shining like pale spectres low in the east. A third—larger, rounder, and more mellow in aspect—was diving into the westward horizon.

At considerable altitude above the stolid mass of the sprawling city roamed its aerial patrol, a number of tiny, almost invisible dots weaving a tangle of vapor trails. There were more now than there had been a little while ago, as distant craft continued to assemble in tardy response to the laggard alarm that had finally announced the visitor's presence, but the latest arrivals were as confused and concerned as their predecessors.

The dots displayed the irritated restlessness of a swarm of disturbed gnats, for their crews were uncomfortably aware of the strange invader now sitting motionless on the plain far below. Their speculation was driven by a greater urgency than that of the soldiers on the ground, for they were acutely aware that they had missed something, and would be called to account for it sooner rather than later.

It was not that any one of them had been derelict in his duty, which was to serve as the homeworld's last line of defense against suspicious intruders. Their mission was to watch the immediate vicinity of the planet, to query any artificial object that came within a certain distance, and to reduce it to glowing gas and powder if adequate explanations for its presence were not immediately forthcoming. As a rule this was a task they carried out with great skill and pride. The tiny vessel now resting undisturbed on the surface below was a very visible debunker of the first accomplishment and impugner of the latter.

Now there was nothing the pilots and their crews could do about it. They were up in the stratosphere, the intruder was safely down on the ground: an altogether unacceptable state of affairs. Indeed, they would have intercepted it had that been possible, which it wasn't.

How can one block the path of an unexpected and unannounced object moving with such stupendous rapidity that its trace registers as a mere flick on an advanced predictor screen some seconds after the source has passed? The patrol's integrated systems were only now beginning to generate figures on the intruder's size and velocity. Data on the first seemed to fluctuate, which made no sense at all. The second . . . the second made considerably less than zero sense. The fact that a dozen different sets of instruments confirmed the figures rendered them no less nonsensical. The patrol's ranking officer ordered all findings withheld until some sense could be made of them. He was not about to risk what had up to that time been a distinguished career by giving the stamp of approval to such lunacy.

Blessed by a refreshing lack of any need to display drive and intelligence, the troops on the ground suffered no such pangs. They kept careful watch and awaited the arrival of someone who was permitted the initiative that they were denied. This was an entirely comfortable state of affairs that, as far as they were concerned, could last until the millennium. As long as no activity was evident on the part of the little ship, correspondingly little reaction was demanded of them. This constituted a battlefield condition with which they were reasonably content.

All of them had either four legs and two arms or four arms and two legs, according to the need of the moment. That is to say: the front pair of underbody limbs could be employed as either feet or hands, like those of a baboon. Superior life does not establish itself by benefit of brains alone; manual dexterity is equally essential. The quasi-quadrupeds of this world had a barely adequate supply of the former compensated by more than enough of the latter.

Where multiple limbs protruded through simple, dun-colored clothing they were covered in short, bristly light-brown fur. Darker ruffs were present at wrists and ankles as well as along the broad reach of shoulders and sternum. Their skulls were mounted on thick but flexible necks that emerged from between the fore pair of shoulders. Two dark, efficient eyes that were better at close-up work than at seeing for distance flanked a unique pattern of small multiple nasal openings above the wide slit of a mouth.

White teeth were sharp and pointed in front, flat in back. Fine hairs screened the nasal portals, filtering the cool air as it was inhaled. The rear feet were heavily shod in thick boots; the center pair were sheathed in thick gloves, while the upper were left free. They were tailless and large-rumped. Short pants, center-body vests, and upper torso garments were fastened with invisible closures. These boasted a variety of pockets and pouches in addition to insignia and other marks of individual identification. Overlaid on the entire arrangement was a network of wide but light straps resembling a dray animal's harness, which was designed to support a variety of military equipment.

Although it was not for them to decide what action to take against this sorry-looking object from the unknown, they had plenty of curiosity concerning it, and no little apprehension. Much of their nosiness was stimulated by the knowledge that the vessel was of no identifiable type, despite the fact that they could recognize all the seventy basic patterns common to their entire region. Of course, none of them were specialists and there was always the possibility of a recent discovery or two that had yet to be included in the regularly reviewed journals. In addition, there was also the possibility it might be an experimental device of their own invention.

Granting all this, the complete lack of external protrusions was disconcerting. The flattened ovoid showed no weapons port, no communications antenna: nothing. There was a suggestion of a single, narrow port at one end, but it was not transparent, and those who strained for a look could see nothing inside.

The possibility of it being a remotely guided or purely mechanical vehicle was not to be discounted. Drones were used extensively by both sides, both for surveillance and communications. Of one thing they could be certain: thus far it was being anything but wildly communicative.

As for their apprehension, that was a consequence of the sheer nonchalance of the visitor's arrival. Ever since its presence had been noted, communications of every kind, from panic to unbridled fury to open curiosity, had been burning up the comm systems. The little vessel had burst like a superswift projectile through the overlapping system of detectors that enveloped the planet, treated the outlying orbital stations and atmospheric patrols with disdain, and sat itself down not in some obscure canyon or camouflaging forest, but within clear view of the capital city.

Something drastic would have to be done about it. On that point one and all regardless of position or rank were agreed. But the appropriate tactics would be defined by authority, not by underlings.

So they hung around in dips and hollows and behind rocks, and scratched and held their weapons, and hankered for their superiors in the city to wake up and come running.

Circumstances have an importunate way of forcing themselves upon the noncommittal. Time, unlike a great many individuals, is impatient. In much the same way that the planetary defenses had been brought to naught by bland presentation of an accomplished fact, so were the guards now similarly disturbed. Giving distant sluggards no time to make up their minds and spring into action, a gap appeared in the side of the ovoid and a thing came out.

This small movement had a way of focusing the attention of the surrounding hexapods wonderfully. They abruptly sprang into action. Or rather into position, no other action being immediately required. Superbly prepared, each individual took his place according to training. Small and heavy portable weapons were tuned to maximum, inter-sextet communications engaged, and shielding activated. The result was a condition of armed readiness sufficient to make superiors proud and adversaries think twice before doing anything that might be interpreted as a hostile move.

The creature looked around, sniffed the air, and then stepped down to the gravelly surface. As a sample of unfamiliar life it was neither big nor fearsome. If it possessed any natural integral armament it was not immediately apparent. There were no long fangs, no sharpened claws, no massive musculature or threatening tentacles. It carried nothing that could not fit in a pocket.

A biped with two arms and a beige-hued face, wearing a one-piece suit of pale green, close-fitting clothing, it was no taller than any of the onlookers and not more than one-third their weight. There was some short fur atop the egg-shaped skull, but otherwise the flesh that was visible was naked. Slim arms terminated in a succession of smaller digits. It was impossible to tell if the shod feet consisted of a similarly subdivided arrangement or a single hoof or pad. Its eyes were small but bright; and the curved protrusions on either side of the head were most likely external ears of indeterminate sensitivity.

A peculiar creature in no way redoubtable. In fact, it looked soft. One could jump on it with all four feet and squash it. Relaxing in spite of themselves, the armed troopers searched in vain for a third set of limbs. Unless the creature was a multiple amputee, the diminished physiology it displayed must be its natural condition. Though this engendered a certain amount of sympathy on the part of several of the soldiers, they did not let down their guard. The fact that no weapons were visible did not mean that none were present.

Nevertheless, despite its inoffensive appearance, one could not hold it entirely in contempt. There were aspects that gave one reason to pause and think. Most notable among these was the absence of readily recognizable ordnance. Moreover, though they had no way of interpreting the meaning of this particular alien's posture and gestures, it was moving about with the subtle assurance of one who had reason to view weapons as so much useless lumber.

In the second place, it was mooching airily around the ship, hands in pockets, inspecting the scarred shell for all the world as if this landing marked a boring call on tiresome relatives. Most of the time it had its back to the ring of troops, magnificently indifferent to whether or not anyone chose to blow it apart. The initial tension among said soldiers was beginning to give way to a distinct feeling of bemusement.

Apparently satisfied with its survey of the vessel, the creature suddenly turned and walked straight toward the concealed watchers. The gap in the flank of the ship from which it had originally emerged remained wide open in a manner suggesting either criminal carelessness or supreme confidence, more probably the latter. Completely at peace with a world in the midst of war, the biped ambled directly toward a small cluster of guards, bringing the need for initiative nearer and nearer, making them sweat with anxiety and creating such a panic that they forgot to itch. Each found himself praying to his private deities that the alien would not change course and swerve in his direction. Most were greatly relieved to see that it did not.

Turning to its left with studied casualness, the intruder came face-to-face with Yadiz, a common trooper momentarily paralyzed by sheer lack of an order to go forward, go backward, shoot the alien, shoot himself, or do something. This resulted in a complete lack of movement on the part of the soldier, who gawked at the biped in utter helplessness.

The alien scrutinized the trooper as casually as if different life-forms in radically different shapes were more common than pebbles on a shingle beach. This inspection continued for several minutes, during which time communications flew across the ether but no one took any action. All waited to see what the alien would do next.

As for the trooper yclept Yadiz, he became so embarrassed by his own futility that he began swapping his weapon from hand to hand and back again.

"Surely it's not that heavy," remarked the alien with complete and surprising fluency. As he spoke he eyed the weapon and sniffed.

Startled, the trooper dropped the gun, which promptly went off with a high-pitched, ear-splitting *crash*. A piece of rock flew into shards and something whined shrilly through the air. The alien turned and followed the whine with its eyes until the sound finally died out.

Then the creature said gently to Yadiz, "Wasn't that rather silly?"

There was no need to formulate a reply. It was a conclusion the trooper already had reached about one second before the bang. He picked up the weapon with a foot-hand, transferred it to a primary hand, found it upside down, turned it right way up, got the strap tangled around his fist, had to reverse it to get the limb free, turned it right way up again.

Some sort of answer seemed to be necessary, but for the life of him Yadiz could not conceive of one that was wholly satisfactory. Wheels spun within his mind, producing friction but no movement. Struck dumb, he posed there holding his weapon by the muzzle and at arm's length, like one who has recklessly grabbed a mamba and dares not let go.

In all his years as a trooper, of which there were more than several, he couldn't recall a time when possession of a firearm had proved such a handicap.

He was still searching in vain for a verbal means of salvaging his self-respect when his immediate superior arrived to break the spell.

A little breathless with haste, the newcomer looked askance at the biped, said to Yadiz, "Who gave you orders to shoot?"

"What business is it of yours?" asked the biped, coldly disapproving. "It's his own gun, isn't it?"

This interjection took Yadiz's superior aback. He had not expected another life-form to speak with the accentless fluency of a native, much less treat this matter of wasting a charge from the angle of personal ownership. The thought that a trooper might have proprietary rights to his weapon had never occurred to him. And now that he had captured the thought he did not know what to do with it. He hefted his own weapon and stared at it as if it had just miraculously appeared in his hand, changed it to another hand by way of insuring its realness and solidity. His pupils were flexing in time to his thoughts.

"Be careful," advised the biped. He nodded toward Yadiz. "That's the way *he* started."

Turning to Yadiz, the alien said in calm, matter-of-fact tones, "Take me to Markhamwit."

Yadiz couldn't be sure whether he actually dropped the gun again or whether it leaped clean out of his hands. Anyway, it did not go off.

The species with whom the biped was conversing were not subject to stuttering. Nevertheless, both troopers looked as if they would have been more than willing to give some form of verbal dislocation a try.

Initial appearances to the contrary, Yadiz was clearly the

more sagacious of the pair. He demonstrated his superior intelligence by keeping his mouth shut while his newly arrived colleague declared with assurance, "That's impossible."

"No it's not," the alien replied confidently.

"Do you know who Markhamwit is?" the trooper inquired, slightly goggle-eyed. In contrast, Yadiz, experienced soldier that he was, kept silent.

"No," responded the biped. "I want you to take me to someone whom I don't know who is. That's logical, isn't it?"

The trooper started to reply, hesitated, and managed to duplicate Yadiz's game of confused cat's cradle with his thoughts instead of his hands. The resulting confusion saw him on the verge of a sudden breakdown.

The biped took pity on him. "I'll make it easy for you. North, south, east, or west. Markhamwit must lie in one of those general directions. Kindly lead me in the appropriate one. You will not be required to analyze my request further."

Yadiz was motioning frantically with his eyes, not daring to open his mouth. His colleague took note, registered an affirmative reply by means of a subtle gesture, and then motioned with his own weapon.

"You are now our prisoner."

The biped sighed. "Oh, all right. If you insist. But let's get on with it."

Feeling a little better (but only a little), the trooper seemed to regain some of the energy he'd had when he arrived. "I will go and find an officer."

"That doesn't do me any good," the alien declared.

"I am not here to do you any good." The soldier was feeling much better now. He flicked a glance at his colleague. "Keep an eye on him while I try to find someone better equipped to deal with this. Don't let him out of your sight." As soon as Yadiz nodded, the other soldier whirled and scampered off on four limbs.

This left Yadiz confronting the alien by himself. The biped stared at him. After a minute of this Yadiz began to sweat.

"Well," said the biped finally, "are you going to take me to Markhamwit?"

"I am supposed to wait here until Bazari returns with an officer."

"Because he told you to wait?"

"Yes."

"Does Bazari rank you?"

Yadiz hesitated only briefly. "No. We are of the same rank."

"Does he have more experience than you?"

"Nooo. Actually, I think I have more experience."

"Then you're obviously better equipped to deal with the situation than he is. So take me to Markhamwit."

"I am not qualified to make such a decision."

"I understand." The biped's lips parted to expose its teeth. It was a most disconcerting expression. "Let me make it simple for you. We try very hard to keep things simple."

Yadiz felt some of the tension ooze out of him. "I would appreciate that."

ii

They met what in another and infinitely earlier time and place would have been called the High Brass about one-third of the way to the outskirts of the city. There was an assorted truckload varying considerably in rank. In addition to far more elaborate attire they boasted insignia that were elegant and decorative as well as descriptive.

Bowling along the perfectly smooth guide track on some sort of maglev system that supported the vehicle about an arm's length above the pavement, the transport zoomed past the two isolated figures. It was nearly out of sight when it halted, pivoted on its central axis, and returned to hover directly opposite the strollers. With a soft, almost imperceptible whine it settled to the surface of the track.

A hyperbolic dome retracted to fully expose the passengers within. Two dozen multi-nostriled, wide-eyed, furry faces peered down from their positions slightly above that of the walkers. A couple of the coddled boasted patches of darker fur that had been carefully groomed and high-lighted to emphasize their coloring.

An outlet appeared on the right-hand side of the craft and a paunchy individual struggled out from his seat beside the driver to confront the ill-matched pair. It was immediately evident that obesity was not unknown among the hexapods. Jowls and facial lines hinted at advanced age, along with a distinctively russet-hued shoulder and sternum growth not unlike the comb of a rooster. It quivered along with the jowls as the owner addressed the hikers. A red metal sun and four silver comet-shapes glistened on the middle shoulder of his harness.

Noting that the trooper was standing in front of the alien instead of behind it and that he held his weapon casually in both hands with the muzzle aimed not at his presumed prisoner but at the ground, the officer prepared to deliver a succinct and daunting reprimand. But first he snapped, "Who told you to desert the perimeter and come this way?"

"Me," informed the alien, airily. He slouched by the side of the vehicular guideway, his attention focused as much on the surrounding scrub-dominated landscape as on the airtruck. Yadiz he ignored completely.

The portly officer jerked as if stuck with a pin, shrewdly eyed the creature up and down, and said, "I did not expect that you could speak our language."

"I'm fully capable of speech," assured the biped. "I can read, too. In fact, without wishing to appear boastful, I'd like to mention that I can also write." Kneeling, it leaned forward to examine a small hard-shelled creature with a segmented body that was struggling to bury itself in the loose soil. Unable to ignore everything without turning his back to the vehicle, which might have felt better but would have constituted an unforgivable insult, Yadiz found himself watching the alien out of the corner of one eye.

"That may be," agreed the officer, willing to concede a couple of petty aptitudes to the manifestly outlandish. He had another careful look, taking mental note of size, shape, color, number of limbs and other external organs, style of clothing and its possible method of manufacture. It made a decidedly unimpressive picture. "Can't say that I'm familiar with your kind of life."

"Which doesn't surprise me," replied the alien. Its responses were not only fluent but quick, couched in colloquial rather than formal dialect. "Lots of folk never get the chance to become familiar with us."

The other's color heightened, a consequence of increased blood flow coupled with a particular endocrinological response. Repressing his initial instinctive reaction (and acutely aware of the truckload of high brass that was watching his every move) he added, with a show of annoyance, "I don't know who you are or what you are, but you're under arrest."

"Sire," put in the aghast Yadiz, unable to keep silent any longer, "he wishes to . . ."

"Did anyone tell you to speak?" demanded the officer, burning him down with his eyes. The last thing he needed at such a delicate moment was interference from some common trooper.

"No, sire. It was just that . . ."

"Shut up!"

Yadiz swallowed hard, considered, and then kept his mouth closed as ordered. He also took on the apprehensive expression of one unreasonably denied the right to point out that the barrel is full of powder and someone has lit the fuse. He did, however, manage to keep a firm grip on his weapon, to the point where his knuckles were starting to turn white beneath the druzy brown fur.

"Why am I under arrest?" inquired the alien, not in the least disturbed as it rose from its crouch to confront the hexapod. By now the segmented burrower had completed its escape.

The officer was becoming used to the creature's astonishing fluency. Unable to explain it, he chose simply to accept it. "Because I say so."

"Really?" The alien's eyelids fluttered. "Do you treat all arrivals that way?"

"At present, yes," explained the officer, on comfortable ground again. "You may know it or you may not, but right now this system is at war with the system of Nilea. We're taking no chances."

"Neither are we," remarked the biped, enigmatically.

"What do you mean by that?"

"The same as you meant. We're playing safe." The thin brows of the creature drew together. "You just admitted that I can speak your language. Are you having difficulty with it now?"

"Not at all." The other licked satisfied lips. His initial unease at the creature's unclassifiable appearance had passed and he was once more completely comfortable with the situation. "You are what I suspected from the first, namely, an ally the Nileans have dug up from some very minor system that we've overlooked. Well, it's not surprising. The galaxy is a vast place and even in the midst of war new minor species are constantly being encountered."

"Your suspicions are ill founded," the alien told him. "An unavoidable consequence of upbringing, no doubt. However, I would rather explain myself higher up."

Ignoring the not-so-subtle dig at his background (and not realizing the comment went considerably deeper than that), the officer's tone darkened menacingly.

"You will do just that," he promised. "And the explanation had better be satisfactory." Yadiz started to say something, but the incipient comment withered under the officer's murderous stare.

He did not care for the slow smile he got from the alien

by way of reply. Though he could not be certain of the meaning since the source was unclassified, it still succeeded in suggesting that someone was being dogmatic and someone else knew better. Neither had he any difficulty in identifying the respective someones. The alien's apparently baseless show of quiet confidence unsettled him far more than he cared to reveal, especially with a dopey guard standing nearby and a truckload of higher-ups looking on. If he lost control of the conversation there were plenty of witnesses who'd never let him live it down.

It would have been nice to attribute the two-legger's *sangfroid* to the usual imbecility of another lesser life-form too dimwitted to know when its scalp was in danger. There were plenty of sentients like that: seemingly brave because they were unable to realize a predicament even when they were in it up to the neck. Many of the lower ranks of his own forces had that kind of guts.

Nevertheless, he could not shake off the uneasy feeling that this case was different. He had no proof, of course, and the creature was anything but offensive (except perhaps verbally). But the alien looked too alert, too sharp-eyed to actually be as ignorant of circumstances as its behavior suggested.

The officer had not survived years of combat and internecine conflict and risen to his present position by underestimating the opposition, either among the enemy or his own kind. The important thing here was to not make a mistake, especially in front of his immediate superiors. He was not required to evaluate, or to render any final decisions; only to expedite. In that respect the alien's brashness and arrogance did not trouble him. It would be for others to induce proper respect in the creature.

Besides, he told himself again, it could easily be and probably was acting out of ignorance of its actual situation.

When reality came down hard on its lightly furred skull, the officer reflected, the creature's attitude would undergo a rapid and respectful change.

Another and smaller hovering vehicle was humming up the guideway. Waving it to a stop, he picked four two-comet subofficers from his own group to act as an escort, shooed them into the new craft along with the biped who entered without comment or protest. He didn't mind the arrogance so long as the creature was cooperative.

Through a side port he said to the senior of the four equally ranked soldiers, "I hold you personally responsible for its safe arrival at the interrogation center. Tell them I've gone on to the ship to see whether there's any more where this one came from."

The nearest subofficer gestured back understandingly, glancing over both shoulders to where the alien sat placidly between two of his colleagues. It ignored them as they patted down its slim body with thick, powerful fingers.

"Should we expect any trouble?" the subofficer asked his superior.

"You saw me conversing with it. It understands our language quite well, so it should understand any orders or warnings. I don't think it'll give you any difficulty."

He glared meaningfully back at the creature only to be rewarded with another disconcerting smile.

"No discernible weapons, sire," declared one of the subofficers in the back as soon as the quick, professional inspection was completed.

"Keep a close watch on it anyway," the officer ordered him. "It looks pretty non-threatening, but that doesn't mean it's incapable of sudden movements or other surprises." The alien did not comment, leaving the officer to wonder about the truth of his observation.

Well, in a few seconds it would no longer be his concern.

He stepped back and watched from the edge of the pathway as the vehicle pivoted. A low whine rose from its underside as it accelerated, heading back toward the city. As soon as it was out of view he clambered back into his own transport. The dome descended and it departed at high speed for the source of all the irritation.

Devoid of instructions to proceed toward town, return to the alien ship, stand on his head or do anything else, Yadiz leaned on his gun and patiently awaited the passing of somebody qualified to tell him. Near his feet, a second segmented burrower commenced a fresh excavation.

As the small, efficient ground-suspension craft entered the outskirts of the city, the subofficer in charge resumed his inspection of the alien. Though unfamiliar to him, it was not necessarily a new type. Species identification not being his specialty he was reluctant to hazard a guess as to its origins. While he had been assured that the thing was conversant with the dominant language, it did not seem interested in engaging in casual colloquy.

In fact, it did not seem interested in much of anything, which spoke poorly for its level of intelligence. Not being privy to the remarkable details of its arrival, the subofficer found himself wondering what all the fuss was about. Usually offworlders brought into the great city, even those from sophisticated worlds, marveled at its massive towers and edifices, its overarching communications loops and bustling crowds of intent, busy citizens. But not this innocuous biped. It simply sat silently, its eyes half closed (normal resting position, he wondered?), and said nothing.

While it was hardly incumbent on him to make conversation, the subofficer had the usual amount of curiosity. It wasn't every day someone in his position got to meet a new type.

"Are you male, female, neuter, hermaphroditic, or

other?" he asked. He made the inquiry forcefully, demanding a response and quite indifferent as to whether or not
the biped might find this line of inquiry offensive.

Taking no umbrage at his tone the biped replied casually. "Male. We're traditionalists."

Unsure exactly what the prisoner meant by that, the
subofficer continued. "What do you think of the city? This
is the capital, you know. The center of administration and
power. Representatives from dozens of different species
strive their whole lives just to visit here once. From these
towers the fate of entire systems is determined and the
course of the war guided. Obviously coming from some
lesser world I don't expect you to grasp the significance of
all this immediately upon arrival, but I'd be interested in
your opinion nonetheless."

As if deigning to notice the immense metropolis for the
first time, the biped leaned slightly forward and let its small,
intense eyes flick about their immediate surroundings.
They were on a priority guideway now, racing along twice as
fast as the more mundane, surrounding traffic.

"Crowded," he finally replied. "Noisy."

After a moment the frustrated subofficer snapped,
"That's all? This is the heart of the most advanced civilization known, and that's all you have to say?"

"Oh, very well," murmured the biped irritably. "It's
also quite big."

" 'Big'," echoed the subofficer. He mulled this over and
decided that the alien was insufficiently intelligent to appreciate the marvel of contemporary engineering through
which he was traveling. This reasoning made perfect sense.
It wasn't that the creature was unawed; he simply did not
possess adequate concepts with which to understand his
surroundings. Definitely a classic lower form. The subofficer was much pleased with this evaluation.

Certainly the creature was not talkative. Perhaps its kind communicated largely by gestures. By way of experiment he flashed a couple of choice obscene ones in the biped's face. The subofficers sitting to either side of him snickered but the biped did not react. Unless you could call the slight parting of its mouth a reaction. The subofficer wasn't sure. It might simply have been a component of normal respiratory function.

And here he'd thought that the alien would provide some entertainment, if not real excitement. Instead, they might as well have been escorting a plant. Disappointed, he folded all four arms against one another and turned to gaze idly out the dome.

When they reached the Interrogation Center he dutifully handed over his charge to a pair of burly guards clad in dull-colored but glossy uniforms. They hustled the biped down a side corridor, away from the glances of curious passersby. The subofficer watched them go, then turned to rejoin his three colleagues.

"Well," one of them asked him, "what do you think that was all about?"

"Nothing," said the other. "A new species or one that's known and insignificant. How it got where it did is much more important than what it is."

His colleague gestured positively. "They'll deal with it."

"Speedily, I should think," said a third. "In any case, it's obviously nothing of much significance." They exited the vast structure and returned to their vehicle. The morning was still fresh and work of actual importance awaited them.

The interrogation center viewed the alien's advent as less sensational than the arrival of a Joppelan five-eared munkster at the city zoo. Data drawn from a galaxy were at the disposal of its large staff. Said information included sometimes exhaustively detailed descriptions of millions of separate and distinct life-forms, a few of them so fantastic that the cogent material was more deductive than demonstrative.

In the unlikely event that requisite material was not readily available, the staff had access to additional files elsewhere on the planet and offworld. Priority hyperaccess allowed them reach into private as well as public sources with a speed private organizations could not hope to duplicate.

Among the millions of cataloged or referenced life-forms were approximately four hundred that possessed some degree of sentience. So far as the researchers were concerned this newly arrived sample brought the record up to four hundred and one. In another century's time it might be four hundred twenty-one or fifty-one. They had been traversing space for so long that such discoveries no longer elicited much in the way of reaction, either among the specialists or the general public. Listing the lesser lifes was so much routine.

Interviews with those life-forms sufficiently intelligent to respond to questioning were equally a matter of established custom. They had devised a standard technique involving queries to be answered, forms to be filled out, conclusions to be drawn. This presupposed a minimal amount of cooperation on the part of the respondent. The degree of cooperation could be adjusted or modified as needed.

Their ways of dealing with recalcitrants were quite flexible, demanding various alternative methods and a modicum of imagination. Some hesitant life-forms responded with pleasing alacrity to means of persuasion that other life-forms could not so much as sense. It required experience and ingenuity on the part of the staff to invent new methods suitable for the persuasion of new species. It was a testament to their expertise that they rarely failed to devise a suitable course of action. The trick was to make sure that the one being probed did not expire during the course of the interrogation. The only difficulty they could have with this new specimen was that of thinking up an entirely new way of making it see reason.

So they directed him to a desk, giving him a chair with four armrests and ten centimeters too high. A bored official took his place opposite. He was dressed differently from the soldiers but not dramatically so. Most notable was the absence of visible insignia. A compact electronic device partially wrapped around and entered one small ear opening. They sat off to themselves at the far end of a large, busy chamber that had been subdivided by means of movable partitions into individual cubicles. Other officials, visiting military personnel, and assorted flunkies of indeterminate importance ignored the mismatched pair as they went about their own work.

The official looked the unprepossessing alien up and down, accepting in advance that it could already speak the local tongue or communicate in some other readily understandable manner. Nobody was sent to this place until educated sufficiently to give the required responses. When first informed of the creature's presence and impending arrival he'd hoped for something a little more exciting, an entity that might be at least visually if not intellectually arresting. Instead, the biped turned out to be ordinary in the extreme.

As he switched on his desk, a tightly packed cluster of instruments rose from one side and aimed itself at the alien. Automatics locked in on the subject, visuals focused, other sensitive devices began taking measurements and making comparisons.

None of this had the slightest effect on the alien. It did not even glance in the instruments' direction, blissfully indifferent to any unseen sonics or beams that might be scanning him. Studying the creature closely, the interrogator was unable to tell from its reaction, or rather, non-reaction, if it regarded the instrument package as a bevy of weapons, torture devices, or harmless sensory devices. Well, he'd been informed in advance that its dominant characteristic was bland indifference. Whether this emotional/mental condition arose out of ignorance or something else was one of the things that would be up to him to determine.

"What is your number, name, code, cipher, or other means of verbal identification?" The interrogator was neither hostile nor cordial. At this point everything, including his attitude, was strictly business.

"James Lawson," the creature replied in a voice as pure and accentless as that of any native speaker.

Demonstrated fluency was no proof of anything, the interviewer knew. There were at least three species whose intelligence level barely met the minimal criteria for sentience but who were superb mimics. They could talk your aural opening off without making any sense whatsoever.

"Sex, if any?" he continued.

"What, again?" The alien sighed as it fiddled with the multiple armrests. "Male."

The interrogator was in no mood to suffer attitude from a lower life-form. He had learned early on that it was useful to establish respective positions at the beginning of any session. It saved time, argument, and was invariably better for the state of one's liver. "See here, you," he told the biped in no-nonsense tones. "This is important. Far more so to you than to me, if you will take a moment to think about it. I strongly advise that you consider your situation and act accordingly, and with proper respect. I suggest also that you pay attention." Unable to tell if this admonition had any effect on the specimen, he continued.

"Age?"

"None."

"There now," said the interrogator, scenting coming

awkwardness and opting for the pleasant approach. "You must have an age."

"Must I?"

"Everyone has an age."

"Have they?"

"Look," insisted the interviewer, very patient, "nobody can be ageless."

"Can't they?"

He gave it up, murmuring, "It's unimportant anyway. His personal time units are meaningless until we get his planetary data." Or the confusion might result from some minor semantic misunderstanding that could more easily be resolved later. It was hardly a question fraught with military import. At least the creature showed no hesitancy to respond, and at this point, that was the most important thing. Analysis of its responses could be performed after the interview had been completed.

Glancing down at his list of questions, which glowed brightly within the transparent window set in his side of the desk, he carried on. "Purpose of visit?" His eyes came up as he waited for the usual boring response such as, "Normal exploration, development of commercial and trade ties" or "Informal contact." When none was forthcoming he reiterated, "Purpose of visit?"

"To see Markhamwit," responded James Lawson.

The interviewer yelped, *"What?,"* deactivated the instrument package and breathed heavily for a while, not sure he'd heard correctly. Certainly the alien was fluent, but between representatives of any two different species, no matter how well educated, there was always still room for mispronunciation and misunderstanding. His fingers moved as he replayed the last statement through his earpiece. When he found voice again it was to ask, "You really mean that you've come specially to see the Great Lord Markhamwit?"

"Yes," the alien replied without hesitation.

The interviewer hesitated uncertainly. "By appointment?"

"No."

That did it. Recovering with great swiftness, the interviewer became aggressively officious and growled, "The Great Lord's time is precious and despite the best efforts of the finest metaphysicians our society has produced, an individual can be kept awake and attentive for only so long. I can tell you with complete assurance that the Great Lord Markhamwit sees nobody without an appointment."

Delivered in measured, careful tones designed to brook no argument, this pronouncement did nothing to disturb the alien's composure. "Then kindly make one for me."

"I'll find out what can be done," promised the other, having no intention of doing anything of the sort. Not for the first time was he glad that the finer points of semantics were not his field. Aliens tended to say one thing when they meant another, which was why the preliminary interview was designed to focus on easily comprehensible basics. At least, that was the intent. Some species proved incapable of handling even that much. A few were downright obstreperous. He was not quite ready to relegate this frustrating biped to that category.

Turning the instrument package on again, he resumed with the next question. "Rank?"

"None."

For a second time the eyes came up. "Now look here . . ."

"I said *none,*" repeated Lawson.

"I heard you. We'll let it pass." The interviewer rubbed tiredly at his forehead. Not yet midday, already he was fatigued, and this alien wasn't helping the digestion of his morning meal one bit. "It's a minor point that can be brought out later." With that slightly sinister comment he tried the next question. "Location of origin?"

"The Solarian Combine."

Flip went the concealed switch as the unlucky instrument package again got put out of action. Leaning backward, the interviewer shut his eyes as he rubbed his forehead with two hands and his belly with the others. A passing official glanced at him, stopped.

"Having trouble, Dilmur?"

"Trouble?" he echoed bitterly. He stared at his softly glowing desk. "What a morning! Query after query on top of a whole season's worth of analysis to summarize. One thing after another! Now this."

"What's the matter?" The new arrival glared at the alien. "Being uncooperative, are we? That's not very nice. Not a good idea, either. You're lucky they assigned you to Dilmur. You could have done a lot worse." The visitor's tone darkened. "You still can." The creature did not reply.

The interviewer jabbed an accusing finger at Lawson. "He's being obtuse. I'm not sure if it's intentional, but you know how basic the preliminary queries are. There shouldn't be any confusion."

"Language problems? Maybe somebody down the line slipped up and sent you a specimen who should have been kept in Basic."

"Oh, he's fluent enough. Comprehension is another matter. First he pretends to be ageless. Then he gives the motive behind his arrival as that of seeing the Great Lord without prior arrangement." His sigh was deep and heartfelt.

"And you wonder why I'm looking tired?" He leaned back in his chair. Internal jets hissed softly as air was pumped in to compensate for the redistribution of weight.

"I don't have time for this sort of nonsense. There's the seasonal summation to finalize. If they thought he was going to be difficult, why did they bring him to this level? And why to me?"

36 ■ Alan Dean Foster & Eric Frank Russell

"You know the procedure," the visitor reminded him.

Another sigh. "Yes, I know. It's just frustrating not to be able even to get past the essentials with some of these lower types. Your failure means more work for somebody else, a waste of time and resources."

"It's not your fault," the other sympathized with his colleague. "You can only do so much."

"And that's not the worst of it," Dilmur continued.

The other's thick brows lifted. "You mean there's more?"

"Wait till you hear this one. On top of everything else he claims that he comes from the 'Solarian Combine.' "

"Hm! Another theological nut," diagnosed the passerby. "Don't waste your time on him. Pass him along to the mental therapists. They're paid to take care of these cases and you're not. Why should you have to put up with the inconvenience? I've always said that you were too conscientious for this job, Dilmur. You should ask for a transfer out of Interbeing Contact and request a position in Research." Giving the silent subject of their mutual discussion a cold look of reproof, he continued on his way.

"You heard that?" The interviewer felt for the instrumentation switch in readiness to resume operation. "Anything you didn't understand?" When the alien didn't respond, he continued, "Now do we get on with this job in a reasonable and sensible manner or must we resort to other, less pleasant, methods of discovering the truth?"

The alien shifted its backside and legs, striving for a comfortable position on a chair that had been designed to accommodate a much bulkier and more complicated pelvic region than his own.

"The way you put it implies that I am a liar," said Lawson, displaying no resentment. His tone and expression had not changed. He showed neither fear nor anger.

The interviewer considered before replying. "Not exactly. Perhaps you are a deliberate but rather stupid liar whose prevarications will gain him nothing. Perhaps you may have no more than a distorted sense of humor. Or you may be completely sincere because completely deluded. We have had visionaries here before. They can be more irksome than the usual visitor but eventually they are dealt with appropriately. We pride ourselves on our egalitarianism. It takes all sorts to make a universe."

"Including Solarians," Lawson remarked.

"The Solarians are a myth," declared the interviewer with all the positiveness of one stating a long-established fact. It was not a matter open to dispute. No sensible, knowledgeable being would attempt to assert otherwise. No *rational* being. He continued to watch the biped closely.

"There are no myths," the alien replied calmly. "There are only gross distortions of half-remembered truths."

"So you still insist that you are a Solarian?"

"Certainly."

"And nothing I could say or do would induce you to change your mind, or alter that assertion?"

"Of course not."

The other stabbed resignedly at the concealed switch and the instrument package promptly sank back down into the body of the desk. "Then I can go no further with you. Just remember that I gave you every opportunity to behave sensibly and that whatever happens from now on is a direct consequence of your own intransigence, or however you prefer to interpret your actions here. I take no responsibility." He touched another switch and several large attendants appeared as if from out of nowhere. Resigned but clear of conscience, he gestured at the seated biped.

"Take him to Kasine."

iii

———————————————————————■———————————————————————

There followed a long walk down a lightly traveled corridor, followed by a subsequent shift via some kind of elevator or motion capsule that was capable of horizontal as well as vertical travel. The capsule was armored and impervious to common weaponry, as was the new, smaller corridor the trio emerged into. The entire procedure was designed not only to transport someone from one place to another but to impress upon them the significance of that journey. If this at all intimidated or otherwise affected the biped, he gave no sign of it. The only emotion he manifested during the trip was a kind of quiet impatience.

There were even fewer individuals present in the large, windowless antechamber they entered, and none at all in the dark office situated off to one side. Upon presentation of compact credentials, the two guards led their smaller charge into a still smaller room that was not only devoid of windows but of much illumination of any kind. In this decidedly gloomy cubicle they left him to confront a singular individual seated behind a much larger desk than Dilmur's.

The door closed behind the guards with a thick, muffled *thunk* suggestive of heavy soundproofing.

Kasine suffered from some medically untreatable maladjustment that made him grossly obese. The advanced technology of this world could fabricate entire starships and communicate between systems, but it had manifestly been unable to do anything for him. He was just one great big bag of fat relieved only by a pair of deep-sunk but brilliantly glittering eyes. Physically immobile, he was mentally alert. Neither the eyes nor the mind behind them overlooked any aspect of the biped's appearance as they pondered and analyzed the information that had been supplied.

Those optics looked at Lawson in much the same way that a cat stares at a cornered mouse. Completing the inspection after allowing a suitable amount of time for contemplation to pass, he activated his own desk instrumentation. The package that emerged from the slick surface was more intricate than the one that had been utilized by Lawson's previous interrogator.

Touching a concealed switch, he listened carefully to a playback of what had taken place during the previous interview, watching the visuals on a small screen positioned intentionally out of his prisoner's line of vision.

Then a low, reverberating chuckle sounded in his huge belly and he commented, "Ho-ho, a Solarian! And lacking a pair of arms at that! Did you mislay them someplace?" Leaning forward with a manifest effort, he licked thick lips and added, "What a dreadful fix you'll be in if you lose the others also!"

Lawson gave a disdainful snort. "For an alleged mental therapist you're long overdue for treatment yourself."

It did not generate the fury that might well have been aroused in another. Kasine merely wheezed with amusement and looked self-satisfied. Giving his visitor ample time to contemplate his surroundings and situation, the interrogator reached beneath the desk and removed the end of a long transparent tube of slight diameter. This he placed between his lips and began sucking upon. Green fluid raced up the tube to vanish down that busy mouth.

When he'd imbibed his fill he offered the end of the tube to Lawson, who declined with a slight smile. Shrugging, Kasine let the tube retract into its holder and settled back into his chair.

"So you think I'm sadistic, eh?"

"Only at the time you made that remark. Other moments, other motivations."

"Ah!" Kasine's expression yawed to the left, assuming a condition anyone familiar with his species would immediately have recognized as a satisfied grin. "Whenever you open your mouth you tell me something useful."

"You could do with it," Lawson opined.

"And while I could very well be wrong," the interrogator went on, refusing to be baited, "it seems to me that you are not an idiot."

"Should I be?"

"You should!" Kasine was emphatic. "Every Solarian is an imbecile. It's a self-defining condition to which we have found no exceptions." Again he gave his guest a careful once-over. "I see no reason to anticipate that you will be any different."

"I might surprise you."

"I doubt it, though I would like to be surprised. You see, I so rarely am. Types like yourself, other self-proclaimed 'Solarians,' and individuals suffering from related syndromes eventually manage to categorize themselves, thus saving me the trouble." His gaze narrowed deliberately. "So far as I am concerned, the only question to be settled here is whether in your case this will occur sooner or later." He ruminated a moment, then went on.

"The last 'Solarian' we had here was a many-tendriled

octoped from Quamis. An extremely eloquent representa-
tive of his kind, whose vocal capabilities were the equal of
his inherently florid gestures. This being an unusual condition for the Quamisians, it made this particular individual
something of a celebrity among his people, though not necessarily an admired one. As we later found out, the authorities on his home planet wanted him for causing an
end-of-the-world panic. They were as profoundly delighted
to be rid of him as we eventually were." Kasine shook his
head at the memory of it.

"For a little while we found him to be quite entertaining, until his dementia grew repetitive and we decided to
resolve the matter. His illusion of Solarianism was strong
enough to make the credulous believe it. Many of the lesser
races are vulnerable to such convictions, particularly when
they are propounded by convincing speakers. But we aren't
foolish octopeds here. We have not become dominant by
accident. Feeling that it would have been impolite not to
assist our friends the Quamisians, we determined to provide
them with the benefits of our superior insight insofar as this
troublesome individual was concerned. That is to say, we
cured him in the end."

"How?"

Kasine organized the recollection precisely before
resuming. "I was only marginally involved in that particular
matter, but the final report naturally had to pass my desk
prior to filing. A complete physiological as well as mental
workup was performed on our many-limbed visitor, subsequent to which, if I remember aright, we fed him a coated
pellet of sodium and followed it with a jar of water. Whereupon he surrendered his stupidities with much fuss and
shouting. As I have already mentioned, he was an articulate
individual. His eloquence was never more inspired than at
that time.

"He confessed his purely Quamistic origin shortly before his insides exploded." Kasine wagged his head in patronizing regret. "Unfortunately, he did not long survive his confession. The Quamisian authorities were very understanding. So that you cannot possibly misunderstand my meaning, as you seem to have done with Dilmur, I will tell you that he died. Very noisily, too."

"Bet you enjoyed every instant of it," said Lawson.

"As I told you, I was only marginally involved and was not present at the resolution. I dislike a mess."

Lawson eyed the enormous body. "It will be worse when it's your turn."

"Is that so? Well, let me tell . . ." He stopped as something that sounded like a little gong boomed softly in the depths of his desk. Feeling around his right ear, he adjusted his inserted receiving module and listened. Lawson waited patiently, legs crossed, hands folded against his stomach, blissfully uninterested in whatever unseen figures might or might not be saying about him.

After a while Kasine blinked and his thick fingers fell from the tiny insert. He stared across the imposing desk, his tone ominous. "Two officers tried to enter your ship."

"That was foolish."

All pretext at jovial banter gone, the interrogator said heavily, "They are now lying on the ground outside, to all appearances completely paralyzed. Their companions on the scene are reluctant to attempt recovery of the bodies without some explanation of what happened for fear of suffering the same fate."

"What did I tell you?" commented Lawson, rubbing it in.

Smacking a fat hand on the desk, Kasine made his voice loud and his manner threatening. "What caused it?"

Lawson gazed thoughtfully ceilingward. "Like all your kind, they are allergic to formic acid. It's a fact I had ascertained in advance."

"Then it's not fatal?" said Kasine, exhibiting surprising knowledge of a field outside his immediate realm of expertise.

"Not in the slightest. At least, not in the doses your two nosy-types received." He gave a careless shrug. "A shot of diluted ammonia will cure them and they'll never have your species' equivalent of rheumatics as long as they live. Given your number of limbs, I'd regard that as a fair trade for a brief moment of inconvenience. When they come around they'll be more disoriented than anything else." He smiled softly. "I wouldn't give them their weapons back for a day or so. They might have a tough time telling old friends from perceived enemies. Nothing to mess up friendship like a little panicky shooting."

"I want no abstruse technicalities." Kasine's tone had turned harsh. "I want to know what caused it. I want to know the exact cause and method of delivery, if it was mechanical or organic or something else."

"Probably Freddy," thought Lawson, little interested. "Or maybe it was Lou. Or possibly Buzwuz."

"Buzwuz?" Kasine's eyes came up a bit from their fatty depths. He wheezed awhile before he said, "The communique informs me that insofar as observers were able to determine, both comatose officers were stabbed in the back of the neck by something tiny, orange-colored, and winged. What was it?"

"A Solarian."

His self-control beginning to slip, Kasine became louder. "If you are a Solarian, which you are not, this other thing cannot be a Solarian too."

"Why not?" Lawson inquired curiously.

The interrogator calmed himself with an effort. Like Dilmur, he accepted this biped's fluency because it was a demonstrable fact, and like the interviewer he found himself experiencing serious doubts as to its mental competence.

"I should think the answer intuitively obvious. Because it is a totally different kind of being. It has not the slightest resemblance to you in any one respect."

"Afraid you're wrong there."

Kasine was fighting to control his breathing. "Why?"

"It is intelligent." Lawson examined the other as though curious about an elephant with a trunk at both ends. "Since you seem to find the basic notion so remarkable, let me tell you that intelligence has nothing whatever to do with shape, form, or size. It has nothing to do with coloration, or the number of limbs, or the design of one's eyes. It is wholly an unquantifiable characteristic."

"Do you call it intelligent to stab someone in the neck?" asked Kasine pointedly.

"In the circumstances under which the action took place, yes. Besides, the resulting condition is harmless and easily curable. That's more than you can say for an exploded belly."

"It is not my department so it's not for me to say what will happen, but one thing you can rest assured of: We'll do something about this." The interrogator made the lightly veiled threat openly.

"It won't be easy," Lawson assured him. "Take Buzwuz, for instance. One tough little arthropod. Though he's small even for a bumblebee from Callis, he could lay out six horses in a row before he had to squat down someplace and generate more acid."

"Bumblebee?" Kasine's brows tried to draw together over thick rolls of flesh, his expression as knotted as his thoughts. "Horses?"

"Forget them," advised Lawson. "You know nothing of either. Exposition would take time and do you no good anyway."

"Maybe so, but I do know this: Whatever they are, they

won't like it when we bring up an armored vehicle and use it to fill your ship with a lethal gas."

"Not only won't they mind, they'll laugh themselves silly. And it won't pay you to make my vessel uninhabitable."

"No?"

"No! Because those already out of it, and knowing the guys I assure you that some of them have already been enjoying your cool if depressingly overcast climate, will have to stay out. Most of the others will get out fast in spite of anything you can do to try to prevent their escape. After that, they'll have no choice but to settle down and live here. I would not like that if I were you. I wouldn't care for it one little bit."

"Wouldn't you?"

"Not if I were you, which, fortunately, I am not. A world soon becomes mighty uncomfortable when you've got to share it with hard-to-catch, highly intelligent enemies steadily breeding a thousand to your one." He looked thoughtful. "I don't believe any of them have bred in quite a while. I think they'd take to the task with real enthusiasm."

Kasine twitched, queried with some apprehension, "Mean to say they'll actually remain here and increase that fast?"

"What else would you expect them to do once you've taken away their sanctuary? Go jump in the lake just to please you? On board the ship there are factors present, both chemical and social, that serve to inhibit their natural reproductive tendencies. Take the ship and those influences away and you remove all restraints. They'll reproduce like mad and revel in every minute of it." He looked meaningfully around the room.

"It may not be Callis, but this world would provide a suitable home. They're intelligent, I tell you, and more adaptable than you can imagine. The harder you'd strive to repress them, the faster they'd breed and the more actively they'd react. Take it from me, the result would be a most uncomfortable environment for any non-Callisian. Render their present home untenable and they will survive even if they have to paralyze every one of your kind and make it permanent.''

"How then if we dropped a thermonuclear device on the site?''

Lawson shook his head sadly. "You really do have a one-track mind, don't you? Narrow gauge, to boot. I told you, no matter what you try, some of them will escape. Anything you can think of they've already thought of and discarded as unworkable. Keep in mind that a Callisian doesn't offer much of a target to track, and I can guarantee you any trackers would be worse than discouraged after a few of them suffered repeated jolts. Nor would Lou and the others make a dash for open country. Callisians are quite comfortable in an urban habitat. They'd likely head straight for the nearest city and take up residence there before spreading out to other areas. Try exterminating them and you'd have to take your own habitat apart . . . and that still wouldn't stop them.''

The images this scenario called forth were sufficiently graphic to force the interrogator to stifle a rising twitch. He was rescued from the need to formulate a reply by the muffled gong within the desk. Fingering his earpiece, he listened again, scowled, and then dropped his hand. For a short while he sat silently, glowering across the desk. When he finally did speak it was with fresh irritation.

"Two more," he said. "Flat out."

Registering a thin smile, Lawson suggested, "Why not leave my ship alone and let me see Markhamwit?''

"Get this into your head," retorted Kasine. "If any and every crackpot who chose to land on this planet could walk straight in to see the Great Lord there would have been trouble long ago. The Great Lord would have been assassinated ten times over."

"He must be popular."

"You are impertinent. Regardless of the survival status or offensive capabilities of any small, winged things that may presently happen to inhabit your ship, it remains that they are there and you are here. While they may be temporarily able to defend their vessel and protect themselves, there is nothing they can do for you. You do not appear to realize the peril of your own position. This does not upset me because I understand and therefore am willing to exercise a certain degree of patience. It is a common failing among delusional types such as yourself, for which we have an extensive variety of cures." Leaning forward with a grunt of discomfort, the interrogator hushed his tones in sheer awe at himself.

"Outside that door are those empowered merely to obey orders or ask questions. They will respond without questions or qualms to whatever directives I may choose to issue. They are obedient and responsive, efficient and thorough. Nothing more. Here, within this room, it is different. Here, I make decisions."

"Takes you a long time to get to them." Lawson was unimpressed.

Ignoring his tone, the other went on. "I suggest you pay closer attention to me. Also, a more respectful attitude would go a long ways toward assuring your continued good health." Thick fingers rapped expectantly on the smooth surface of the desk.

"It is wholly up to me to decide whether or not your mouth gives forth facts. If I deem you a liar, I can decide whether or not it is worth turning to less tender means of obtaining the truth. If I think you and your particular delusions too petty to make even your truths worth having, I can decide when, where, and how we shall dispose of you." He slowed down by way of extra emphasis. "All this means that I can order your immediate death."

As phlegmatic as ever, the alien replied without hesitation. "The right to blunder isn't much to boast about."

"I do not think your effective removal would be an error," Kasine countered. "As mentioned, those creatures in your ship are impotent so far as this room is concerned. Even if you could activate some kind of signal or alarm they could not arrive in time to help. What is to prevent me from having you destroyed?"

"Nothing," Lawson informed him simply.

"Ah!" Slightly surprised by this frank admission, the fat face became gratified. "You agree that you are helpless to save yourself?"

"In one way, yes. In another, no."

"Your intentional obtuseness tries my patience."

"And your insistence on refusing to see reason tries mine."

Kasine sighed. "You have stated that you cannot save yourself from any action we may choose to take as regards your personal existence. Then you seem to contradict yourself. Explanation?"

"There's nothing complicated about it. You can have me slaughtered if you wish. It will be a little triumph for you if you like that sort of thing." Lawson's eyes came up, looked levelly at the other's. "It would be wisest if you enjoyed the triumph to the full and made the very most of it, for it won't last long."

"Won't it?"

"Pleasure is for today. Regrets are for tomorrow. After the feast, the reckoning."

"Oho? And who will present the bill?"

"The Solarian Combine."

"There you go again! I would prefer that you argue with me. At least then you are rational." Kasine rubbed his forehead wearily. "The Solarian Combine. I am sick and tired of it. You'd think that our assorted fanatics and zealots would tire of it also and find a new fetish to fixate upon, but no! The same thing, over and over again. It's not the only such infection, but it's certainly among the most popular. Inventions which are the most difficult to prove are consequently the hardest to trace, which makes them favorites among the credulous." He leaned back and his chair creaked.

"Forty times have I faced so-called Solarians, all of whom proved to be maniacs in varying stages of mental deterioration who were recently escaped or expelled from some not-too-faraway world. Despite their often colorful individual variations they all clung to the same basic obsession, until they were cured or otherwise disabused of such notions. Such repetition and lack of imagination dulls the mind and spoils the days of those like myself who have to deal with them. Even in my specialty one hungers for variety, or at least innovation.

"But I'll give you your due for one thing: You're the coolest and most collected of the lot." He fiddled with a control beneath the rim of the desk and a glow filtered upward from the slick surface. Kasine gazed at it for a few moments, perusing information and trying to decide on a further course of action, before sitting back to consider the biped once more.

"I suspect that it is going to be rather difficult to bring you to your senses. We may have to concoct an entirely new technique to deal with you. I regret that this will require an allocation of resources better employed elsewhere."

"Too bad," said Lawson, sympathetically.

"Therefore I . . ." Kasine broke off as the single heavy door opened and a five-comet officer entered in a hurry. He was advancing on all four legs and breathing hard, having come a respectable distance in a great rush.

"What is this?" Kasine was more than a little irritated.

"It is standard procedure for me not to be interrupted at such times." He folded his lower hands. "I hope you have a good excuse."

"Apologies, sire. There has come down to us a message from the Great Lord." The newcomer shot an uneasy glance at Lawson before he went on. "Regardless of any conclusion to which you may have come, you are to preserve this arrival intact and unharmed. With regard to its interrogation, normal proceedings are to be suspended forthwith and until further notice."

"That's taking things out of my hands," grumbled Kasine. "Is there no chance that I might be permitted even a half day with him?" He stared hard at Lawson. "I could guarantee at least minimal results."

The officer was emphatic. "The communique was quite clear. He is to be left alone and unevaluated."

The interrogator sniffed disappointedly. "Am I not supposed to know the reasons?"

Hesitating a moment, the officer said, "I was not told to keep them from you."

"Then what are they? Don't interpolate. Let me make my own decisions. Speak up."

"This example of other-life must be kept in fit condition to talk. Reports have now come in from the Central Defense Nexus and elsewhere. We want to know how his ship slipped through the outsystem detection net, how it got past the orbital and atmospheric patrols. We want to know why the vessel differs in design and appearance from all known types, where it comes from, what gives it such tremendous velocity as well as the ability to decelerate almost instantaneously without its occupants suffering any ill effects. In particular and as quickly as possible, we must find out the capabilities and military potential of those who built the craft."

Kasine blinked at this recital. Each of these questions, he felt, was fully loaded and liable to go bang. The mind behind his ample features worked overtime. For all his gross bulk he was not without mental agility. Unlike some, he had not reached his present position by chance or through personal contact. In some ways his skills exceeded his waistline. And one thing he'd always been good at sniffing was the smell of danger.

As the anxious officer waited, words and phrases whirled through Kasine's calculating brain: slipped past, origin, type of ship, tremendous velocity, bumblebees, the coolest and most collected. His brilliant and sunken eyes examined Lawson again, noting the indifferent posture, the relaxed expression. In the light of the news the officer had brought he could now perceive more clearly the characteristic of this strange biped that inwardly had worried him most. It was a somewhat appalling certitude.

His mind continued to race. As he had told the alien, decisions were made in this room. Now was not the time for vacillation.

In the end he felt impelled to take a gamble. If it did not come off he had nothing serious to lose.

If it did he would get the credit for great perspicacity.

Very slowly, Kasine informed the officer, "I think I can answer those questions in part, though without adequate interrogation time not in any specific detail. This creature claims that he is a Solarian. I consider it remotely possible that he may be."

"May be! A Solarian!" The officer stuttered a bit, backed on all fours toward the door. "The Great Lord must know of this. I will tell him of your decision at once."

"It is not a decision," warned Kasine, hastily insuring himself against future wrath. "It is no more than a modest opinion. It must be borne in mind that normal procedures have been interrupted prematurely and that information gathering has been confined to a brief time-period. Given such limitations it is really impossible to render any kind of decision with finality."

"I will convey that information also," the officer assured him.

Kasine watched the other go out. Already he was beginning to wonder whether he had adopted the correct tactics or whether there was some other as-yet-unperceived but safer play. He had been hit hard and fast with a great deal of data impossible to analyze on the fly. Under such circumstances rendering any kind of assured conclusions was fraught with risk. Yet the Great Lord was famed for his abhorrence of equivocation, and he'd been compelled to take that into account.

Gradually his gaze turned back toward the subject of his thoughts.

Lawson said, very comfortingly, "You've just saved your fat neck."

iv

Markhamwit went through the reports for the fourth time and set the portable reader aside. Rising from the massive chair, he began to pace restlessly up and down the audience chamber.

"I don't like this incident. I don't care for it at all. I view it with the greatest suspicion. It's nebulous around the edges and you can't get a proper grip on it." He halted sharply. "I fear we may be victims of a Nilean trick. It would be just like them to try and distract us from truly serious matters with a clever sideshow like this. Much easier and cheaper to sit around devising diversions than to come to grips in honest battle."

"That is possible, my lord," endorsed First Minister Ganne.

Markhamwit turned pensive. "Let's suppose they've invented an entirely new type of vessel they've reason to think invincible, but questions remain about certain aspects of its performance that cannot be evaluated via simulation. The obvious next step is to test it as conclusively as can be done at minimal risk to themselves and to their current strategic position. They must try it out under severe conditions before the design can be adopted and manufactured in large numbers.

"The simple approach would be to equip it with appropriate weaponry and send it out to participate in combat. This would provide a useful, but not conclusive, test of its capabilities. To be certain of the design's success this approach would have to be utilized on multiple occasions. In addition to being time-consuming, it is not always easy to assess the results of such confrontations. Combat conditions make it difficult to draw accurate conclusions about equipment performance.

"But there is another way. If it can penetrate our innermost, most sophisticated, and elaborate defenses, namely those that safeguard the homeworld, land here and get out again without suffering incapacitating damage to itself or its crew, it qualifies as an indisputable success. They will have achieved all their aims quickly and at minimum risk to personnel and material. And they can do all this with one ship and a clever story taking the place of an entire squadron."

"Quite, my lord." Ganne had built his present status on a firm foundation of consistent agreement.

"But they can't be too obvious about it. For example, it would be a giveaway if it arrived with a Nilean crew aboard. Their intentions would be immediately manifest." Markhamwit's expression turned sour. "So they hunt around for and obtain the cooperation of a non-Nilean, unorthodox life-form as ally. He comes here hiding himself behind a myth." He smacked one pair of hands together, then the other pair, the concussive sounds echoing through the sparse but elegantly decorated chamber.

"All this is well within the limits of probability. Yet, as Kasine thinks, the arrival's story may be true."

"It was offered as a 'modest opinion' only, my lord. Kasine apparently was adamant on that point."

"Cautious as always," Markhamwit muttered. "Given the outlandish circumstances one cannot blame him for that."

Ganne did not respond. Nor did he offer any direct comments of his own on Kasine's opinion. Privately he doubted it but refrained from saying so. Now and again the million-to-one chance turned up, to the confusion of all who had brashly denied its possibility. Better to equivocate as positively as possible. Better still to say nothing at all.

"Get me Zigstrom," decided Markhamwit abruptly. Ganne withdrew a small cylinder from a pocket and murmured into it, softly but firmly. Very little time passed before the minister looked up and gestured appropriately.

The Great Lord fitted his own aural plug and accepted the cylinder from Ganne. "Zigstrom . . . never mind the platitudes now, listen to me . . . we have many self-proclaimed authorities on the Solarian Myth. While I have somewhat more important things on my mind these days I do occasionally take the time to sample extant developments in popular culture. In the course of such samplings I have heard it said there are one or two such specialists who believe this myth to have a real basis. Who is paramount among these?"

He listened a bit, then growled, "Don't hedge with me. I want his name. He has nothing to fear." A pause, followed by, "Alemph? Find him for me. I must have him here without delay."

Passing the communications cylinder back to Ganne, he grumbled to himself, "I really don't have time for childish distractions."

"No, my lord," the minister murmured.

"But unless this ship turns out to be a most remarkable

and unprecedented illusion or clever three-dimensional projection, and I'm not discounting such possibilities, there is something here that needs to be investigated. It should not take long to get to the bottom of things."

"I quite agree, my lord."

Markhamwit turned to gaze out the specially shielded window that wrapped around one entire curved end of the chamber. The city spread out below, teeming and alive. Except for moments of state when he allowed himself to be exposed to its adulation, its streets and byways must be forever closed to him.

The multitudes outside and their brethren elsewhere on the planet as well as on other worlds relied on him to keep them safe and properly looked-after. It was a daunting responsibility and he had no intention of shirking that duty, even if it meant having to take the time to personally investigate minor ploys of the Nileans. Behind him Ganne looked on in silent admiration. This he did out of love and respect for the Great Lord.

Also, there were concealed devices watching.

They put the minor matter out of their minds and proceeded with business vital to the smooth operation of the state and the conduct of the war. The required expert turned up in due course, sweaty with haste, disheveled and obviously ill at ease. Having been wrenched with little in the way of explanation from his daily routine and conveyed posthaste to the famous tower, his condition was understandable. He came hesitantly into the room, trying not to gawk at the surroundings, and sometimes forgetting to bow low at every second step.

The Great Lord looked up from his endless work and fastened his famous glower on the new arrival. "So you are Alemph?"

"My lord, if Zigstrom has given you the impression that I

am a leader of one of these foolish cults, I must assure you that . . ."

"Don't be so jittery," Markhamwit snapped. "I wish to pick your mind, not deprive you of your bowels." Rising and moving to an elaborately engraved chair fashioned from an especially lustrous material, he placed all four upper limbs on its slightly concave rests and fixed authoritative eyes upon the other. "I understand that you believe that the Solarian Myth is something more than a frontier legend. I want to know why."

The newcomer swallowed and looked involuntarily at Minister Ganne, who urged him on with a slight but reassuring gesture.

Alemph cleared his throat. "It is my contention, and that of several colleagues of like mind, that the story has repetitive aspects that are too much for mere coincidence. There are also other and later items I consider significant. As you can imagine, these are difficult to research, but there is an extensive literature relating to the subject that has been built up over a considerable period of time."

"I have no more than a perfunctory knowledge of the tale," Markhamwit informed him. "In my position I've neither the time nor inclination to study the folklore of our galaxy's outskirts. There are more pressing demands on my waking moments. Be more explicit. You say there is an extensive literature. Very well. I wish examples, not allegory. And try to relax. You have been brought here to talk, not to suffer."

Alemph plucked up courage. "There are many stories I could relate, sire, but awareness of the value of your time induces me to restrict myself to the most striking.

"At one edge of our galaxy are eight populated solar systems situated fairly close together and arranged in a rough semi-circle. This local gravitational grouping has a total of thirty-nine planets. At what would be the approximate center of their circle lies a ninth system. This one is quite remarkable in that it boasts a total of thirteen worlds, seven of which are inhabitable. However, all are devoid of any life higher than the Second Order animals."

"Being quite familiar with all pertinent galactic demographics, I am aware of that much," commented Markhamwit. "However, the knowledge sparks nothing of note in my memory. Go on."

Lowering his upper body, a tired Alemph assumed a more informal and comfortable four-footed stance and was not reprimanded. Thus encouraged, he continued.

"The eight populated systems have never developed space travel, even to the present day. Their respective technological accomplishments run the gamut from fortified keeps and towns to advanced electrical engineering, but none has yet to reach even their proximate moons. Yet when we first visited them we found they knew many things about each other impossible to learn by mere astronomical observation. When confronted with this seeming paradox they had a strange story to account for this knowledge.

"They said that at some unspecified time in the distant past they'd had repeated visits from the ships of the El-mones, a life-form occupying this ninth and now deserted system. All eight believe, and their respective legends contend, that the Elmones ultimately intended to master them by ruthless use of superior technology. Their distant ancestors were to be subdued and could do nothing effective to prevent it."

"But they weren't," Markhamwit observed.

"No, my lord. They weren't. It is at this point that the myth really begins. The inhabitants of all eight systems tell essentially the same story. That is an important thing to remember. That is what I call too much for coincidence."

"Get on with it," ordered the Great Lord, showing a

touch of impatience. "I'm quite capable of following your reasoning."

Continuing hurriedly, Alemph said, "Just at this time a strange vessel emerged from the mighty gulf between our galaxy and the next one and made its landing in the El-mones' system, the most highly developed in that area. It carried a crew of two small bipeds. They claimed the seem-ingly impossible feat of having crossed the gulf. They called themselves Solarians. There was only one piece of evidence to support their amazing claim: their vessel had so tremen-dous a turn of speed that while in motion it could neither be seen nor detected. Admittedly these Elmones could not have had access to the kind of advanced sensor technology we are familiar with today, but still . . ."

"Yes, yes. And then?"

"According to the inhabitants of the other eight sys-tems, the Elmones were by nature incurably brutal and am-bitious. They slaughtered the Solarians and pulled their ship to pieces in an effort to discover its secret. They failed absolutely. Many, many years later a second Solarian vessel plunged out of the enormous void. It came in search of the first and soon suffered the same fate. Again its secret re-mained inviolate."

"I can credit that much," said Markhamwit. "Alien techniques are elusive when one cannot even imagine the system of logic from which they've arisen. At such times pa-tience is of even greater value than perception and skill. Why, the Nileans have been trying . . ." He changed his mind about going on, snapped, "Continue with your story."

Alemph gestured readily. "It would seem from what oc-curred later that this second ship had borne some means of sending out a warning signal for, many years afterward, a third and far larger vessel appeared but made no landing. It merely circled each Elmone planet, broadcasting repeated messages saying that where death was concerned it is better to give than receive. Maybe it also bathed each world in an unknown beam, or momentarily embedded it in a force field such as we cannot conceive of, or dropped bacteria or viruses encoded with genetic variations. Nobody knows.

"By the time the vessel reached the third world in their system the alerted Elmones commenced attempts to bring it down or otherwise blast it out of the sky. For reasons that are not clear in the legends, but that can be imagined, they failed utterly. The ship vanished back into the dark chasm whence it came and to the present day the cause of what followed has remained a matter for speculation and the source of multiple but harmonious sagas on the eight other proximate systems."

"And what did follow?"

"Nothing immediate. The Elmones made a hundred crude jokes about the messages that, because of their periodic visitations, soon became known to the inhabitants of the other eight systems. Meanwhile the Elmones proceeded with preparations to enslave their neighbors.

"A year later the blow fell, or it would be better to say began to fall. It dawned upon them that their females were bearing no young, were indeed not even producing any eggs. Ten years later they were frantic. In fifty years they were numerically weak and utterly desperate. In one hundred fifty years they had disappeared forever from the scheme of things. The Solarians had killed nobody, injured nobody, shed not a single drop of blood. They had contented themselves with denying existence to the unborn. The Elmones had been eliminated with a ruthlessness equal to their own but without their brutality. They have gone. There are now no Elmones in our galaxy or anywhere in Creation.

"Meanwhile their seven planets remain, to all outward intents and purposes hospitable and inviting. Since our original contact with them the inhabitants of the eight other systems have learned to utilize space travel and gone voyaging and trading. But as one might imagine, nothing can persuade them to go anywhere near the worlds of the Elmones.''

The Great Lord was silent a moment, then snorted condescendingly. ''A redoubtable tale, ready-made for the numerous charlatans who have tried to exploit it. It would be difficult to invent a more convenient myth with which to threaten the recalcitrant and unbelieving.'' Markhamwit folded his primary hands. ''The credulous are always with us. On another hand, the majority of us are not easily taken in by tall tales of long ago. We require considerably more consequential proof. Is this all your evidence?''

''Begging your pardon, my lord,'' offered Alemph. ''There are the seven inhabitable but deserted worlds still in existence. Allowing for individual species and societal variations, there is precisely the same story told by the inhabitants of eight other systems who remained out of touch with and unaware of each other until we arrived. And, finally, there are these constant rumors that my modest but energetic organization has kept careful track of since we first were made aware of them.''

''What rumors?''

''Of small, biped-operated, and quite uncatchable ships occasionally visiting the smallest systems and loneliest planets within our sphere of exploration.''

''Bah!'' Markhamwit delivered himself of a forthright and urbane gesture of derision. ''We receive such a report or something similar every hundredth day. Despite the waste of time and energy involved our vessels repeatedly have investigated and found nothing. Formal scientific probing has generated absolutely nothing in the way of factual confirmation of any of these anecdotes.'' He shifted in his great chair.

"The lonely and isolated will concoct any fanciful incident likely to entice company, in the hope that they will benefit from the contact. The Nileans doubtless fabricate a few themselves, trying to draw our forces away from some other locality, hoping to isolate them to the point of vulnerability. Why, we blew apart their mothership *Narsan* when it went to Dhurg to look into a most elegant story we'd permitted to reach their stupid ears."

"Perhaps so, my lord." Having gone so far under a declared umbrella of immunity, Alemph was not to be put off. "But permit me to point out that well as we may know a great deal of our own galaxy, we know nothing of others. That they are composed of similar forms of matter, of stars and gas clouds and measurable energy, this much we can determine. Unimaginable distance renders anything less massive than stellar phenomena invisible to us."

Markhamwit considered, then eyed Minister Ganne. That worthy straightened self-consciously under the omnipotent stare. "Do you consider it possible for an intergalactic chasm to be crossed?"

"It seems incredible, my lord." Ganne was more than anxious not to commit himself. "Even were it possible to overcome the physical constraints, the sheer amount of time involved would seem to preclude any degree of practicality. Not being an astronautical expert I am hardly qualified to give an opinion."

"A characteristic ministerial evasion," scoffed Markhamwit. Resorting to his earpiece and voice transmitter again, he asked for Sector Commander Yielm. As soon as that worthy was put through he demanded, "Regardless of the practical aspect, do you think it theoretically possible for anyone to reach us from the next galaxy?" Silence while he listened, then, "Why not?" Another pause, subsequent to which he flicked off the transmitter and turned back to the others.

"That's his reason: Nobody lives for ten thousand years."

Alemph was respectful as ever. "How does he know, my lord?"

Half a dozen guards conducted James Lawson to the august presence. Uniforms immaculate, marching without strain in a bipedal stance while clutching a different weapon in each pair of hands, they drew stares from preoccupied officials and visiting administrators as they strode the length of the antechamber. The quantity of highly trained force involved seemed excessive for one small alien.

Reaching the end of the long, polished walk they positioned him carefully in the traditional spot and then formed themselves into a stiff, expressionless row outside the towering double doorway. Time passed.

Eventually the subofficer in charge relaxed long enough to whisper to the prisoner. "You are to go in." He indicated the doors.

Lawson nodded. "Why didn't you say so?"

"It is obvious," the subofficer informed him brusquely.

"Nothing is obvious," Lawson replied. "Everything requires consideration. For example, the section of floor on which you are presently standing is blue while the one just in front of you is green. Why should you be standing on blue instead of green?"

"Because it is . . ." The subofficer broke off, his heavy brows twisting, his entire expression clearly reflective of the fact that this particular notion had never occurred to him before. Glancing down at the polished surface beneath his feet, he started to take a short step forward, hesitated. His fellow guards were watching him closely out of the corners of their eyes.

Leaving him with both thoughts and feet slightly twisted, Lawson gave a gentle push on one huge door. It retracted with admirable ease and he stepped inside.

His approach from the entrance to the middle of the room, a respectable hike, was slow and easy, his attitude markedly relaxed. Nothing in his manner betrayed the slightest consciousness that he was very far from home and among a strange kind. Indeed, he mooched in casually, as if sent on a minor errand to buy a kilo of crackers.

Indicating another of the too-large chairs, Markhamwit spent most of a minute sizing up the visitor. Suitably unimpressed and not trying to conceal it, he proceeded to voice his skepticism.

"So you are a Solarian?"

"I am."

"You come from another galaxy?"

"That is correct."

Markhamwit shot a now-watch-this glance at Minister Ganne before he asked, "Granted the truth of both statements, which I do not, is it not remarkable that you can speak our language?"

"Not when you consider that I was chosen for that very reason." It was manifestly evident that Lawson was not in the least intimidated by his surroundings.

"Chosen? By whom?"

"By the Combine, of course."

"For what purpose?" Markhamwit demanded to know.

"To come here and have a talk with you."

"About what?"

"This war you're having with the Nileans."

"I knew it!" Entwining his primary arms, the Great Lord looked satisfied. "I knew the Nileans would come into this somewhere." His chuckle was harsh. "They are amateurish in their schemings, but what can one expect of such an unimaginative species? The least they could have done for you was think up a protective device better than a mere myth. As armor it strikes me as appallingly inadequate."

"I am little interested in protective devices," said Lawson carelessly. "Theirs or yours."

Markhamwit's face slid into his kind's equivalent of a frown. "Why not?"

"I am a Solarian."

"Is that so?" He showed his teeth: thin, white, and pointed in front. Though omnivores, his people had a tendency to prefer the denser varieties of protein. "In that case our war with Nilea is none of your business."

"Agreed. We view it with splendid indifference."

An unsettling feeling that he was overlooking something significant nagged at the Great Lord. "Then why come to talk about it?"

"Because we object to one of its consequences."

"To which one do you refer?" In truth Markhamwit was no more than mildly curious.

"Both sides are roaming the interstellar reaches in armed vessels and looking for trouble."

"What of it?"

Lawson spoke carefully to insure that he was perfectly understood. "The void between worlds is free. It belongs to everyone and anyone with a desire to explore, trade, share cultural peculiarities, or simply wander about in search of nothing in particular. Space is vast, but finite. Within that vastness small, artificial objects like ships are easily distinguished. They should not be interfered with. No matter what proprietary rights a species may claim for a planet or system, the void between stars is common property, if one accepts the definition of near-vacuum as a form of property. It belongs to Life itself, not to this or that particular life-form just because it happens to have a bigger stick or more advanced technology than its neighbor. Where the void is concerned, existence confers equality."

"Who says so?" demanded Markhamwit, scowling.

"We say so."

"Really?" Amazed and amused by the sheer impudence of it, the Great Lord invited a further display by asking, "And what makes Solarians think they can lay down the law?"

"We have only one reason." Lawson's gaze took on a certain rarefied coldness. "We have the power to enforce it."

The other rocked back, glanced at Minister Ganne, found that worthy studiously examining the ceiling.

"You're very assured," Markhamwit commented evenly.

"We have reason to be."

"And I suppose that you have codified this little principle you have so helpfully compounded for the sake of others?"

"I'll keep it as simple and straightforward as possible so that anyone can understand it," Lawson replied readily. "The law we have established and intend to maintain is that every space-traversing vessel shall have the right of unobstructed passage between worlds, regardless of species or world of origin, regardless of philosophical or theological bent, regardless of any other alliances or partnerships it may have otherwise established.

"What happens once it enters the outer atmosphere of any planet does not concern us unless it happens to be one of our own." He paused a moment, glacial-eyed, and added, "Then it does concern us very much."

Markhamwit did not like that. He didn't like it one little bit. It smacked of an open threat and his natural instinct was to react with a counter-threat. But the interview with Alemph was still fresh in his mind and he could not rid his thoughts of certain phrases that kept running around and around like a dire warning.

"Fifty years later they were weak and desperate. In a hundred fifty years they were gone . . . forever!"

He found himself wondering against his will whether even now the ship in which this singular biped had arrived was ready to broadcast or radiate an invisible, unshieldable power designed to bring about the same result. It was a horrid thought. As a method of coping with incurably antagonistic life-forms it was so perfect because so permanent. It smacked of the appalling technique of Nature herself, who never hesitates to exterminate a biological error. There was a finality to it that took hold of one's thoughts and would not let go.

That was the beauty of it, of course. As a new type of threat he had no ready parry for it. Perhaps the Nileans deserved more credit than he had given them.

Contrariwise, one tended to think that this biped was talking out of the back of his neck. The tendency was born of hope that it was nothing but a tremendous bluff waiting to be called. One could call it all too easily by removing the bluffer's head and tearing his ship apart.

As the Elmones were said to have done.

What Elmones? There were none!

Suppose that it was not bluff?

Much as he hated to admit it even to himself, a situation he had expected to require no more than a few moments of his time was shaping up into a tough one. If in fact it was a cunning Nilean subterfuge it was becoming good enough to prove mighty awkward. It was astonishing what could be accomplished with incredible gall and a clever line of patter. If nothing else, the perpetrators had succeeded not only in tying up his invaluable attention but in actually worrying him. He conceded the fact with great reluctance.

Consider what was known: a ship had been dumped on this world, the governmental center of a powerful system at war. On the strength of an ancient fable and its pilot's glib tongue it claimed the ability to sterilize the entire planet. Therefore it was, in effect, either a mock-bomb or a real one. The only way to ascertain its true nature was to hammer on its detonator and try to make it explode.

Could he dare?

Playing for time, Markhamwit pointed out, "War is a two-sided affair. Our warships are not the only ones patrolling in space."

"We know it," Lawson avowed. "Did you think we believed you were fighting with yourselves? The Nileans are also being dealt with."

Markhamwit sat up straighter. "What do you mean they're being 'dealt with'?"

"I mean that the same common sense I'm trying without much luck to pass along to you is simultaneously being conveyed to your erstwhile foes."

"So you've another ship there?"

"Yes." Lawson registered a faint grin. "The Nileans are stuck with the same problem, and doubtless are handicapped in their reactions by the dark suspicion that it's another of your tricks."

The Great Lord perked up. It gave him malicious satisfaction to think of the enemy in a jam and cursing him for it. Then his mind suddenly perceived a way of at least partially checking the truth of the other's statements. Keeping his eyes on the biped to check its reaction, he turned to Ganne.

"That neutral world of Vaile still has contact with both sides. Are their communications facilities considered up to the current norm?"

"I believe so, my lord, though it would require a moment to ascertain that fact for certain."

"Go beam it a query. Explain that we have a formal diplomatic request that will in no way compromise their neutrality. As a favor to us, have them ask if the Nileans are presently dealing with the crew of a vessel claiming to be of Solarian origin."

"Immediately, my lord." Ganne went out. Despite the speed at which subspace communications traveled, a reply could not be expected before nightfall. It would take time for the Vaileans to receive the query, ponder the request, compose the requested communication, shift it to Nilea, and wait for a response.

Yet the minister was back in a few moments.

Shaken and nervous, he reported, "Communications Central says that a message was received from Vaile a short time ago. A similar question has been put to us at the request of the Nileans."

"Hah!" Despite a natural reluctance, Markhamwit found himself being unwillingly pushed toward Alemph's way of looking at the matter. Folklore, he decided, might possibly be founded on fact. Indeed, it was more likely to have a positive basis than not. Long-term effects had to have faraway causes. Were there not ample examples within his own culture of tales dismissed as legend, only to be resurrected as truth by industrious archaeologists and historians? How many times had diligence and a refusal to be swayed from one's beliefs turned fancy into fact?

Then, just as he was nearing the conclusion that Solarians actually did exist, it struck him with awful force that if this was a crafty stunt pulled by the Nileans they could be depended upon to back up their stooge in every foreseeable manner. This meant they would have done their best to anticipate every possible, reasonable reaction on the part of their foe. The call through Vaile that had just come in could be nothing more than a carefully planned byplay designed to lend verisimilitude to their deception. If that was the case, it meant that he was correct in his initial assumption: the Solarian Myth was rubbish.

These two violently opposed aspects of the matter had him in a quandary. His irritation mounted because one used to making swift and final decisions cannot bear to squat on the horns of a dilemma. And he was so squatting.

With a gesture he could shift the spatial position of dozens of warships and thousands of highly trained fighters. A few words from his lips could cause the populations of entire continents to tremble or cheer. With an expression, he could alter the destinies of powerful individuals of many species. All this he accomplished with skill, intelligence, and great cunning.

Now he was being asked to take extraordinary action based solely on the veracity of a fable. It was an incredible situation.

Obviously riled, he growled at Lawson, "The right to unobstructed passage covers our vessels as much as anyone else's."

"It covers no warship bearing instructions to track, intercept, question, search, or detain any other craft it considers suspicious," declared the alien. "Violators of the law are not entitled to claim protection of the law."

"Can you tell me how to conduct a war between systems without sending armed ships through space?" asked Markhamwit, bitterly sarcastic.

Lawson waved an indifferent hand. "We aren't the least bit interested in that problem. It is your own worry."

"It cannot be done!" Markhamwit shouted.

"That's most unfortunate." Lawson was a font of false sympathy. "It creates an awful state of no-war."

"Are you trying to be funny?"

"Is peace funny?"

"War is a serious matter," bawled Markhamwit, striving to retain a grip on his temper. He would not let this absurd conversation get the better of him. "It cannot be ended with a mere flick of the finger."

"That fact should be borne in mind by those who so

nonchalantly start them." Lawson was quite unmoved by the Great Lord's ire.

"The Nileans started it."

"They say that you did."

"They are incorrigible liars."

"That's their opinion of you, too."

A menacing expression on his face, Markhamwit snarled softly, "Do you believe them?"

"We never believe opinions."

"You are evading the question." Markhamwit felt much more comfortable with this line of inquiry. He was used to driving home a point with all the force and energy of a spear thrust. His persistence was razor-sharp and few could wiggle free of it. He was determined that this devious alien would not be among the exceptions.

"I am not asking you to confirm an opinion, only to render one," he continued relentlessly. "Somebody has to be a liar. Who do you think it is?" Fully alert, he awaited a reply.

The biped considered. "We haven't looked into the root causes of your dispute. It is not our woe. So without any data to go upon we can only hazard a guess."

"Go ahead and do some hazarding, then," Markhamwit invited. He licked expectant lips.

Undeterred by the other's attitude, Lawson complied. "Probably both sides have little regard for the truth. It is the usual setup. When war breaks out the unmitigated liar comes into his own. His heyday lasts for the duration. After that, the victorious liars hang the vanquished ones."

Had this viewpoint been one-sided Markhamwit could have taken it up with suitable fury. A two-sided opinion is disconcerting. It's slippery. One cannot get an effective grip on it.

Having failed to receive a response he could deal with in traditional terms, he changed his angle of attack. "Let's suppose I reject your law or principle or whatever it is and have you shot forthwith. A less elegant solution than continued philosophical discourse, perhaps, but gratifyingly conclusive. What happens then?"

"You'll be sorry."

"I have only your word for that."

"If you want proof you know how to get it," Lawson pointed out.

It was an impasse over which the Great Lord brooded with the maximum of disgust. He was realizing for the first time that by great daring and an apparent disregard for personal consequences, one creature could defy a world of others. A threat backed up by weapons was easy to deal with. You countered with weapons of your own.

But a threat backed up only by another threat, which in turn was backed up by still another, could only be countered with threats of one's own. It became a battle of words, in which thousands of heavy weapons and highly trained soldiers were rendered extraneous. It was pregnant with possibilities of which he had never previously thought. Some ingenious use could have been made of it, to the great discomfort of the enemy . . . assuming that the enemy had not thought of it first and was now using it against him.

There was the real crux of the matter, he decided. Somehow, anyhow, he had to find out whether the Nileans or one of their allies had a hand in this affair. If they had, they would make every effort to conceal the fact. If they had not, they would be only too willing to show him that his troubles were also theirs.

But then again, how deep was their cunning? How well had they thought this out, how many possibilities and reactions had they considered and prepared for? Was it more than equal to his own perceptive abilities? Despite the endless reams of propaganda, despite all the insults and name-calling he knew that they respected his skills. They would never precipitate a ploy of such deviousness if it required underestimating his competence.

How long had they prepared for this? As to any request for proof, might they not be ready and willing to hide the truth behind a smoke screen of pathetically eager cooperation?

If this new ship actually was a secret Nilean production or even a clever technical illusion of some kind, it followed that those who could construct one could equally well construct two. Also the unknown alien world that had provided a biped stooge plus some winged, stinging creatures could as easily provide a second set of pseudo-Solarians.

Even now another fake extra-galactic vessel and crew might be conveniently grounded on Nilean territory, awaiting the inspection of his own or some mutually agreed-upon neutral deputation; everything intricately staged and orchestrated to convince him that fiction was fact and thereby persuade him to recall all warships from their patrol assignments.

Even if all vessels so recalled were maintained on active standby, that would leave the foe a clear field for long enough to enable them to grasp the final victory that had eluded both sides for so long. He and his kind would know that they had been taken for a ride only when it was too late. Almost the sole crumb of comfort he could find was the thought that if this was not an impudent hoax of colossal proportions, if all this mystic Solarianism was genuine and true, then the Nileans themselves were being tormented by exactly the same processes of reasoning.

At this very moment they might be viewing with serious misgivings the very outfit that was causing all this bother, wondering whether or not the alien ship and crew they were dealing with were supporting evidence born of the Great Lord's limitless foresight.

This picture of the Nileans' predicament served to

soothe his liver sufficiently to let him ask, "In what way do you expect me to acknowledge this law of yours?"

Lawson said, "By ordering the immediate return of all armed vessels to their homeworlds, orbital docking stations, satellite staging areas, or other bases."

"They'll be a fat lot of use to us just sitting on their home stations."

"I don't agree. They will still be in fighting trim and ready to oppose any attack. We deny nobody the right to defend themselves."

"That's exactly what we're doing right now," declared Markhamwit. "Defending ourselves."

"The Nileans say the same."

"I was given to understand that you were fluent in our language. Did you not just hear me tell you that they are determined and persistent liars?"

"I know, I know." Lawson brushed it aside like a subject already worn thin. "Since for the sake of convenience we'll also make the assumption that *you* are fluent in your own tongue, I will spell it out one more time in terms not even a professional administrator could confuse.

"So far as we are concerned you can smother every one of your own worlds under an immense load of warships ready to annihilate the first attacker that pokes a hostile nose or other applicable organ into your system. But if these vessels fight at all it must be in defense of their own territory. They must not roam around wherever they please and carry the war someplace else."

"But . . . , "

"Moreover," Lawson went on, "you can have a million ships meandering freely through space if you wish. Their numbers, routes, or destinations will be nobody's business, not even ours. We won't object so long as each and every one of them is a peaceful trader or explorer going about its lawful business and in no way interfering with other people's ships."

"You won't object?" Again Markhamwit found his temper sorely tried by the other's airy self-confidence. "That is most gracious of you!"

From his seat in the oversized chair Lawson eyed him coolly. "The strong can afford to be gracious. We consider it among the highest of obligations."

"Are you insinuating that we are not strong?"

"Reasonableness is strength. Irrationality is weakness."

"Are we now to have argument by aphorism?"

"Many words seem to have no effect on you. Instead of lengthy detail, perhaps still greater simplicity is in order."

Banging a fist on a gleaming chair arm Markhamwit declaimed, "There are many things I may be, but there is one thing I am not: I am not irrational."

"It remains to be seen," murmured Lawson significantly.

"And it will be seen! I have not become the ruler of a great system by virtue of accident. I did not achieve my present exalted status through fortuitous timing and sheer good luck. My people do not serve under a leader whose sole qualification is imbecility. Nor am I credulous. Given time for thought and introspection plus the loyal support of those beneath me, I can cope with this situation or any other that may come along."

"I hope so," offered Lawson in pious tones. "For your own sake."

Markhamwit leaned forward, exposed his teeth once more, and spoke slowly. "No matter what decision I may come to or what consequences may follow, the skin presently in danger is not mine. It is yours!" He straightened up, made a motion of dismissal. Ganne immediately snapped to attention. "I will give my answer in the morning.

Until then, I suggest you do plenty of worrying about your-self.''

Rising, Lawson turned and sauntered unhurriedly toward the immense doorway. Both the Great Lord and the First Minister followed him with their eyes.

At the portal he turned to look back. ''A Solarian deeply concerned about his own fate would be rather like one of your hairs bothered about falling out.'' He stared hard at the Great Lord. ''The hair goes and is lost and becomes one with the dust, but the body remains.''

''Meaning . . . ?'' snapped Markhamwit. He was sick and tired of these pithy alien axioms, convinced he'd wasted too much time on the matter already.

''You're not dealing with me as an individual,'' Lawson explained. ''You are dealing with my kind.''

V

―――――――――――――――■―――――――――――――――

A lert and waiting, the impressive escort accompanied Lawson to the interrogation center and left him at the precise spot where they had first picked him up. Going through the barrier, he closed it behind him, thus shutting himself off from their view. In a leisurely manner he ambled past desks and large workstations where examiners and processors looked up from their assignments to watch him uncertainly. He had reached the main exit before anyone saw fit to dispute his progress.

An incoming three-comet officer barred his way. "Where are you going?"

Lawson smiled pleasantly. "Back to my ship."

The other showed vague surprise. "You have seen the Great Lord?"

"Of course. I have only now just left him." With a confiding air he added, "We had a most interesting conversation. A great many matters of vital importance were discussed in an atmosphere of freedom and mutual respect. Unfortunately, nothing was resolved and so the discourse will have to be continued. He wishes to consult with me again first thing in the morning.''

"Does he?'' The officer's eyes hugely magnified Lawson's importance. It did not take him more than a split second to conceive a simple piece of logic: to look after Markhamwit's guest would be to please Markhamwit himself. So with praiseworthy opportunism he said, ''I will get a vehicle and run you back.''

"That is very considerate of you.'' Lawson looked at the three comets as if they were six.

It lent zip to the other's eagerness. While he moved off and spoke into a voice cylinder, other officers, common troopers, and administrative personnel came and went through the entrance. Only a few bothered to glance longer than a second in the biped's direction. Strange life-forms were a frequent presence in the tower and nothing to lose worktime over.

The aircar was forthcoming in double-quick time, sped away before Dilmur or Kasine or anyone else could intervene to question the propriety of letting the biped run loose. The vehicle's speed was high, its driver inclined to be garrulous. Lawson relaxed in contemplation of the urban environs and shortly thereafter, the somewhat desolate countryside. Why otherwise apparently sentient beings should choose to pack themselves into such ponderous concentrations as cities was a continuing mystery to him. It could not be pleasant.

"The Great Lord is a most exceptional person,'' the driver was saying, hoping it might be repeated in his favor on the morrow. Privately he thought Markhamwit a pompous stinker. "He is famed as much for his discerning intellect as for his administrative abilities. We are most fortunate to have such a leader in these trying times.''

"You could have one worse,'' agreed Lawson, blandly damning Markhamwit with faint praise.

"He is a most exceptional personage," the officer continued obsequiously. "A unique personality."

"I won't argue with you on that one."

"I remember once . . ." The other broke off and brought the vehicle to an abrupt stop, scowling toward the side of the guideway while the powerful engine hummed softly. In a rasping voice he demanded of the new object of his attention, "Who gave you orders to stand there?"

"Nobody," admitted Yadiz dolefully.

"Then why are you there?"

"He cannot be somewhere else," remarked Lawson.

Clearly, the officer had not expected that the alien might choose to comment on the matter of a common trooper's current disposition. He blinked, studied the view forward for a while, then twisted to face his passenger.

"Why can't he?"

"Because wherever he happens to be *is* there. Obviously he cannot be where he isn't." Lawson smiled pleasantly and sought confirmation from Yadiz. "Can you?"

Something snapped, for the officer promptly abandoned all further discussion, activated the aircar's door, and snarled at the soldier. "Get inside, you gaping idiot!"

Yadiz got in, handling his weapon as if it could bite him with both ends. The driver manipulated controls and the door closed with a soft hiss, whereupon they accelerated forward. For the remainder of the trip the officer hunched over the controls, chewed steadily at his thick bottom lip, and said not a word. Now and again his eyebrows knotted with the strain of thought as he made vain attempts to sort out the unsortable.

At the now heavily patrolled perimeter that had been set up a goodly distance from the tiny alien ship, the paunchy individual who had first consigned the arrival to the interrogation center watched the aircar ease to a stop and settle to the ground. Frowning, he came over to confront the occupants as they emerged.

"So they have let it go?"

"Yes," said the driver, knowing no better.

"Whom did it see?"

"The Great Lord himself."

The other gave a little jump, viewed Lawson with embarrassed respect, and took some of the authority out of his tones.

"They didn't say what is to be done about these four casualties we've suffered?"

"Made no mention of them," the driver replied. "Maybe they should be moved."

"We can't do that without authority. Until then local treatment will have to suffice, although I can't say as how our team medics are having any luck."

Lawson chipped in, "I'll tend to them. Where are they?"

"Over there." The portly officer gestured toward a protected dip in the rocks. "As I said, we couldn't shift them pending instructions."

"It wouldn't have mattered. They'd have recovered by this time tomorrow anyway."

The officer looked relieved. "It isn't fatal, then?"

"Not at all." Lawson was most reassuring. "I'll go get them a shot of stuff that will bring them to life in two ticks."

He went toward the ship. The driver climbed moodily into his vehicle and headed back toward the sprawling metropolis. On the way back, his forehead would occasionally twist and furrow as he tried and failed to shake free of a persistent mental itch.

The creature perched on the rim of the little control room's single small observation port was the size of Lawson's fist. Long extinct Terran bees would have thought it a mutant giant among their kind, though the relationship was more visual than biological. Modern Callisians might have regarded their ancient Terran counterparts as backward pygmies had there been any real consciousness of Callisianism or Terranism or any other form of planetary parochialism.

The Callisians somewhat resembled Terran hymenoptera in shape, general coloration, and their ability to deliver a potent sting. Internally they were very different. Convergent evolution, some might have called it. Lawson preferred the more pungent term "depraved," which the Callisians accepted with good humor. They had their own piquant descriptions for endoskeletal, soft-bodied, ground-bound bipeds.

At this far-advanced stage in the development of an entire local grouping of worlds, there had ceased to be an acute awareness of worldly origin, shape, or species. A once essential datum in the environment had been discarded and no longer entered into the computations of anyone. The biped was not mentally biased by his own bipedal form; the insect not obsessed by its insectile condition. They knew themselves for what they were; namely, Solarians, and two aspects of one colossal entity that had a thousand other facets elsewhere.

Indeed, the close-knit relationship between life-forms far apart in shape and size but sharing a titanic oneness of psyche had developed to the point where they could and did hold mental intercourse in a manner not truly telepathic. It was "self-thinking," the natural communion between parts of an enormous whole.

So Lawson had no difficulty in conversing with a creature that had no aural sense adequately attuned to the range of his voice, no tongue with which to speak. The communication came easier than any vocal method, was clear and accurate, left no room for linguistic or semantic booby traps, no need to explain the meaning of meaning. It proceeded with the clarity of truth and the utter absence of deception, hesitancy, or uncertainty. The Solarians would have found none of this in any way especially remarkable. If you didn't think, you didn't have anything to say, and anything you thought could not be misconstrued.

He flopped into the pilot's seat, gazed meditatively through the narrow port, and opined, "I'm not sanguine about their being reasonable."

"It does not matter," commented the other. "The end will be the same."

"True, Buzwuz, but unreasonableness means time and trouble. There are other matters of importance that need attending to, other kinds of life to be lived."

"Too much conscientiousness is bad for the circulation. Time is endless; trouble another name for fun," declared Buzwuz, being profound. He employed his hind legs to clean the rear part of his velvet jacket.

Lawson said nothing. His attention shifted to a curiously three-dimensional image invisibly fastened to the nearest wall. It depicted four bipeds, one of whom was a swart dwarf; also one dog wearing sunglasses, six huge bee-things, a hawklike ornithorp with grasping digits positioned halfway along each wing, a tusked monster vaguely resembling a prick-eared elephant, something else like a land crab with long-fingered hands in lieu of claws, three peculiarly shapeless entities whose natural radioactivity had fogged part of the sensitive image, and finally a spiderlike creature jauntily adorned in silken booties, shimmering vest, and feathered hat.

This characteristically Solarian bunch were facing the image recorder in the stiff, formal attitudes favored by a bygone age, and so obviously were waiting for the birdie that they were unconsciously comical. He treasured this scene for its element of whimsy; also because there was immense significance in the amusing similarity of pose among creatures so manifestly unconscious of their differences. It was a picture of unity that is strength; unity born of a handful of suns and worlds and a double-handful of planets circling a common gravitational core.

The image was full of old friends, companions, colleagues who were much more than that. When a Solarian said that a friend was part of him, it was not a metaphor but a statement of fact. The depth of this was something non-Solarians had considerable difficulty comprehending. Another pseudo-bee-mind as insidious as part of his own came from somewhere outside the ship. "Want us back yet?"

"No hurry."

"We're zooming around far beyond the city," the thought went on. "Not the venue I'd choose for sightseeing, but we didn't choose this world. It chose us. The city itself is the usual predictable, boring exposition of technological prowess. The sheer size of the population is depressing, but there are a very few interesting parks filled with plants obviously long exterminated from this vicinity."

"I'm glad you're not totally bored," Lawson thought. "It's nice just to be outside. Satisfaction can be found anywhere one is willing to look." Lawson shifted in the comfortable seat. "How are the locals reacting to your recreational sortie?"

"We've shown ourselves within reach of a few of them. They swiped at us without hesitation. And they meant it!" A pause, followed by, "They have instinctive fear of the unfamiliar. It accords with their social conditions as well as their current political situation. On a group basis it might be different, but I doubt it. Reaction time about one-tenth. Choice of reaction: that which is swiftest rather than that which is most effective. They're physically powerful and reasonably agile given their bulk and design, but not quick.

"Visual acuity is good . . . for a mammalian-based physiology. Hearing less so, decreasing substantially with modest distance. You have to make considerable noise to attract their attention if they're not looking directly at you."

"I've been having similar problems," Lawson confessed.

"Grade eight mentalities lacking unity other than that imposed upon them from above. It's sad."

"I know." Lawson squirmed out of his seat as instruments conveyed the sounds of heavy hammering on the ship's shell somewhere near the single airlock. "Don't go too far away, though. You may have to come back in a rush."

Making his way back through the ship, which given its modest size did not take very long, he cycled the portal and moved to the rim. Not quite level with the ground, he found himself looking down at a five-comet officer. The caller had an air of irateness tempered by apprehension. The fingers of his middle hands rubbed nervously against one another, as if they'd much rather be wrapped around the hafts of the two sidearms conspicuously holstered at his upper waist.

His eyes kept surveying the area above Lawson's head or straining to see past the biped's legs lest something else spring out to the attack. As soon as the lock had opened he had retreated several paces.

"You're not supposed to be here," he informed the alien.

Lawson affected some bemusement. "Aren't I? Why not?"

"Nobody gave you permission to return."

"I don't need permission," Lawson told him.

"You cannot come back without it." The officer was adamant.

Registering an expression of mock bafflement, Lawson said, "Then how the deuce did I get here?"

"I don't know. Someone blundered. That's his worry and not mine."

"Well, what *are* you worrying about?" Lawson invited.

"It's plain that something's worrying you. Your expression's a dead giveaway."

The officer's face twisted. He finally concluded warily, "I've just had a message from the city ordering me to check on whether you are actually here because, if so, you shouldn't be. You ought to be at the interrogation center."

"I've been to the interrogation center. They had me for a while and I answered their questions and now I'm back here."

"You should be there," the officer insisted.

"Doing what?"

"Awaiting their final decisions."

"But they aren't going to make any." Lawson spoke with devastating positiveness. "It is we who will make the final ones."

The officer didn't like the sound of that. He considered retiring to report the gist of his conversation with the alien to higher authorities, then decided that could be done later. He scowled, watched the sky, and kept a wary eye on what little he could see of the ship's shadowy interior.

"I've been instructed that if you were found here, I should send you back to the city at once."

"By whom?"

"Military headquarters."

"Not another one of *those.*" Lawson sighed heavily, as if he'd just been presented with the offer of an utterly tasteless meal. "Tell them I'm not going before morning."

Sensing forthcoming awkwardness, the officer took another precautionary step backward. The four troopers who had been laid out by the brightly colored flying creatures had fully recovered thanks to the biped's efficient ministrations, but that didn't mean the officer desired to replicate their experience. Fatal it might not have been, but according to the troopers it had been something other than enjoyable.

"You've got to go now," he insisted.

"All right," replied the biped agreeably. "Invite your superiors at headquarters to come and fetch me. I'll wait for them."

"They can't do that."

"I'll say they can't!" agreed Lawson, with hearty emphasis.

This was even less to the visitor's taste. He found himself in the uncomfortable position of having to threaten a being who had already treated threats as so much irksome babbling on the part of unruly infants. His fingers hungered for the solidity inherent in his twin sidearms.

"If you won't go voluntarily, you'll have to be taken by force."

"Try it."

"My troops will receive orders to attack."

"That's all right with me. You go shoo them along. Orders are orders, aren't they?"

"Yes, but . . ."

"And," Lawson continued firmly, "it's the order-givers and not the order-carry-outers who'll get the blame, isn't it?"

"The blame for what?" inquired the officer, very leerily.

"You'll find out!"

The other stewed a bit. What would be found out, he decided, was anyone's guess, but his own estimate was that it could well be something mighty unpleasant. The biped's attitude amounted to a guarantee of that much.

Thus far his team had suffered no permanent casualties. The alien's reaction had been almost as convivial as coercive. Though the biped had declined to comply with orders, the requisite message had been delivered and accepted. Beyond that the officer's latitude of action was limited. How much initiative was he expected to show? How far was he supposed to go to force compliance? Not only had the biped refused to be forced, it had implied that attempts to do so would be met with something rather more vehement than a temporarily paralyzing sting to the neck.

His troopers and subofficers looked to him to make decisions that would not jeopardize their lives. That was something his superiors back at headquarters tended to overlook. They had only reports to peruse. It was very different when you were crouched under cover close to a totally alien vessel trying to avoid the attentions of incredibly fast-moving little flying creatures equipped with immobilizing hypodermics in their tails.

There was such a thing as mental as well as physical initiative.

"I think I'll get in touch again, communicate the gist of our conversation, tell them you refuse to leave this vessel and ask for further instructions." It sounded rather lame even to his ears.

"That's the boy," endorsed Lawson, showing hearty approval. "You look after yourself and yourself will look after you." He stepped back inside and the lock closed noiselessly behind him.

The officer pondered the shiny, oddly depthless surface of the alien ship for a long moment before turning away to file his report.

vi

———————————————•———————————————

The Great Lord Markhamwit paced up and down the
room in the restless manner of one burdened by an
unsolvable problem. Every now and again he made a vicious
slap at his intricately tooled and embossed harness, a sure
sign that he was considerably exercised in mind and that his
liver was feeling the strain.

It was an intolerable situation. He felt like a traveler
trapped in the center of a bridge both ends of which had
washed out. This unaccustomed mental condition had kept
him up most of the night, and as a consequence he was in a
foul mood. Those around him sensed his frustration, with
the result that even his most trusted advisors were taking
pains to avoid him.

First Minister Ganne was not allowed that option. Designated to serve as the primary interface between the Great
Lord and the rest of an anxious civilization, he could not
call in sick or beg off his duties for personal reasons. He was
expected to be at Markhamwit's side at all times, as ready
and alert as a finely tuned instrument. This responsibility he

bore with great skill and discipline. It gave him great power but also put him at constant risk. Despite the rewards it was not a post eagerly sought after. The Great Lord was notorious for his outbursts, the adverse repercussions of which tended to rain down most heavily on those closest to him at the time. Ganne handled these flare-ups with a smooth professionalism that was the envy of the less assured. Presently he stood passively off to one side, composed and poised, seemingly half asleep but in reality utterly alert as he waited for whatever might come.

Eventually Markhamwit ceased his contemplative pacing and turned a bilious gaze on his most trusted advisor. "Well," he snapped at him, "have *you* been able to devise a satisfactory way out?"

"I assume you are referring to the riddle posed by this self-proclaimed Solarian, my lord?"

The Great Lord's expression turned sour. "No, Ganne. I was thinking of what the dominant grain should be during the autumnal planting. If you were as sagacious as you are adept at playing for time we should have been done with this and a dozen related matters in half the time-period."

"I regret to say, my lord, that intensive contemplation has generated no helpful insights," the First Minister admitted ruefully.

"Doubtless you retired on a hearty meal and enjoyed a good night's sleep without giving it another thought."

"Indeed, no, I . . ."

"Never mind the lies. I am well aware that everything is left to me. Well then, let it be so. I expected nothing less when I reached this position. It would be agreeable to have some intelligent assistance, but if not then I will rely, as I have always had to do in the end, on my own expertise."

Ganne offered no comment. Leaping to one's own defense under such circumstances would have been grossly counterproductive. When the Great Lord was in such moods even ready agreement could be ruinously misconstrued.

Protracted silence might not be especially helpful, but neither could it put one in more trouble than already existed. If nothing else, Ganne had confidence in the knowledge that the crisis was not of his making; therefore he saw no way he could be faulted for it. In his infinite capacity for discernment, the Great Lord would find someone else to blame.

Going to his desk, Markhamwit employed an earpiece and speaking tube. "Has the biped started out yet?" Getting a response, he resumed his pacing. His lips were tight, his expression grim. Lesser officials might well have lost consciousness on the spot had they but momentarily encountered that ferocious glare. Not Ganne. Just as one did not become Great Lord by indecision so one did not reach the status of First Minister if easily intimidated.

With a start he realized that Markhamwit was staring at him. He relaxed when he saw that there was no malice in the Great Lord's gaze. Instead, he was concentrating on the words of the unseen talker.

Eventually he set the communications device aside. "At least he condescends to come and see me. If he can be believed, he will be here in half a time-unit. It will be interesting to discover if his impudence is born of power or pure audacity."

"He refused to return yesterday," remarked Ganne, treating disobedience as something completely outside all experience. "He viewed all threats with open disdain and practically invited us to attack his ship. I spoke with the commander in charge and he was equally confounded. He was desperate to know if he had conducted himself properly and I had to confess to him that I didn't know myself what would constitute appropriate reaction under those circumstances. The situation is as unprecedented as it is infuriating.

"In at least one thing we know that the alien was as good as his word: the four paralyzed soldiers that he treated subsequent to his return to his ship have recovered completely. The medics are puzzled but concur that they have suffered no debilitating aftereffects.

"The alien was not entirely truthful, however. Or perhaps he was merely inaccurate when he said they would be perfectly all right. Though physically normal, they now absolutely refuse to leave the safety of their armored personnel carriers, and spend much of their time continuously watching the sky. The slightest humming or buzzing sound causes them to jump about frantically in search of unseen enemies. So while they may be as good as new physically, they have been victimized mentally in a manner the biped did not predict. Whether he deliberately withheld this information from us I cannot say. Perhaps he simply could not foresee it."

"I know, I know." Markhamwit dismissed it with an irritated wave of the hand. "But then, all that would be in keeping with his story. Verisimilitude must be maintained throughout. If he were to show uncertainty or fear or even concern at this point it would undercut his entire tale. If this is truly a gigantic sham it is an all-or-nothing business for those most intimately involved. His life and those of his winged allies depend on his convincingness." Markhamwit halted in midstride to gaze out the weapons-proof window.

"If our garrulous biped is a barefaced bluffer it can be said to his credit that he is a perfect one. As he would have to be, with much more than just his insignificant life on the line. And there is the real source of all the trouble."

Ganne intuited that he was about to hear one of those cogent, unforeseen speeches that explained why Markhamwit was the Great Lord and he only a minister. "In what way, my lord?"

Markhamwit turned to him, a more thoughtful expression on his face than Ganne could recall seeing in some time. "Look, we are a powerful life-form, so much so that after we have defeated the Nileans we shall be complete masters of this entire section of our galaxy. We are highly scientific and technologically advanced. In addition, we have produced a society whose cultural achievements are second to none among the known sentient races. We have vessels capable of traveling between star systems, advanced communications facilities that enable us to maintain contact with and guide vast armadas of those vessels, and formidable weapons of war.

"To all intents and purposes we have conquered the physical elements and bent them to our will. Any who have stood in our way or otherwise attempted to restrain us have been co-opted or brushed aside, which will be the fate of the Nileans unless we can compel them to see reason. All this makes us strong, does it not?"

"Yes, my lord, very strong."

"It also makes us weak," growled Markhamwit. "When focus narrows one loses sight of developments outside the immediate range of one's concern. In concentrating on the macrocosm it is possible to lose sight of what is happening right under one's feet."

"I am not sure I follow, my lord," Ganne was forced to confess.

Markhamwit was speaking to him but looking at something else. Something only he could see. "This problem dumped in our laps proves that we are weak in one respect; namely, we have become so conditioned to dealing with solid physicalities that we don't know how to cope with intangibles. In perfecting ships and weapons we have forgotten the power of words and ideas. And fable, and myth. We match rival ships with better ships, enemy weapons with more powerful weapons, improved shields and detection devices with enhanced versions of our own.

"But we are stalled the moment a foe abandons all recognized methods of warfare and resorts to what may be no more than a piece of sheer, unparalleled impudence. Instead of a theater of war, we have war become theater. If we were not trapped in the midst of it, like a bug in oil, I would be applauding the entire conceit as well as its perpetrators. Oh yes, Ganne, this is clever! I am not flattered that the Nileans do not underestimate me, and I am not about to underestimate them. One is far more apt to go down to ignominious defeat at the hands of an enemy one forgets to respect."

"Surely," Ganne said, "there must be some positive way of checking the truth and . . ."

"I can think of fifty ways." Markhamwit resumed his trudging and glared at the minister as if that worthy were personally responsible for the predicament in which they found themselves. "And the beauty of it is that not one of them is genuinely workable."

"No, my lord?"

"No!" He stopped again, suddenly this time. "I will give you some examples. They might as well trouble your thoughts also, since they kept me from sleeping most of the night.

"We could check on whether Solarians actually do exist in the next galaxy if our ships could get there, which they can't. And neither can any other ship, according to Yielm. We could make direct contact with the Nileans, call off the war, and organize mutual action against Solarian interlopers, but if the whole affair is a Nilean trick they will continue to deceive us to our ultimate downfall. They will have a ready answer to every possible question we might raise because they will already have played out identical scenarios over and over in their simulation chambers.

"Or we could seize this biped, strap him to an operating table, and cut the truth out of him with a scalpel. If it is all so much bluff I would think he would be hard-pressed to maintain the fiction by the time we began to extract his internal organs."

"That ought to be the best way," ventured Ganne, seeing nothing against it. He'd always been a believer in directness, when his own personal interests weren't involved.

"Undoubtedly, if his story is a lot of bluff. But what if it is not? What if the unlikely is reality and the impossible, for just one time, turns out to be the truth?"

"Ah!" Ganne felt for an itch and pinched deep into his thick hide.

"The whole position is fantastic," declared Markhamwit. "This two-armed creature comes here without any weapons identifiable as such save the ability of some small winged accomplices to deliver a temporarily paralyzing sting. Not a gun, not a bomb, not an energy-beam projector of any kind. So far as we know there isn't so much as a spearthrower on his craft. His kind have killed nobody, maimed nobody, shed not a drop of blood either now or in our recorded past, yet he claims powers of a kind we hesitate to test."

Ganne was visibly uneasy. "Do you suppose that we are already sterilized and therefore doomed, like the Elmones?"

"No, certainly not. Even granting that there's a morsel of truth to the fable, if he had done such a thing he would have lifted off during the night because there would be no point in dickering with us any longer."

"Yes, that's true." The minister felt vastly relieved without knowing why.

Markhamwit continued. "Anyway, he's said nothing whatever about such methods of dealing with us. It would be interesting to confront him with the story and observe his reaction. But of course if it is a Nilean ploy they would have researched all the Solarian legends and coached their puppet accordingly. He would react to the query as glibly as he has to every other question that has been put to him.

"As to the reality of such a threat, we know of it only fictionally, as part of the overall Solarian Myth. Seven habitable but empty worlds do not constitute proof of anything concerning the former existence of possible inhabitants. Intelligent life does not evolve on all habitable planets."

"What of the coincidence?" Ganne reminded him. "Of the fact that the inhabitants of all eight proximate systems tell the same tale?"

"Alemph was brought here as an expert on a myth, not as a historian. I am not about to alter the conduct of the war on the opinion of a fable-tracer. While I do not dismiss his conjecture, it remains only that. More facts are needed. We must have some kind of hard evidence. It is impossible to make any kind of decision based solely on words, either this biped's or ours.

"As to any actual danger posed by our self-proclaimed Solarian, the sole threat he has made is that if we destroy him we shall have to cope with those winged creatures who will remain here to outbreed us. I believe he has already made one error by letting slip the fact that their toxin is non-fatal."

"That is so, my lord. Unless he feels that the fact is irrelevant to his purpose."

Markhamwit went on. "In addition, he claims that if by some means we succeed in destroying them also, we shall still have to face whatever his theoretical Combine may bring against us later on. Assuming for the moment that it actually exists, I cannot imagine the true nature of that particular menace except that by our standards it will be unorthodox.''

"Their methods may represent the normal ways of warfare in their own galaxy," Ganne pointed out. "Perhaps they never got around to inventing energy beams and high explosives.''

"Or perhaps they discarded them a million years ago in favor of techniques less costly and more effective.'' Markhamwit cast an impatient glance at the chronograph whirring on the wall. "Trickery or not, I have learned a valuable lesson from this incident. For that I offer thanks whether to magical Solarians or perfidious Nileans.''

"What lesson might that be, my lord?'' an uncertain Ganne inquired.

"I have learned that tactics are more important than instruments, wits are better than warheads. If we had adopted a similar carefully devised approach and used our brains a bit more we might have persuaded the Nileans to knock themselves out and save us a lot of bother. As soon as this incident is resolved I intend to see that funding for our psychological warfare department is greatly increased.'' He put all four palms together to form a meaningful pyramid shape. "All that was needed was a completely original approach. I intend to see to it that we formulate a few of our own.''

"Yes, my lord.'' Privately Ganne prayed that he would not be commanded to suggest one or two original approaches.

"What I want to know,'' Markhamwit went on, bitterly, "and what I *must* know, is whether the Nileans have reached a similar conclusion first and are egging us on to knock ourselves out. So when this self-professed Solarian arrives I'm going to . . .''

A soft musical tone sounded, the towering door parted, and the captain of the guard showed himself, bowing low as he stepped inside.

"My lord, the alien is here."

"Show him in."

Plumping heavily into his chair, Markhamwit tapped restless fingers on four armrests and glowered at the door. Ganne prudently took up a stance to the Great Lord's right and just behind his field of vision. In addition to subscribing to the universal theory "out of sight, out of mind," Ganne knew that the massive carved chair would provide excellent cover in the event of any genuinely unexpectedly Solarian surprises.

Entering blithely, Lawson approached without waiting for permission, smiled at the expectant pair with his usual insouciance, and asked, "Well, does civilization come to these parts or not?"

It riled the Great Lord, but he ignored the question and the attitude behind it, controlled his temper, and said heavily, "Yesterday you returned to your vessel contrary to my wishes."

"Today your warships are still messing around in free space contrary to ours." Lawson heaved a sign of resignation. "If wishes were fishes we'd never want for food."

"You appear to forget," Markhamwit reminded him, "that in this part of the cosmos it is my desires that are fulfilled and not yours! This is an undisputable fact that you would do well to remember."

"But you've just complained about yours being ignored," remarked Lawson, pretending surprise.

Markhamwit licked sharp teeth. Despite his lack of sleep he was feeling much better today, having had time to mull over a great many possibilities. He had determined that whatever the outcome of this confrontation it would proceed far differently from its predecessor. He was in charge and intended to remain so for the duration of the conversation. Solarians or no, it was he who held the high ground, and he fully intended to keep it.

"It won't happen again. Certain individuals made the mistake of letting you go, unchallenged and without question. Eagerness is often the shortest path to stupidity. They will pay for that. We have a way with fools."

"So have we."

Having had time the day before to consider the biped's manner and the nature of his possible reply, Markhamwit was no longer so easily taken aback. He replied firmly and without hesitation.

"That is something of which I require proof. You are going to provide it." His voice had regained its familiar authoritative tone. Nearby, Ganne swelled with confidence. This was the Great Lord he knew and served.

"And what is more," Markhamwit continued, "you are going to provide it in the way I direct, to my complete satisfaction."

"How?" inquired Lawson.

"By bringing not representatives but members of the Nilean High Command here to discuss this matter face-to-face."

"They won't come."

"I guessed you'd say that. It was such a certainty that I could have said it for you." Markhamwit displayed satisfaction at his own foresight. "So much for the vaunted Solarian omnipotence."

"It has nothing to do with that."

"It has everything to do with that." The Great Lord was immensely pleased with himself. "They've thought up an impudent bluff. Now they're called upon to support it in person by chancing their own precious hides. That is too much. That is taking things too far. So they won't do it. They'll prepare for the eventuality of the question and supply their stooge with all manner of evasions and excuses, but when all these have been dismissed and it comes right down to one or more of them putting their own necks on the line, we at last reach the point where clever words and sophistries no longer suffice." He threw a glance at Ganne. "What did I tell you?"

"I don't see how the Nileans or anyone else can bolster a non-existent trick," offered Lawson mildly.

"A good try, biped, but now that I am familiar with the logic of the situation it is I who runs in the lead. They do not need to convince me of your existence. They need only appear before me to argue the problem. That would be convincing as far as I am concerned."

"Precisely!"

In spite of himself Markhamwit frowned. "What do you mean, 'precisely'?"

"If it's a stunt of their own contriving in which they believe deeply why shouldn't they back it to the limit and risk a few lives on it? The war is on and they've got to suffer casualties anyway, even among the High Command. If they can dig up volunteers for one dangerous mission they can find them for another."

"So? That doesn't tell me why they won't send one or more of their own number here to confront me in person."

"Of course it does. They'd probably comply, albeit reluctantly, if they thought there was half a truth in the tale worth resolving. But they won't gamble one life on a setup they suspect to be of your making. There's no percentage in it. That's why the question of our 'omnipotence' has no relevance."

"It is not of my making. You know that."

"The Nileans don't," said Lawson.

"You claim to have another ship on their world. What is it there for if not to persuade them?"

"You're getting your ideas mixed."

"Am I?" Markhamwit's grip was tight on the arms of the chair. He'd almost had enough of this biped and his glib verbal byplay. It was a dance he hadn't sought and he was just about ready to step out. Noting the expression on the Great Lord's face, Minister Ganne took another surreptitious step backward. "In what way?"

"That vessel is there solely to tell the Nileans to cease cluttering the void . . . or else! We're not interested in your meetings, discussions, or wars. You can kiss and be friends or fight to the death and it will make not the slightest difference to us one way or the other. All that we're concerned about is that space remain free, preferably by negotiation and mutual agreement. If not, by compulsion."

"Compulsion?" snapped Markhamwit. "You toss nonspecific threats about like so much grass seed. I would give a great deal to learn exactly how much power your kind really does possess. Perhaps little more than iron nerves and wagging tongues."

"Perhaps," admitted Lawson, irritatingly indifferent.

"You're just full of little lectures and obscure information, aren't you? No hesitation whatsoever in telling others how to behave and what to do next. Well, I've listened to everything you've had to say and now it's my turn. I'll tell you something you don't know." Markhamwit leaned forward in the chair, staring at him. "Our first, second, third, and fourth battle fleets have dispersed. Temporarily I've taken them out of the war. It's a risk, but worth it. There's been something of a hiatus in the fighting lately and the dispersal was carried out progressively and in utmost secrecy. If the Nileans do take note of this operation it will take them some time to confirm it, decide on a course of action, and react. Meanwhile I have obtained a breathing space for the crews of those fleets, one which I am having them put to good use. What do you have to say to that?"

"Doesn't alter the situation if your ships are still chasing around here, there, and everywhere with belligerence on their minds and arrogance in their actions."

"On the contrary, it may alter the situation very considerably if we have a fair measure of luck." Markhamwit continued to watch the alien closely. "Can you imagine why I have ordered this extraordinary maneuver?"

"Far be it from me to imagine why you would do anything," Lawson replied with maddening lack of concern.

Markhamwit was not about to be baited. "Every ship of these fleets has been redirected into a colossal, intensive hunt. I now have a total of seventeen thousand vessels scouting all cosmic sectors recently settled or explored by the Nileans or their close allies. Know what they are looking for?"

"I can guess."

Markhamwit reserved the satisfaction of delineating it to himself. "They're seeking a minor, unimportant, previously unnoticed or overlooked planet populated by soft-skinned bipeds with hard faces and gabby mouths. If they find it," he swept an arm in a wide, expressive arc, "we'll blow them clean out of existence and the Solarian Myth along with them."

"How nice."

"We shall also deal with you in a suitable manner. Not everyone under me is a fool. Some are quite efficient and extraordinarily inventive. That is something for you to ponder. In addition we'll deal with your winged stingers as the need arises, and we'll settle with the Nileans once and for all."

"Dear me," offered Lawson meditatively. "Do you really expect us to sit around forever while you play hunt the slipper?"

For the umpteenth time thwarted by the other's appalling nonchalance, Markhamwit lay back without replying. For a wild moment he toyed with the notion that perhaps the Nileans were infinitely more ingenious than he'd first supposed and were taking him for a sucker by manning their ship with exceptionally sophisticated, reactively programmed or remotely controlled robots. That would account for this biped's unnatural impassivity. If he was nothing more than the terminal instrument of some incredibly complicated and extraordinarily well shielded array of electronic apparatus created by Nilean science, it would account not only for his attitude but for a great many other unsettling aspects of his condition. There would be no need to simulate emotions in a talking machine. A more alien (i.e., Solarian) mien would be hard to achieve. No unreported allied species, however well prepared, could match it.

But it just wasn't possible. Long ago, before the war started, a subspace message to the nearest fringe of Nilea's petty empire had to be relayed from planet to planet, system to system, took a long time to get there, an equally long time for a reply to come back. It was completely beyond the power of any science, real or imaginary, to control an automaton across many light-years to a degree so fine that it could respond conversationally with no time lag whatsoever.

Similarly, it was impossible to conceive of a device that could carry on an unpredictable dialogue without noticeable hesitation. There was no way the most sophisticated mechanical could be programmed in advance to deal with everyone from a common soldier to the Great Lord himself.

As to the possibility of Nilean specialists controlling it from within the bowels of the little ship squatting out on the plain, that vessel had been scanned and checked by every device known to contemporary physics. It was under round-the-clock observation by dozens of specialized monitoring devices. Frequently updated reports indicated that it was emitting no radiation whatsoever. Not only were familiar communications frequencies blank, according to the observers it was emitting not so much as a lingering hiss. Communications and control-wise, it was a null.

Lawson, he decided uneasily, was robotic in some ways but definitely not a robot. Rather he was a life-form possessed of real individuality plus a queer something else impossible to describe. A creature to whom an unknown quantity or quality had been added and who was therefore unlike anything formerly encountered.

Emerging from his meditations, which the biped tolerated in hopeful silence, he growled, "You'll sit around because you'll have no choice about the matter. I have ordered that you be detained pending my further decisions. Or until the word I am waiting for is transmitted by one of my questing warships."

"That doesn't answer my question," Lawson pointed out.

"Why doesn't it?"

"I asked whether you expect *us* to sit around. What you see fit to do with this portion can have no effect upon the remainder."

"This portion?" Markhamwit's air was that of one not sure whether he had heard aright. "I have got *all* of you!" He pressed a stud set in the chair's lower left armrest.

Lawson stood as the guards came in, smiled thinly and said, "I can tell you a fable of the future. There was once an idiot who picked a grain of sand from a mountain, cupped it in the palm of his hand, and said, 'Look, I am holding a mountain!' "

"Take him away," bawled Markhamwit at the escort. "Keep him locked up until I want him again. Secure him behind multiple doors and make sure no one is allowed access to him without my specific permission!"

"As you order, my lord." The head of the escort bowed crisply as he acknowledged the injunctions.

Watching them file out and the door close behind the

biped, the Great Lord fumed a bit. "Creating cockeyed problems for others is a game at which two can play. In this existence one has to use one's wits. If the Nileans think they can deceive us so easily they are in for a most uncomfortable surprise." He flicked a glance at the elegant wall chronograph, which displayed the time not only within the city but throughout the system.

"Let the biped lose sleep contemplating my words for a change. Isolation focuses the mind wonderfully. Perhaps after he realizes his powerlessness, and that whatever happens to him depends on my whim, he may choose to be informative rather than merely voluble. Meanwhile he can have no contact with the Nileans or those winged things or anyone else. I do not think it will take long for him to come to his senses."

"Undoubtedly, my lord," endorsed First Minister Ganne, dutifully admiring him.

vii

James Lawson carefully surveyed his cell. It was large and fairly comfortable, with an odd-shaped bed wide enough to accommodate three of him, a thick air-filled mattress, the inevitable four-armed chair, and a long, narrow table. There were no electronic devices of any kind and the only visible switch or button proved to control the overhead light, which was sealed behind a translucent ceiling panel. There were no utensils or tools or anything sufficiently portable and sturdy enough with which to simulate same. Nothing that a prisoner could modify to stab at the floor, the door, or himself.

The walls were coated with a thick swirl of flatulent green and puce, a color scheme not particularly to his liking. A generous basket of fruit stood on the middle of the table alongside a shallow bowl piled high with some brownish objects resembling wholemeal cakes. There was a soft plastic pitcher full of water and a thick, wide mouthed tumbler of matching material. He tested the water, made a face. It was tepid.

He was as amused by the sight of the food as he had been by the rough courtesy with which the guard had conducted him here. Evidently Markhamwit had been specific in his instructions. Put him in the brig. Don't harm him, don't starve him, but put him in the brig.

The Great Lord wanted it both coming and going. Always looking ahead, he was establishing a claim to kindness as a form of insurance against whatever might befall, while at the same time keeping the victim just where he wanted him until thoroughly satisfied that nothing dreadful could or would be called down upon him.

There was a small barred window set in the western wall seven meters above the floor, more for ventilation than for light. Even without the bars it was far too narrow for him to squeeze through. The only other opening was the big, tightly woven grille across the entrance. A very large guard sat on a stool on the other side of the bars boredly perusing a narrow but thick rectangle of electronics that backed up a small, glowing screen. At frequent intervals he glanced over to check on the occupant of the cell. Lawson smiled at him but failed to elicit any reaction whatsoever.

Turning, Lawson walked over to the heavy chair. Taking a seat he tilted back, stretched out his legs, and rested his heels on the base of the bed. Closing his eyes and ignoring the indifferent guard, he had a look at his ship. This was fully as easy as staring at the blank, coated walls of the cell. All that was necessary was for him to readjust his mind and look through other eyes elsewhere. Not only can it be done, it becomes second nature when the mind behind the other eyes is to all intents and purposes a part of one's own. When one is personally close to the owner of these alternate oculars, the switch is made even easier.

He got a multiple picture because he was looking through multiple lenses, but he was accustomed to that. As well as being informative, it made for interesting variety.

Meeting and knowing other shapes and forms is as nothing compared with the experience of actually sharing them, including those employing organs stranger than eyes.

There was no gradual changeover of vision, no blurring or focusing required. One minute he was staring at the walls of his prison, the next he was outside, back on the dry plain east of the city.

The ship was resting exactly as he'd left it. Its lock still stood wide open but having learned respect the hard way, nobody was entering or attempting to do so. The recently reinforced ring of guards maintained their perimeter, watching the vessel in the perfunctory manner of those already sick of the sight of it. Those nearest affected an alertness born of unpleasant experience, their attention directed as much at the cloud-laden sky as at the ship itself. Meanwhile their colleagues played at various games, rested, drilled, or performed routine maintenance on weapons and other equipment.

Not exactly a bucolic scene, Lawson decided. More one that reeked of somnolent threat.

As he studied the terrain the swiftly moving eyes through which he was looking swung low, dived toward an officer who loomed enormous with sheer closeness. Looking up suddenly and flashing an expression of complete panic, the officer made a wild swipe at the eyes with a ceremonial short sword curved two ways like a double sickle. Involuntarily Lawson blinked, for it came like a slash at his own head. His neck went taut as the shining blade whistled through the space that would have been occupied by his gullet had he been there in person.

"Someday, Lou," he thought, "I'll do as much for you. I'll give you a horrible nightmare."

The bee-mind came back. "Ever looked through somebody landbound, trying to escape danger on legs and without wings? Thumping along metabolizing calories at a fantastic rate yet hardly covering one's own body-length at a breath? Chained to the earth, in utter thrall to something as prosaic as mere gravity? That *is* a nightmare!'' A pause as what could be seen through his optics showed him to be zooming skyward. ''Want out yet?''

''No hurry,'' Lawson answered.

''How about a wider perspective?'' The view tipped, revealing the entire area and occasionally, the city beyond. In essence, Lawson was looking back at himself. Only a Solarian could truly see himself as others saw him.

''Doesn't look like much of anything has changed,'' he commented.

''Nope. They haven't tried much since you left. They're not above taking a few potshots at us, though, when they can see us.''

Lawson didn't have to ask if anyone had been hit. Nor would they have had to inform him. He would have known instantly.

''As you're already aware,'' the Callisian continued, ''their reaction time leaves a lot to be desired. They're strong, but when it comes to speed of movement they make a human look swift. They've tried to compensate a few times by setting automatic weapons' trackers on us and locking in the firing mechanism.''

''What happened?''

''We just dodged out of the way until we got tired of putting up with it. Then a couple of us dipped behind one of them just as his eager comrade was preparing to let loose. With the automatics locked on his buddy had to dodge pretty fast. That put a quick stop to those fun and games. Since then they've been pretty quiet.''

''Keep me posted,'' Lawson informed the other. The bee-mind's response took the form of an intentionally patronizing mental pat on the head.

Withdrawing from that individual he re-angled his mind

and let it reach outward, tremendously outward. This, too, was relatively easy. The velocity of light is sluggish, creeping along on little cat's photons when compared with near-instantaneous contact between the mental components of a psychic whole. Thought is energy, light is energy, matter is energy, but the greatest of these is thought. As becomes immediately apparent if one takes the time to think about it.

Someday his enormously advanced multikind might prove a thesis long evolved: that energy, light, and matter are creations of superthought. They were getting mightily near to it already; just one or perhaps two more steps to godhood when they'd have finally established the mastery of mind over matter by using the former to create the latter according to their needs. It was a fascinating as well as momentous project that kept a large percentage of the Combine fully occupied. Far, far from his present location there was a whole lot of contemplating going on.

Similarly there was no time lag in his reaching for the central world of Nilea, nor would there have been one of any handicapping duration had he reached across the galaxy and over the gulf into the next. He merely thought "at" his objective and was there, looking through eyes exactly like his own at the interior of a ship that differed little from his own except in one respect: it harbored no big bees.

This other vessel's crew consisted of one biped named Edouard Reeder and four of those fuzzy, shapeless entities who had fogged his souvenir image. A quartet of Rheians, these, from a planet-sized moon of a ringed planet. Rheians in name only; Solarians in long-established fact.

Callisian bees wouldn't be of much avail in coping with Nileans who were likely to hang around inviting hearty stings for the sheer pleasure of resulting intoxication. Their peculiar makeup enabled them to get roaring drunk on any acid other than hydrofluoric, and even that corrosive stuff was viewed as a liquid substitute for scoot berries.

But the Nileans were south-eyed, scanning a band of the spectrum that ran well into the ultraviolet. And one has to be decidedly north-eyed to see a Rheian with real clarity. So far as local life-forms were concerned, this reputed Solarian vessel was crewed by one impertinent biped and a handful of near-ghosts. Several suitably eerie encounters subsequent to the little vessel's unexpected arrival had left them feeling more than skittish. Like most creatures suffering optical limitations, the Nileans suspected, disliked . . . aye, feared . . . living things never more than half visible.

It might have been the same with other Solarians in their attitude toward such peculiar fellows from a moon of another system but for one thing: that which cannot be examined visually can be appreciated and understood mentally. The collective Rheian mind was as much an intimate component of the greater Solarian mass-mentality as was any other part. The bipeds and the bees had phantom brothers.

Reeder was thinking "at" him. "I've just returned from the third successive interview with their War Board, which is bossed by a hairy bully named Glastrom. He's completely obsessed by the notion that your Markhamwit is trying to outsmart him. I've tried everything I can think of short of drawing pictures to make them see reason but it doesn't seem to make any difference. And on the rare occasions when it looks like I might be making some progress with him, one of his companion idiots is quick to jump in with the usual paranoid objections."

"Sounds frustrating."

"There's an understatement. At least you only have to convince one blockhead. I'm stuck with a whole row of 'em. Every time it looks like I might be making some headway, somebody's head gets in the way. They're frantic that the foe's about to pull a fast one on them and that fear swamps any notion that I might be telling the truth."

"Similar reaction at this end," Lawson told him. "I've been stuck in the pokey while Markhamwit waits for destiny to intervene in his favor. I don't know how much patience he has but I get the distinct feeling he'd rather live out his natural life span than make what he perceives to be a too-hasty decision on this one."

"They've come near trying the same tactic with me," Reeder's mind informed him, showing strange uninterest in whether or not his counterpart was being made to suffer during his incarceration. "Chief item that has made them hesitate is the problem of what to do about the rest of us." His gaze shifted a moment to the shadowy, shapeless quartet posing nearby.

"The boys put over a mild demonstration of what can be done by wraiths with the fidgets. They switched off the capital's light and power and so forth while cross-eyed guards fired at the minor moon. The Nileans didn't like it. They still thunder and threaten, but their attitudes are much subdued and they've lowered their voices. It's not exactly respect, but at least I don't have to smell their breath every time we have a talk. They won't go near the ship." Intimations of amusement accompanied the mind picture.

"It's kind of sad to see them twitching and jerking all the time as they look to their rumps, under their bellies and beneath every vehicle in search of one of the guys. You should've seen their faces when I told them it was a mild demonstration and that I had to do everything in my power to restrain my companions from taking serious steps."

"Can't say they're overfond of our crowd here, either." Lawson paused thoughtfully before continuing. "Chronic distrust on both sides is preventing conformity with our demands and seems likely to go on doing so until the crack of doom. The Great Lord is in a great mental jam and his only solution is to play for time. He's trying to be as subtle as possible about it, but that's not his forte."

Reeder's response was as clear as if he'd been sitting on the other side of the expansive bed. "Same way with Glastrom and the Nilean War Board. I get the feeling they'll let me talk into the next millennium before they'll break down and actually make a decision. At this point it doesn't much matter what I say, or what the boys do. They've made up their minds not to make up their minds."

Lawson considered. "Well, we can't sit around here and wait for their stars to go nova. Neutral commerce is being interfered with."

"Limit their time," interjected the four laconic but penetrating thought-forms of the shapeless ones.

"Limit their time," simultaneously endorsed several bee-minds from a source much nearer.

"Give them one time-unit," confirmed a small and varied number of entities scattered through the galaxy.

"Give them one time-unit," decided an enormous composite mentality far across the gulf.

"Better warn them right away." Reeder's eyes showed him to be making for the open lock of his ship. His mind held no intimation of any personal peril that might arise from the deliverance of this ultimatum to a group of hostile, bellicose beings who had already taken a personal dislike to him. This was because he was as ageless as that of which he was part, and as deathless because, whether whole or destroyed, he was part of that which can never die. Like Lawson he was human plus humans plus other creatures. The first might disappear into eternal nothingness, but the plus-quantities remained for ever and ever and ever.

For the same reasons Lawson followed the identical course in much the same way. The intangible thread of his thought stream snapped back from faraway places and the eyes he now looked through were once more solely his own. Taking his heels off the bed he stood up, yawned, stretched himself, sauntered up to the welded grille, and addressed himself to the sentry.

"I've got to speak to Markhamwit at once."

Putting down the softly humming electronic reader, the guard registered the disillusioned expression of one who hopes everlastingly for peace and invariably hopes in vain. His aspect was lethargic but his eyes were alert.

"The Great Lord will send for you in due course. Meanwhile you could rest and have a nap. Are your sleeping arrangements inadequate?"

"No; they're irrelevant. I do not sleep."

"Everybody sleeps sometime or other," asserted the guard, unconsciously dogmatic. "They have to. It is a natural law to which all representatives of the higher orders subscribe. It is vital to rejuvenation and energy."

"Speak for yourself," advised Lawson. "I've never slept in my life and don't intend to start now. It's an outmoded concept we discarded quite a while ago. What I recall of the activity strikes me as a distinct waste of time."

"Even the Great Lord sleeps." The guard delivered this assertion with the air of one producing incontrovertible evidence.

"You're telling me?" Lawson deposed.

The other gaped at him, sniffed around as if seeking the odor of a dimly suspected insult. It fled before his mind could fasten on it.

"My orders are to keep watch upon you until the Great Lord wishes to see you again. You should be flattered. It is an honor to be confined to the tower. If you had been returned to the interrogation center you would be shut up in a closed chamber with instruments to keep constant watch over you and no one for company."

"The concern on my behalf is touching, but I am mine own company, thank you."

"You will see the Great Lord when he wishes it," the guard insisted, "and not a moment before."

"Well then, ask him if he so wishes."

"I dare not. I would not have the temerity."

"You don't need temerity. Just use your mouth."

The other hesitated. "It would be exceeding my authority even to consider the notion. I could get into a lot of trouble."

"This whole place is already in a lot of trouble, thank you very much. If you're too reduced in psychological circumstances to make the effort, ask someone who does dare."

"I'll call the captain of the guard," decided the other with alacrity.

Carefully turning off the reader and setting it on a small shelf next to his chair, he disappeared down the passageway, came back in short time with a larger and surlier specimen who glowered at the prisoner and demanded in no-nonsense tones, "Now, what's all this rubbish?"

Eyeing him with exaggerated incredulity, Lawson said, "Do you really dare in front of witnesses to define the Great Lord's personal affairs as rubbish?"

The captain's pomposity promptly hissed out of him like gas from a pricked balloon. He appeared to shrink in size and went two shades paler in the face. Even his fur seemed to curl in on itself. The guard edged away from him like one fearful of being contaminated by open sedition.

"I did not mean it that way," the officer stammered.

"I sincerely hope not," declared Lawson, displaying impressive piety. "It is an assumption almost not to be believed."

"I was misunderstood," the captain added in haste, trying to recover lost ground he hadn't even been aware that he'd been standing on. "While you are fluent in our language you cannot hope to understand some of its more subtle overtones.''

"Very subtle," Lawson replied agreeably.

Recovering with an effort, the captain asked, "About what do you want to speak to the Great Lord?"

"I'll tell you after you've shown me your certificate."

"Certificate?" The officer was mystified. "Which certificate?"

"The document proving that you have been appointed the censor of the Great Lord's conversations."

The captain said hurriedly, "I will go and consult the garrison commander."

He went away with the pained expression of one who has put his foot in it and must find somewhere to scrape it off. The guard warily resumed his seat on the stool, picked up the reader, put it down again, gawked at Lawson, hunted through his fur until he found the parasite that had been irritating him. As Lawson looked on impatiently the other crunched it between two thick fingers.

"I'll give him a hundred milliparts," Lawson finally remarked. "If he's not back by then, I'm coming out."

The guard stood up, hand on gun, face showing alarm. "You can't do that."

"Why not?"

"You are locked in."

"Hah!" said Lawson, as if enjoying a secret joke.

"Besides, I am here."

"That's unfortunate for you," Lawson sympathized. "Either you'll shoot me or you won't. If you don't, I'll walk away and Markhamwit will be most annoyed. If you do, I'll be dead and he'll be infuriated." He shook his head slowly, full of mock empathy. "Tsk, tsk! I would not care to be you!"

His alarm mounting to a near-unbearable point, the

guard tried to watch the grille and the far end of the passageway at the same time. Meanwhile the biped stood gazing pleasantly back at him, hands out in plain sight, doing nothing that could be construed as remotely hostile. The guard would have been much happier had the prisoner begun fiddling with a tiny piece of plastic, or the metal of the grille, or the walls of his cell. Those were identifiable actions to which he could have responded with an appropriate reaction. The fact that he was simply standing there projecting an unshakable confidence was far more unnerving.

So the guard's relief was intense when the captain reappeared and ordered him to unlock. He passed the electronic key over the seal on the grille and stepped hurriedly out of the way, as though letting out something large, fanged, and poisonous. As he emerged from the cell, Lawson nodded agreeably and the guard flinched.

The officer eyed the alien guardedly. In his absence Lawson's status had apparently risen a notch, since his manner now hovered somewhere between deference and admonition.

"The commander passed along your request. While I personally do not approve I have no say in the matter. I am merely an administrator."

"Do I get to see Markhamwit?"

The captain harrumphed noncommittally. "That is not for me to know. You will, however, be permitted to talk over the line to First Minister Ganne. The rest is up to him."

Leading the way with the guard in the rear he conducted the prisoner to a small nearby office, signed for an earpiece and speaking cylinder. An intermediary manipulated the controls on a board, then gestured at the alien. Picking up the communications devices, Lawson held the inadequately shaped plug close to his ear, it being too big to fit in the locally accepted manner. At the same time his mind sent out a soundless call shipward.

"This is as good a time as any."

Then he listened to the plug and heard Ganne saying, "What you want to tell the Great Lord can be told to me."

"It's better that I tell him myself. That way there can't be grounds for confusion or misinterpretation."

"I assure you I will accurately convey anything you have to say."

Lawson gave a mental shrug. "It's your neck. I've been told to pass him the news that he's got seven-eighths of a time-unit." He smiled pleasantly at the functionary monitoring the transmission. "They've wasted the other eighth at this end."

Out of one corner of his eye he noted the listening captain registering surly displeasure. His gaze rose casually and he observed that the door and two windows were half-open. Lou, Buzwuz, and the others would have no trouble, no trouble at all.

"He's got seven-eighths of a time-unit?" Ganne's voice rose a fraction. "To do what?"

"Beam his orders for recall."

"Recall?"

Lawson sighed with tired patience. Even with all its inherent misperceptions and uncertainties spoken language certainly had its place, and it was a basic requirement for development among lower life-forms; but for those who had long since dispensed with it save for novelty's sake it could prove a disconcerting impediment to sensible conversation.

"You're only wasting valuable moments repeating the end of each sentence. A moment in time is like a leaf in a cascade. Once it drops below a certain point it's gone. It'll never turn and flow back up that stream. See, I've just had to waste another explaining the obvious to you."

"The obvious?"

"There you go again." Lawson strove to be patient. "You were there all the time, listening to our talk, your ears as open as your eyes. You're not hard of hearing, are you?''

Ganne snapped, "I'll stand for no gross impertinence from you. You might as well know that my opinion of you is considerably less tolerant than that of the Great Lord, and that if it were up to me this entire business would be resolved a good deal faster and with a lot less babble on your part. However, I remain constrained by my loyalty to the Great Lord and my unending admiration for his analytical abilities.''

"That's two more moments gone," Lawson replied diffidently.

A low growl at the other end. Obviously containing himself, Ganne demanded, "I want to know precisely what you mean by saying that the Great Lord has seven-eighths of a time-unit.''

"It's more like thirteen-sixteenths now. He has got to take action by then.''

"Has he?" sneered the Minister. "Well, suppose he doesn't?''

"We'll take it.''

"That comes well from you. You're in no . . .'' His voice broke off as another sounded authoritatively in the background. More dimly and in another tone entirely he could be heard saying, "Yes, my lord. It's the biped, my lord.''

Behind him in the little office Lawson could also hear something else; a low drone coming nearer, nearer, through the door, through the window. There were exclamations from the locals behind him, a few scuffling, jumping noises, some thin yelps, then successive dull thumps and silence. He didn't bother to look around.

Then Markhamwit was on the line, his voice harsh. "It will do you no good to bait my minister. If you hope to precipitate the issue by further bluff, you are very much mistaken.'' Then with added menace, "Reports from my fleets have now started to come in. These are being scanned and evaluated by our best people. Sooner or later I'll get the one for which I am waiting. I shall then deal with you rather drastically.

"Meanwhile you may make all the mouth-noises you wish. It will do nothing to change my decision, which with each passing moment I am convinced is the correct one."

"I've already spoken to Ganne about passing moments," Lawson gave back. "The two of you might have a profitable discussion concerning that, but I doubt it. You've now got approximately three-quarters of a time-part. At the end of that period we shall take the initiative, do whatever we consider to be for the best. It won't be drastic because we shed no blood, take no lives. All the same it will be quite effective."

"Will it?" Markhamwit emitted his kind's equivalent of a sardonic chuckle. "In that case I will do part of that which you require of me. In other words, I will institute action at the exact moment you have nominated. That is what you desire, is it not? Action on my part?"

"It would be an invigorating change," Lawson conceded.

The Great Lord's voice was low and threatening. "It will be the action *I* deem best fitted to the circumstances."

"Time's marching on," remarked Lawson, unimpressed. The drone had left the room but could still be heard faintly from somewhere outside. He could see the soles of a pair of recumbent footgear lying near his own feet.

"You cannot get to your ship, nor can you communicate with it." Markhamwit sounded quite pleased with the situation. "And in precisely three-quarters of a time-unit there will be no ship to which you can return. The aerial patrol will have blasted it clean out of existence while it sits there, a steady target that cannot be missed."

"Can't it?"

Having finally decided to move, Markhamwit pursued the resolution *he* had determined upon with evident enthusiasm.

"The sterilizing apparatus, if there is such a thing, will be vaporized with the vessel before it can be brought into action. Any winged things left flying around will be wiped out one by one as and when opportunity occurs. They may be highly intelligent, as you say, but I do not think they can sting through armor, and no matter how quickly they can breed, development of any egg to maturity still takes time." He snorted conspicuously.

"Since you've seen fit to push this matter to a sudden conclusion I am prepared to take a chance on anything the Solarian Combine may do." Finally, with sarcasm, "*If* there is a Solarian Combine and *if* it can do anything worth a moment's worry, a prospect that I am increasingly inclined to doubt."

He must have flung aside the earpiece and cylinder at his end, for his voice became less distinct as he said to Ganne, "Get Yielm for me. I'm going to show those Nileans that attempted hoodwinking is a poor substitute for bombs and bullets."

Dumping his own end of the line, Lawson turned, stepped over several bodies unable to do more than curse him with their eyes. Proceeding down a short, deserted corridor he soon found himself confronted by a wide, translucent door. It was not sealed. He pushed it aside and stepped out into a large yard. There were transplanted trees, hedgerows, walking paths, and running streams. Spigots were set among artfully camouflaged holders.

He ignored them as he crossed diagonally under the direct gaze of half a dozen guards patrolling walls and rooftops. Curiosity was their only reason for watching him, the interesting spectacle of a life-form not listed among the many with which they were familiar. It was his manifest confidence that fooled them, his unmistakable air of having every right to be going wherever he was going. Nobody thought to question it, not a momentary notion of escape crossed their minds. No one escaped from this place.

Indeed, one of them obliged by operating the lever that opened the end gate, and lived to damn the day when he permitted himself to be misled by appearances. Not to be outdone, another whistled down a passing aircar that stopped for the fugitive. The driver, too, later found reason to deplore the pickup.

Lawson said to the driver, "Can you take me to that ship out on the plain?"

"The alien vessel? I'm not going that far." The other scratched himself and mooted the request.

"It's a matter of major importance," Lawson informed him in profound tones. "I've just been speaking to First Minister Ganne about it."

"Oh?" The driver perked up. "What did he say?"

"He put me on to the Great Lord who told me I've got little more than half a time-unit to spare."

"The Great Lord," breathed the other, with becoming reverence. He nudged controls, turned the aircar, and sent it whistling onward. "I'll get you there in plenty of time."

"That is very good of you," Lawson told him.

The driver knew the city well, darting along pathways far less congested than those farther in, taking clever shortcuts, occasionally racing along high-priority paths reserved for military or administrative traffic. The aircars and larger craft they passed on the way spared them not a passing glance. Since most of the traffic this time of day seemed to be heading into the city, there was very little to slow them down. As they reached and passed the outskirts, traffic thinned out still further, allowing the driver to accelerate even more. Soon the aircar was barreling along the empty guideway, vibrating from the increased velocity.

"Nice vehicle," Lawson commented conversationally.

"Thanks," replied the driver. He was a comparatively svelte, youngish individual, resilient and adaptable, eager to do his part to help win the great war and defeat the hated Nilean plague. Or so he would readily have said had he been asked. Lawson didn't ask him. He didn't need to. Inculcated fanaticism is a trait as obvious to the trained observer as a bright blue stain.

"Yours?"

The other blinked at him. "Of course not." He tapped the control dash. "Government issue."

"Good. I wouldn't want you to risk your own property on my behalf." Lawson peered forward. "No need to slow when we get there. Everything's been cleared through the Great Lord himself and time is of the essence. Time *is* the essence."

"I understand," responded the driver, not really understanding at all.

There was no need to burst through the guard ring; it no longer existed. All troops together with their heavy weapons, transports, and monitoring equipment had been withdrawn to a safe distance. Assembled in a solid bunch behind the best cover available, the soldiers were resting on their arms like an audience awaiting a rare spectacle. A couple of slightly more alert officers danced and gesticulated as the aircar swept into view alongside the ship, but they were far off, well beyond calling distance, and the driver failed to notice them.

"Thanks!" Lawson tumbled out of the cab. "One good turn deserves another, so I'm telling you to get out faster than you came."

The other blinked at him a second time. "Why?"

"Because in about one-fifth of a time-unit a dollop of bombs or the destructive equivalent will land right here.

You'll make it with plenty to spare provided you don't sit there gaping.''

Though puzzled and incredulous, it was to the driver's credit that he saw clearly this was a poor time to probe further into the matter. Taking the offered advice, he got out fast, his vehicle rocking with sheer speed as it sped away over rocks and low brush. Again a pair of officers waved frantically, again the driver failed to notice their frenzied gyrations.

Lawson entered the lock, did not look back as it cycled shut behind him. Similarly, he did not bother to inquire whether all his crew were aboard. He knew that they were there in the same way that they had known of his impending return and intended liftoff.

No one greeted him as he made his way forward. The tiny cockpit was deserted. Dumping himself into the pilot's seat he relaxed while the sensory cocoon enfolded him in its amorphous, accommodating embrace. Throughout the ship the other members of the crew were making similar, though less elaborate, arrangements.

It was really very frustrating, though the outcome could hardly be called surprising. Repetition bred not contempt but a kind of timeworn familiarity. Yet now and again they were surprised. Scarce pockets of rationality and common sense occasionally manifested themselves. These exceptions were treasured by those fortunate enough to encounter them.

This, however, was not one of those places or occasions. More than talk was going to be required. He sighed. No rest for the weary. Or the concerned. And all because hormones continued to hold sway over reason. The ship's chrono politely impressed itself on his consciousness. He'd got just seventy-two milliparts in which to beat the big bang. He took a last look out the port at the dusty plain, the massive city squatting soullessly in the distance. Then he nudged a tiny contact the minimal amount and went out from under.

The vacuum created by the vessel's departure sucked most of the troops' skullgear from their heads. A few small wingless inhabitants of the wide plain found themselves suddenly and unaccustomedly airborne. After a brief spiraling flight they tumbled back to the ground, largely unhurt by the experience but in their limited way universally bewildered.

High above, the aerial patrol swooped and swirled as its pilots cursed softly, held on to their activated weapons systems, and sought in vain for the target.

viii

—■—

As the little ship vanished not only from the humid, cloud-heavy atmosphere of the over-armed world but also from its immediate stellar environs, Lawson found himself reminiscing on how he'd come to find himself in this particular region of this particular galaxy, so different and so far from his own. Not that there was anything notable or extraordinary about the mission in which he was participating. He'd performed similar duties before, but usually much closer to home. Though relatively familiar and extensively mapped, their own galaxy was far from completely explored. This voyage represented something of a reach for him personally, if not for his kind.

Another individual might have found it boring, but not Lawson. For him every moment of existence brought new discoveries, new delights, even on those irritating occasions when one was forced to deal with the unenlightened and obstreperous. From what little he'd seen thus far this encounter was likely to be no different from what he expected.

Which was to say it would require a little more work than one might wish for.

It was his motivation for participating that made him unusually reflective. This arose out of a previous visit he'd made to a different region of this swirl of stars. What he'd seen and observed there had left him with a strong desire to someday return. He knew that he couldn't make up for what had happened that time. No one could. Not even Solarians could change the past. Nor was it a matter of making amends. Some things were beyond the aid of even the best intentioned.

It pivoted on the inescapable fact that what they'd told Markhamwit and Ganne went for other species as well. It was a dictum the Combine held to firmly and it usually served well all the parties involved.

Execution and follow-up was not always flawless, however. Sometimes no matter what you did, no matter how hard you tried, there was a certain amount of failure. Not every procedure, no matter how tried and tested, worked every time. The universe was not a perfect place, nor was it especially sympathetic. Intelligence was a precursor to but not necessarily a guarantee of success.

Just because an individual, or a species, happened to be intelligent it did not follow that it was also smart. Markhamwit was certainly intelligent: whether he was smart or not remained to be discovered. The same held true for Glastrom and the Nileans, as it did for all other independently evolved sentient species.

These thoughts cast him back to another place and another time. It wasn't far from the Great Lord's homeworld as Solarians measured distance. No more than a modest detour from his current intended destination. The more he remembered, the more it seemed he had only just been there . . .

The ship of strange shape hung in low orbit around the exquisite blue-green world while its instruments sampled atmosphere and gravity and assorted other useful indices of whether or not its crew would be happy should they choose to go for a picnic. Sensors also took the measure of the massive single moon, large enough to cling to a substantial atmosphere of its own.

Meanwhile the vessel's crew of four pondered the consequences of this careful mechanical attention while chatting among themselves. They vocalized their conversation because of their close proximity to one another, because it was traditional, and because it was much easier to hold simultaneous converse among four entities in that fashion.

Lawson was the youngest member of the group. Cognitively he was as much a part of the quartet as the eldest adult, maturity having more to do with experience than any abstract measure of intellectual capacity. Though Nafasi was considerably his senior there was no feeling of mental distance between the two men. Nafasi simply projected heavier thoughts, the result of the weight of experience. It was like a stronger, deeper taste to a particularly rich dessert. Over time Lawson would acquire his own distinctive mental flavor.

It was the same with Toyo and Alma. There was the usual distinctive feminine tinge to their thoughts that both intrigued and pleased him, just as they responded to the masculine tints of the two males aboard. The differences were very subtle and noticeable only to other Solarians. The fact that all four crew members of the tiny vessel were Terrans was due to the fact that members of that species were just a tick more curious than their fellows, and therefore slightly better inclined emotionally to the job of exploration.

That was their purpose and intent. Fast-traveling predecessors had recorded some problems in this neighboring galaxy, difficulties that had developed to the point where it might be time to address them with more than observation. Whenever possible the Combine preferred not to interfere, to let other lesser lifes mature and develop on their own. But when, through no fault of those concerned, progress took a turn down a blind alley, it was time to step in.

Simultaneously with Lawson's vessel a couple of other craft driven by similar intent were casting about for information up and down the length and breadth of the same galactic arm. Lawson and his shipmates checked in with them periodically. It was usually left to Alma to do this, since the modest but still singular effort required to establish long-range communication took less out of her than her companions, though any of them including the young Lawson were equally capable of making the necessary connection. In toto a dozen or so Solarians had crossed the gulf to have a look around and file a report. Despite having studied the preliminary information, there was no way any of them could be sure exactly what to expect.

Some of what the first scouts had reported they could already confirm. Two dominant species were reaching out beyond the boundaries of their own systems, extending their reach and influence to worlds beyond their own. Thus far, no problem. But they had demonstrated an inclination to persuade by force where reason failed, and to seek allies to enhance not trade and commerce and cultural exchange but the kind of hidebound militaristic organizations that could frustrate rather than bolster the type of development the Combine sought to encourage.

This did not yet constitute a serious concern, but it was certainly a development that bore watching. That was what the crew of four was there to do: watch, take note, and report back. Eventually more serious steps might have to be taken, but events had not yet devolved to that point. Perhaps the shaky pendulum of cultural evolution would swing back for one dominant life form or the other and interference could be avoided. It was much to be hoped. Not only was it premature for the Combine to take an active role, there were always potential side effects that not even it could foresee.

It wasn't the task of Lawson and his companions to monitor the progress of either rapidly advancing species or render an evaluation of their methods. That job fell to others. Instead they had been directed to carry out a survey of the starfield that lay between the two would-be empires, to see if anything like a substantial third force might be arising between them. Such a buffer species could serve not only to forestall the war that the predictors sadly foresaw developing but also to raise the maturity level of all three concerned.

Thus far no such potentially helpful life-form had been detected. This was a fecund region of youngish to middle-aged stars and the worlds they secured with their gravity had given birth to life aplenty. Some of it was sentient, but so far every one they had touched upon had been quite primitive.

Until now. The signs of technological progress on the surface below were unmistakable, though visible only to the ship's highly advanced sensory equipment.

"I wonder if they realize how lucky they are." Toyo Wowara examined a visual floating in the air near her seat. She plucked it from its resting place and turned it over and over in her fingers.

Schooler was peering at another, more intricate projection. "It's certainly the prettiest place we've visited so far. Oceans and continental masses in classic proportion, temperate to tropical climate, plenty of rivers for irrigation, and tectonically stable. Greenery everywhere. You couldn't ask for a better world on which to evolve."

Toyo nodded. "And as soon as they're ready, they've got a habitable moon beckoning them outward. Talk about having a natural spur to scientific development right on your doorstep."

"It's not home, but it's better than a memory." Nafasi Seguin muttered at the control dais. Within, concealed devices that were as much magic as mechanical hummed responsively. "What do you think, James?" He glanced back at the youngest member of the crew.

Lawson was eyeing the same projection as Alma Schooler, an enhanced representation of the southern continent. As he stared, magnification focused on a long, gently curving cove into which multiple rivers and streams emptied. This handsome bay fronted a gentle, rolling plain that backed up against mountains clad in dense vegetation.

"Looks nice. I wouldn't mind a stroll. What do we do if we encounter any of the locals?"

Nafasi smiled. "They're at an interesting stage. There are urban concentrations but the population is still mostly rural. There's evidence of transoceanic travel by means of both sail and steam, and an equivalent land-based transportation system on at least two of the four continents. The other two seem to be less developed. But there's no question that they understand and utilize science in their daily lives. A couple of the largest cities even show evidence of airborne pollution, probably a consequence of the burning of fossil fuels."

Toyo wrinkled her nose. "Technology stumbles on."

"They have to go through the stage," Nafasi reminded her. "You have to crawl before you can walk."

"Not to mention poop in your collective pants," she added. "They'll grow out of it."

"Or poison themselves," the sometimes somber Alma pointed out. "Some species do."

Nafasi shrugged. "That's not for us to decide. They have to raise themselves by self-determination to the minimum accepted level. Otherwise formal contact will do them more harm than good. They'll either lurch about and try to worship us, or wither away in an orgy of self-pity and racial inadequacy."

He looked over at Lawson. "That doesn't mean we can't yak with them on an individual basis. Experience has shown that isolated encounters have no effect on the body politic, either because reports of such visits aren't believed or because those encountered choose for reasons of their own not to report them. Does that answer your question?"

Lawson's attention remained focused on the slowly shifting projection. "I suppose. It's just that while I've studied plenty of accounts I've never personally interacted with representatives of a non-Combine life form that's achieved this degree of technology. They're sort of in-between."

"A delicate era in their development." Nafasi monitored the ship's readouts with another part of himself. "They're straddling the developmental fence. What they do in the next hundred years or so will determine whether they continue to advance or destroy themselves through inimical technologies." He squinted at a projection.

"There are some real disparities in design if not the level of accomplishment between the paired continents we're stationary over and the other two across the major ocean."

Toyo looked interested. "Different technological response to different conditions?"

Nafasi shook his head. "That's what I would assume, except that according to the sensors there are no significant differences between the four landmasses. Nothing on a scale to require development of an entirely different systemology for development and exploitation."

"Aesthetics?" Alma proposed. "Religion?"

Again Nafasi was negative. "On a continent-wide basis? Unlikely. No, most probably we have two different societies maturing here, separated by an oceanic rift. Not an untypical situation. There is evidence of contact between the two. Certainly some of the sea-faring craft we've imaged are capable of traversing the distances involved. But the differences are striking."

"Something to tickle the mind." Alma clearly relished the challenge of resolving the developmental disparity.

"While we're taking a stroll," Lawson reminded her. He was respectful of his elders but in no way intimidated. He was as much a Solarian as any of them, as much as any wizened ancient or barely sapient toddler.

"I agree," said Nafasi. Though there was no captain on the ship and all were equal in terms of control, Nafasi was senior and therefore accorded the privilege of speaking first, if not of giving orders. It wasn't necessary anyway. He wouldn't have opened his mouth if he hadn't already sensed a consensus.

He turned back to his board. "I'd be astonished if they had anything capable of detecting our presence, much less our approach. We'll pick a quiet area but one that's not on the outskirts. I'd like to have a talk with some of the locals and it'll go easier if they're not true country bumpkins. We want rural but not uneducated types." He poked a manipulative finger into the projection.

"The hills that front the southern portion of this bay look like a good spot. There are sizable farms all over the area, the terrain will offer a place to conceal the ship, and yet it's not too far from a major seaport. We should be able to drop in, have a look around, strike up a conversation or two, and get out without causing any panic."

"I'm for that." Toyo rose from her seat and whispered at the projection. Magnification obediently increased, to the point where they could make out individual structures and a spiderweb of narrow, unpaved roads. "Look at these woods. Almost jungle-like despite the temperate climate."

"I'd like to take a permanent record of the seaport

facilities to the north," Alma said. "Given the size of their moon they must have to deal with some pretty impressive tides. That they've obviously done so is a testament to their abilities."

Nafasi nodded thoughtfully. "All right. We'll make a couple of quick passes and let the sensors soak up plenty of stuff for you to study later. Then we'll drop down for a walk-about in person." He stretched meaningfully. "Myself, I'm ready for some warm, unrecycled air."

"Yes," agreed Lawson. "That last world was chilly."

"Shambling ursine types at the sticks-and-stones level," Alma recalled. "Not much to talk about."

"Give them time," Nafasi reminded her. "Someday they too will be ready, if they choose the right path."

Toyo made a face. She was easily the most irreverent member of the group. "Maybe by then they'll have done something about their body odor."

"They're one step removed from pure animalism," Alma was disapproving. "Don't be so critical."

"Can I help it if I have a more refined sense of smell than the rest of you?"

"You can't help much of anything, Toyo," quipped the other woman unexpectedly.

"I can help myself to some sweet flowers, if there are any," she retorted.

"From what we've seen so far I imagine there'll be blooms aplenty." Nafasi waved at the board and the little ship commenced its descent, aiming for the seaport that so intrigued Schooler.

A couple of multi-masted vessels anchored out in the bay bobbed a little more urgently that morning as an unexpected gust of wind jostled their hulls. Their sails were furled and their boilers cool, which led several of their crew to attribute the disturbance not to unseen sources of wind but to a couple of rogue wavelets.

One sailor who was nearly blown off the end of the long pier took personal offense at the wave theory, and with good reason. He also insisted that he had seen something vaguely oval in shape that was fashioned of material like dull glass appear out of the southwest and rush past not more than a ship's length above his head. It was the force of its passing that had nearly swept him into the waters of the bay, not some mysterious wave.

Upon hearing this explanation his compatriots insisted loudly that his tumble was more likely due to the force of liquid stimulants passing through his body. After participating in several fights in defense of his veracity the lone sailor gave up trying to defend the proof of his eyes and returned to his duties, but his mind would hold on to that image until the day he died.

Scanning passes completed, the little ship settled in a pile of dust in a hollow quite close to a disturbed but stalwart tree. It spread massive branches wide, each thickly festooned with knobby clusters of round green spheres. Though not leaves, they served the same function. While the tree could easily have sheltered the craft beneath its dense boughs there was no need to do so, since air travel of any kind was still unknown to the energetic inhabitants of this world. The only creatures capable of detecting its presence from above were interested solely in more mundane matters like finding food.

Toyo was first out, though her companions were close behind. The air was coy with the sweet musk of growing things. The small flying creatures that had been unsettled by the ship's arrival gradually returned to their branches and their crannies in the rocks, ignoring the glistening bulge that had appeared without warning in their midst. Animals with bright pink skins and short legs scuttled out again in search of fallen nuts and seeds while the modest creek that drained the hollow carried settling dust seaward.

Lawson hopped down alongside Wowara, looked around approvingly. "It's as beautiful on the surface as it was from above. This species has a great start on the future."

"If they don't mess it up," Schooler commented, ever the realist. She knelt to examine a cluster of bright blue flowers with ragged edges.

"All right," said Seguin. "Everyone enjoy themselves and take a different point of the compass. Be back when you've tired of it." Bending to gently pluck a blue blossom, he stuck it behind his right ear and then promptly struck off northward, unarmed but hardly defenseless. Wowara turned southward while Schooler headed east.

That left the west to Lawson. No one had chosen a path or direction. Their choices had been arrived at by mutual, silent consensus. Solarians did everything by consensus, except when someone got hopping exercised about something. Then there was a consensus to let that individual do as he or she pleased. It was a system that worked very well and allowed for fits of excitable individuality. No such incidents were likely to afflict the crew of the little ship. They had been chosen for their compatibility.

Lawson had no worries as he strode down the gentle slope, avoiding bushes and high grasses. Once, he sensed the presence of something large and furry watching him from a cave in the low rock face nearby. Stopping, he stared directly toward it for several long moments. The creature within neither advanced nor retreated. Eventually it returned to the snooze that Lawson had interrupted, and he continued his walk.

Yellow, white, and pink flowers soon overwhelmed the blue, a zephyr-stirred sea of primitive but cheery colors. Small insects darted among the blossoms, assisting the various species in reproduction. His old friends Buzwuz and Lou would have delighted in the untrammeled surroundings, but they were not along for the journey. Their presence was not required.

He was stooping to admire a dense cluster of yellow blooms that together formed a sphere half the size of the ship when a voice interrupted his reverie. Rising and turning without panic or fear, he found himself confronting a native.

The similarities were startling: bipedal, two arms, fingers, a rounded (but hairless) skull, bright black eyes, and a prominent nasal ridge. The external ears were set much higher on the head than in one of his own kind, however, and were pointed like those of a cat. She spoke again, her manner indicative of uncertainty but not fear. A six-legged beast stood nervously nearby, short of face but long of leg and tail, a single saddle cinched between the two front pairs of legs.

Lawson activated the small shiny integral translator attached to his belt, swinging it around so that it pointed in the native's direction. "Hello," he said softly, his lips even.

She started visibly, then relaxed. The lipless mouth moved. "You can understand me?"

He tapped the translator. "Through this device. It would take me a while to master your language to the point where I could speak it myself. Several weeks, at least."

Hesitation, then, "Surely you could not learn so fast?"

Seeing her mouth remain parted he thought he could hazard a smile. "I'm a quick learner and languages are a specialty of mine." Silently he thought to his companions, *"I've met one of the local dominants. She seems wary but willing to continue the conversation. Arrived on some kind of riding animal. Quiet, too. I didn't hear them come up on me."*

Toyo's thought-form reached him. "You're a fast worker, James. Didn't even need an introduction."

"Hey," he cast back, "she spoke first."

"Have a useful chat," Seguin thought. He did not need

to ask if the native was armed because that would have been instantly apparent in Lawson's thought-form.

Similarly, it was clear he was not in any danger. Having learned all they needed to know in a few short, terse thoughts, the others carried on as though nothing more extraordinary had happened than a chance encounter between a couple of mice. They expressed no interest in how the encounter would proceed. That was entirely up to Lawson.

"My name is T'eele. I saw your coach set down," the native told him. "My first thought was to flee, but I was fascinated by your means of transportation. It just appeared." She moved a little nearer, her very round eyes inspecting him closely. "Where do you come from?"

Lawson widened his smile, noting no adverse reaction, and gestured upward with a finger. "Out there. From beyond your sky."

"From Langese?" she asked hesitantly.

"If by that you mean your moon," he inferred, "no. From much farther."

"From farther." She pondered this. "Then your glass vehicle is some kind of sky-boat?"

He nodded approvingly, wondering how she would interpret the gesture. "That's very good. Yes."

She looked around suddenly. "Are there more of you?"

"I have friends with me," he told her simply. "We mean you no harm. We are simply here to have a look around and to enjoy some fresh air. And to meet with you." He extended a hand.

She considered the proffered limb, reached out with one of her own and gently drew the underside of her fingers across the back of his hand. Not only was she a physically attractive being, he mused, but she had courage aplenty.

"You're very bold," he complimented her.

She made a peculiar but not unpleasant whistling sound

in her throat. "There are those who consider me reckless, even for a subordinate matriarch. I accept it as a challenge." She gestured back over a shoulder. "Your sky-boat: how does it fly? By what mechanism can it support itself in the air? I see no smoke, no puffs of steam."

"You wouldn't understand the principles involved, much less the mechanics," he assured her. "What's a subordinate matriarch?"

"One next in line to lead an extended clan. You don't have clans?"

"Not in the same sense. We're all part of one clan, actually. We call ourselves Solarians."

" 'So'larians,' " she echoed, making a good attempt at the alien word.

So even the rumors hadn't reached this world, he thought. These people were truly unvisited. He was pleased. They would be a novelty to one another. He looked forward to enjoying her company as much as his present surroundings.

"Lucky," came the thought-form of Toyo. "I haven't found anything but bugs. Nice bugs, though. They don't try to sting or bite."

Lawson shut her out to concentrate on his visitor. "So you watched us arrive and you didn't run away."

"I couldn't. I was too astonished. I've never seen anything like you before, though you look something like a very peculiar person. Just . . . odd. Not ugly and revolting, like a Denkou."

Lawson's smile subsided. "What are you?"

She straightened, pride evident in her stance. "One of the true people, of course. I am B'eitara." She took a sudden step backward. "You are not some friend of the Denkou?"

"Take it easy. I don't even know what a Denkou is. Maybe you could enlighten me?"

She relaxed visibly. "Truly you are ignorant of our world. So you cannot be blamed for your ignorance."

"Thanks," he said dryly.

She gestured past him. "The Denkou live far from here, across the sea. I know all about them because I live here near the great port of Sere'ili and I listen to the memory-talk of the sailors and soldiers."

Lawson did not tense. Solarians had long ago discarded such reactions as wasteful of energy. But he became more attentive. "Soldiers?"

"Oh yes." She did something with her facial muscles that was not quite a smile but that had the effect of conveying the same feeling. "The armies of the B'eitara are renowned for their spirit and fighting ability. Once, we fought among ourselves, but now we are unified in search of greatness."

"Unification is good," he told her.

"When the grand fleet is finished we will carry the fight to the homelands of the Denkou and put an end to them."

"That's not so good," he said.

Her expression changed, first to one of instinctive anger, gradually shifting to curiosity. "I do not understand. We look so much alike and you say you are no friend of the Denkou."

"I didn't say that. I said that I wasn't familiar with them. My companions and I have just arrived here. We're just learning about you, much less these Denkou. They're not like you?"

"Oh, no!" The mere suggestion clearly shocked her. "The Denkou are horrible, hairy creatures, much bigger than you or me, with dreadful slitted eyes and long poisonous fangs. They suck the life out of their victims and leave them discarded husks."

"Dangerous animals," he suggested.

"Yes, but with a crude sort of raw intelligence."

"How intelligent?" he asked softly.

She seemed a little hesitant. "They have ships and roads, like we do, only much more poorly designed and built. They live in cities where they work endlessly on weapons of war and make plans to enslave the B'eitara. Their art is repulsive to the eye and their music grating to the ear. The world will be well rid of them."

"I see," said Lawson slowly. "How soon until this grand fleet is ready to sail against the Denkou?"

She looked away. "Well, actually it's something that's only been talked about. It would be a very costly undertaking. Denkouar is so very far away some sailors are not even sure a fleet could travel that distance and arrive in good enough condition to fight. At least, that's what the sailors tell me. They also say that the Denkou have strong fortifications along their coasts, just as we do. So this is something that may not happen for a very long time."

Lawson nodded. The western ocean presented quite a challenge for a low steam-and-sail technology. Successfully invading an entire hemisphere and carrying a war to inhabitants possessing equal technology called for more of an investment than these B'eitara seemed capable at first glance of making.

"You hate these Denkou." It was not a question.

"You have only to see them." She shuddered visibly. "Everything about them is hideous: their appearance, their habits, their religion, their philosophy."

"You've seen Denkou, then?"

She hesitated. "Well, not exactly. I've seen one that was killed and stuffed, and I've talked to sailors who've encountered them alive. But I've never actually seen one myself."

It was obvious to Lawson that there was little point in pursuing this line of conversation. A beautiful fanatic was still a fanatic. Perhaps she was no more than that, an exception among her own kind. One could hope.

"Tell me more about the B'eitara," he asked her, ready to change the subject from talk of war and ugliness.

Lawson was not the only one to encounter a sample of the local life. Alma had met a pair of adolescents out for a hike and after overcoming their initial terror had settled in to talk with them. Their responses to her inquiries about the Denkou differed only in the most minor details from the information Lawson had gleaned from the female named T'eele. While both of them carried on with their respective conversations they remained in contact with Nafasi and Toyo, who thus far in their own explorations had encountered only plants and wildlife.

"We have what appears to be an unusual and possibly unique evolutionary situation here," Lawson was thinking.

"Yes," concurred the thought-form of Nafasi. "A world so hospitable it may well have given birth to two distinctly different sentient species. Separated by the major ocean, they seem to have developed independently."

"And now that they're aware of each other," added Toyo, "they've wasted no time learning how to hate each other's guts, apparently for no other reason than that they *are* different."

"A deplorable state of affairs but one we've encountered before," Nafasi went on. "Unfortunately, even though two apparently dissimilar species are involved instead of the usual one, we still can't interfere. Tribal conflicts are beneath our official notice. They'll have to surmount this hurdle themselves before we can step in and offer advice."

"I wouldn't worry too much. They can't make a war of it," Alma declared confidently. "The logistical problems it would involve exceed their ability to solve. With a little luck, trade and commerce will succeed in overcoming their initial fearful reaction to each other and they'll learn to get along. Distance and the lack of technology sufficiently advanced to overcome it should make the difference.''

"I wonder if we really are dealing with two distinct species here," Nafasi offered thoughtfully, "or merely paranoid distortions of sailors' tales. Neither this T'eele or the two adolescents has actually seen a live Denkou. I think it's time we did.''

There was no need to ask for his companions' opinions. They were as plain to him as his own thoughts.

Lawson watched the local sun drop behind a hill as he sat with T'eele beneath the shade of a fragrant-blossomed tree she called *minwitii*. "My friends and I are going to leave soon.''

She looked surprised. "So quickly? But your presence here is a wonder that should be shared with others. I know of many in the city much more qualified than I to speak with you, to answer your questions and ask many of their own.''

"You've done just fine," he told her sincerely. "I appreciate your candor. Not many individuals at your level of achievement would have been able to handle my sudden appearance as gracefully as you have.''

"You are not so very different from us," she told him. "Though it makes me laugh to see someone with ears on the sides of their head instead of on top, as is proper. How can you hear anything with that kind of arrangement?''

"We know how to listen," he assured her. "It's one of the things we do best. Listen and ask questions.''

"I would have liked to have asked more of my own." She put her lean, lightly furred arms around her knees and gazed at the darkening sky. "Are there any other peoples besides you up there, beyond the sky and the moon?''

"More than you can imagine," he told her.

"I would like to meet them too, someday." Her voice and expression turned sad as she lowered her gaze back to him. "That will not be possible for me, will it?''

"I'm afraid not. You're very adaptable, but I think it would be a bit overwhelming for you. And we have a policy about such things. You have to learn how to walk before you can run." Buzwuz, he knew, would have been appalled at the earth-bound analogy and would have put it much differently.

"I am not sure that I understand."

"Your many-times-removed offspring will," he assured her.

"At least I was able to have this time with you. I will look at the stars differently now, when the sun is down. I will know that there are others like the B'eitara out there, others who will be our friends someday." She made a face. "Are there also those like the Denkou out there?"

"I don't know. I keep telling you that I've never met a Denkou."

"Pray that you do not." Reaching out, she stroked the back of his left hand with the fingertips of her own. "This is how we say goodbye, Ja'mes L'awson."

He hesitated, wondering what the others would think, and then decided it didn't matter. Leaning forward in the failing twilight, he put his lips gently against her mouth. She looked startled but did not pull away.

"That's how males and females among my people say goodbye. It's a very ancient ritual. We've changed in many ways, but surprising things hold up under the weight of ages."

She felt of the edges of her mouth with the limber fingers of one hand. "How very peculiar! It seems so unhygienic."

The thought-forms of Nafasi and Alma were grinning at him. Toyo's teasing was more straightforward. "Hey, how come you never said goodbye to me that way, James?"

He cast a cool thought at her. "The opportunity never presented itself."

"Present, indeed," she quipped.

"That's enough ethnological transference for one day." Nafasi's mental tone was brisk. "We've done enough here for now. Let's have a look at these boogeyfolk, the Denkou."

Lawson blinked as his thoughts returned to the grassy place beneath the tree. He rose and stepped back from the native. "Goodbye, T'eele. And good luck with your life. I hope it's a long and happy one."

She made a simple gesture with one hand. "Farewell, Ja'mes L'awson. You have honored me among all my clan."

He ignored Toyo's following thought as he turned and strode off in the direction of the ship.

ix

━━━━━━━━━━━━━━━━ ■ ━━━━━━━━━━━━━━━━

F or a vessel capable of crossing the intergalactic gulf the journey from one side of the great ocean to the other took a literal blink of an eye, though choosing a landing site required a moment or two of study. They set down in a dry creek bed not far from the sea, which here crashed against a much rockier, wilder shore than the one they had left. They were situated not far north of a major city, on the northern crest of the southwestern continent.

An intermittent cold drizzle was swirling when they emerged from the lock, but it soon gave way to a stiff ocean westerly as they headed shoreward. All of them wore the same attire as they had in the much milder land of the B'eitara, fluctuating meteorological conditions being something to which they gave little heed. Within certain climatological parameters many Solarians had the ability to regulate their body temperature. As a consequence the four of them would not freeze, but they would require food at an earlier hour than usual.

The trees on this rugged coast were tall and straight,

with narrow, deeply grooved leaves that were very different from the placid growths that shaded the perfumed, sunny fields of the B'eitara. What flowers were visible hugged the ground and sought protection from the wind in cracks in the rock. In addition to the prolific yellows and whites there was a striking lavender blossom so large Lawson could not span it with his open palm. It emitted a faint stink that was in sharp contrast to its bright hues.

They kept together this time as they walked out of the creek bed and down toward the beach. Crustaceans and mollusk-like creatures scuttled energetically about the scree, migrating between one wave and another. Something with a vast wingspan soared by overhead, watching the shorebreak for edible denizens of the surf line. Sea-soaked logs by the hundreds littered the base of the stunted cliff the visitors descended.

"As lovely as where we were earlier." Alma's gaze pierced the horizon. "Not as warm, but in its stark aspect equally invigorating."

"A comely world," Toyo agreed. "Maybe time will assist these two species in keeping it that way."

"We still don't know that there are two species here," Nafasi reminded her. "We have only the word of three young B'eitara for that. I'd like a little more proof."

Alma had wandered a little ways down the beach. Now she called back to them without turning. "Come and talk to it. Your proof, that is. Five or six of them, from the look of things."

They caught up to her and together the four of them ambled down the shoreline.

There were a half dozen of the shambling, shuffling creatures. For all their apparent clumsiness they handled their fishing gear with dexterity. Three of them stood out in the shallow, choppy surf, a long black net stretched between them. Two others waited on the beach, accompanied by a much smaller individual. Whether it was a child or simply a stunted adult the visitors had no way of telling. Covered in long, stringy, jet-black hair that was lightly curled at the ends, it was an exact duplicate of its larger companions.

The juvenile hypothesis turned out to be correct. When it caught sight of the four approaching Solarians the small individual let out a startlingly loud squeak and rushed to hide behind the legs of one of the larger members of the hirsute retinue. As yet Lawson and his friends were unable to tell if the creatures were male, female, neuter, or assorted. Except for variations in size there were no immediately obvious sexual characteristics or physical differences between them.

The two Denkou on shore immediately assumed a defensive posture that placed them in front of the youngster. One gave forth a series of deeper, more mature squeaks that must have reached those out in the surf. They hurriedly folded up their long net and made their way inshore, striding powerfully through the small waves. Packs on their broad backs jounced and bobbed as their owners rushed to gain the beach.

The four visitors slowed and stopped within speaking distance while the two Denkou protecting the youngster favored them with glowering stares. Their eyes were large and bright, with blue-flecked irises and the long black slitted pupils the B'eitara T'eele had mentioned.

Hands consisted of thick pads set with only two opposable fingers, more like pincers than anything else. Both the arms and legs were truly double-jointed, which gave the creatures great flexibility despite their size. Each of the adults was at least as big as a small bear while the largest of them towered over the tallest of the Solarians. They wore no clothing other than their functional packs and belts. Prominent piercing fangs protruded from the upper jaws even of the child.

Toyo gestured toward a pile of moist, pulpy invertebrates that had been heaped on a wide, waterproof sheet.
"Appropriate food for flesh suckers."

"If those B'eitara knew what they were talking about,"
Lawson conceded.

Hands on hips, she studied the scowling Denkou spec-
ulatively. "Mighty impressive hypodermic cutlery for
vegetarians."

"One cannot deprecate a species because they have
been condemned by nature to the consumption of certain
foods." Nafasi gazed unblinkingly back at the largest native.
"It's quite likely they consider the masticating of protein
solids unbelievably repulsive."

"I'm sure they do." Lawson was put in mind of his liq-
uid-diet Callisian friends.

Two of the largest Denkou took a challenging step forward.

"Time to open up a dialogue." The much smaller Toyo
matched their advance. It did not matter which of them approached the natives. She had simply chosen to act before
any of her companions.

"Hello. How's the fishing?" The rectangle on her service belt squeaked hysterically.

Clearly taken aback, the Denkou immediately set to
squeaking among themselves. Following an incongruous
but brief conversation, the second-largest turned back to
the visitors.

"Thimd am I. Like the hairless B'eitara you look, yet you
are not." He stared hard at each of them in turn. "Your
faces differently are set, you have not even short fur on your
bodies, and your ears . . ."

"Those ears again," chuckled Nafasi. He had the ability
to wiggle his own, a sign not of Solarian control over their
bodies but of one individual's control over his companions'
expressions. "No," he explained through his translator.

"We are not B'eitara. We come from lands much farther away than theirs."

"Are you all cooperative fisherfolk?" Toyo inquired.

Thimd gestured expansively. "This my family is. We fish for only part of our waking time. I am also a builder of boats. My brother Stayv is a machine-maker. We also together have a small garden plot."

"You sound quite successful," Nafasi told him.

"We do well enough." Thimd was being more proud than boastful.

Toyo advanced until she was standing within arm's reach of the much more massive Denkou. Her attitude was one for whom the satiation of curiosity far exceeds any concern for the safety of one's individual self.

"A garden? What do you do with a garden, with teeth like that?"

The Denkou took no offense; indeed, it seemed amazed at her ignorance. "Why, we many crops raise."

"We in *khokoua* specialize," explained another. Lawson was still having trouble trying to separate females from males, if indeed that easy division could be made among the Denkou. "Its core is most sweet and tasteful."

"Plant juices," Nafasi thought. "They liquefy the interior and suck out the result. Maybe they can do it with flesh also, but it's clear they're not exclusively raging carnivores."

"They seem willing, if not eager to talk," Alma pointed out.

"Certainly they're no more or less suspicious than the B'eitara," Nafasi agreed. "Or perhaps hesitancy is simply politeness to them. After all, we're more than total strangers."

"Let's sit and talk." Lawson eyed the slithering mass of netted invertebrates. "But that doesn't mean we have to stay for lunch."

"Are you sure you're not a different kind of B'eitara?" asked one of the Denkou.

"Not at all," Nafasi assured it. "We are Solarians."

"You like B'eitara look," the husky creature declared through its body beard. "Except you some hair have."

"You don't get along too well with the B'eitara, do you?" Toyo chose a seat among the wave-polished rocks. At high tide this entire shoreline would be under water all the way up to the cliffs, Lawson reflected. The danger didn't seem to concern the Denkou family.

"They irritable little creatures are," the largest Denkou explained. "Always ready for a fight. They will at the slightest imagined insult kill, and fire their weapons on the innocent and unarmed at the least provocation."

"Yes," squeaked another emphatically. "Imagine sailing completely across the great ocean only trouble to make, to loot and to murder. They a vicious, barbaric race are. Knowing this you can understand our need to be assured that you are not simply another variety of them, or some close ally we have not encountered before."

"You've seen the B'eitara do these bad things, then?" Alma lazily dipped her feet in a refreshingly cool tide pool.

The Denkou eyed one another. "Well, no, not actually," the first speaker replied. "But we news of such atrocities read more frequently than we would like. Very well documented it all is."

"Your media representatives and your government wouldn't lie about something like that, of course," said Toyo.

The Denkou looked shocked. "Why should they? B'eitara prisoners admit that they find us loathsome to look upon. They abhor our appearance, our manners, our habits, our body odor, even the way we eat."

"Maybe your leaders just want to stir up trouble between you and the government of the B'eitara," Nafasi suggested.

"Why would they do that?" The Denkou appeared genuinely bemused. "It is the B'eitara who want to make discord. Fortunately their raids infrequent are and little harm do because of the distances involved."

"And because your weapons are so primitive," Lawson pointed out.

One of the Denkou took exception to this observation. "Our weapons are *not* primitive! They the most modern and sophisticated are that can be fashioned. Are you trying to tell us that you have better weapons where you come from?" Tension among the locals increased noticeably as they awaited a response to this query.

"Actually, we have no weapons at all." Nafasi spread his hands wide to expose his narrow duty belt.

The largest Denkou eyed him askance. "You are unarmed?"

Nafasi smiled at him. "I didn't say that. I said that we have no weapons. It's not the same thing at all."

"If we decide that you lying are and that you are spies for the B'eitara, we could hold you here while one of us returns in the wagon to notify the authorities. You don't look very fast or strong to me. What's to keep us from restraining you?"

"Not much," admitted Nafasi simply. "But it would be an impolite way to treat guests. If we were spies do you think we'd be sitting here chatting casually with you like this, instead of watching from afar? Besides, what would we be spying on? Family fishing techniques?"

One of the Denkou gave the questioner a rap on the back of his head that would have felled Lawson or any of his companions. "Freemesh! Can't you see that they're telling the truth? See the easy way they look at us? They couldn't be B'eitara."

"They could very clever liars be," insisted the bestricken one, as he rubbed the back of his hairy skull.

"With words, yes. But not with their faces." The big female turned to regard the visitors, draped casually across the rocks. "See how they upon us gaze? There no averting of eyes is, no wrinkling of nostrils, no disgust or contempt in their postures or expressions. No B'eitara would at us like this look."

"Like what?" Alma asked curiously.

"Like another of our own kind. Like people."

Nafasi sighed. "It's abundantly clear that you developed civilization independent of one another, probably unaware of each other's existence until what you would regard as historic times. That's a big ocean separating you and there's no land connection between the east and west hemispheres. The size of your moon guarantees hefty tides." He gestured at the cliff face. "There's plenty of evidence for them right here. Tides like this mean that small craft don't function well close inshore. That would've served to postpone contact between your respective peoples even longer.

"When you made contact you discovered that not only were you utterly different physically but that you didn't like each other either, with the result that now you're fighting over nothing at all."

"Nothing at all?" The main Denkou took exception. "We only defending ourselves against vicious B'eitara attacks are."

"They'd probably claim that they're doing the same thing with regard to you. You're both intelligent, you've got a wonderful world to share that's big enough for the both of you, and you can accomplish a lot more working together than you ever can sniping and raiding each other."

"We can never with the B'eitara learn to work," insisted one of the smaller locals. "They so different from us are."

"Different how?" Nafasi demanded to know.

The Denkou regarded him as though he had just taken a long step into a fresh pile of idiocy. "You seem good eyes to have. If you have upon the B'eitara looked you can see immediately how different we are.''

"I'm sorry,'' said Alma, ''but I don't see that at all.''

The Denkou glared at her. ''I was to that one speaking.'' He gestured at Nafasi.

"Speak to one Solarian, speak to them all.'' Toyo was chucking some sort of mollusk-thing under its almost-chin. It rolled over on its ventral side to give the soothing fingers easier access.

The Denkou gave up, went on. ''We much larger than the B'eitara are. We a proper amount of hair have, while the B'eitara almost totally bald are. They chew solid food instead of sucking it properly. Their pupils round are instead of slitted. There are many other distinctions too numerous to describe. Surely you recognize these?'' The other Denkou looked on anxiously. Meanwhile the juvenile had hesitantly approached Lawson and was examining the fabric of his jumpsuit with much interest.

"Those are simply differences in shape and appearance,'' replied Nafasi. ''They mean nothing.''

"Then how do you 'different' define?'' the Denkou inquired belligerently.

"The only differences lie here.'' Alma tapped the side of her head. ''Both you and the B'eitara are intelligent. That's all the similarity you need. From what we've managed to glean thus far from our brief visit here you're about equal in intelligence.'' The Denkou bristled at this but said nothing.

"That is to say,'' Toyo went on, still playing with the mollusk, ''that you're equally stupid.''

"You claim a friend to be and then you insult us,'' the Denkou growled.

"A statement of provable fact is never an insult, and it's foolish to regard it as one,'' she told her. ''You're stupid because you can't see beyond your skins. This is not entirely your fault. Tell me: in a completely dark room, communicating by means of self-illuminating printed messages passed back and forth, could you tell a B'eitara from a Den-kou?"

"There are different ways of thinking," the female insisted.

"Sure there are. The rational and the irrational. Neither of you is the latter. You're just careless."

"Are you truly saying that we should try to make friends with the B'eitara?" asked an aghast male.

Alma shrugged. "It beats mounting bigger and bigger raids against each other for the next several hundred years. You'd progress a lot faster through cooperation than the stimulus of casual mayhem."

"Progress toward what?" asked one of the Denkou guardedly.

"Cooperation. Maturation. Advancement. Qualification for entry into the Solarian Combine."

"Ah!" One of the Denkou looked satisfied. "That explains it. You come seeking allies to in some greater war of your own participate."

"Not at all," said Nafasi easily. "No one is forced to join the Combine. In fact, no one is asked. Others ask us if they can join."

"And how do you who to let into your precious Combine and who to keep out decide?"

"It's very simple. If a species is mature enough to join the Combine, they don't have to ask. They simply become a part of it. If they're still asking questions about how to qualify, then they're not ready."

This threw the questioner into mental contortions. He tried to decide how to proceed, failed, backed up, got further entangled upstairs, suddenly found himself wondering what a fisherman-gardener was doing trying to formulate such questions anyway.

"This is a matter for the local governor is," he decided abruptly.

"Sorry," said Lawson, "but if we'd wanted to parley with local officialdom we'd have set down in the center of the nearest city. We much prefer talking to regular folks."

"It doesn't matter." The Denkou started cautiously toward the path that could be seen descending the cliff face. "We must the proper officials notify."

"Suit yourselves," said Toyo. "You might tell them that it's time to start thinking about trying to make friends with the B'eitara."

"They won't listen," insisted one of the smaller Denkou.

"A lot of officials don't," agreed Alma. "Not-listening is a qualification for entry into higher levels of officialdom in many primitive societies. But now and again you come across the rare one that goes against the grain. They won't believe you when you tell them about us anyway. But you might tell your friends and neighbors about our conversation here today. Try to explain to them that shape and appearance aren't important at all when compared to intelligence and maturity."

"You all the same as one another look," pointed out one of the female Denkou.

"Not all Solarians do," Lawson explained. "Some of us are small and have wings. Others live in the sea and have fins or flippers. There are Solarians with tentacles instead of hands and others with hardly any manipulative digits at all."

"Now you spinning tales are," asserted the senior female Denkou.

"Not at all," declared Nafasi. "We're spinning some basic truths. Shape means nothing. Physical design means nothing. Color and shading and what sort of limbs you use to get about means nothing. Thought is all-important.

Those who think alike are alike. Those who share the same outlook on reality are real. Everything else strives to reach that point. It's not an enforced uniformity or even a compelled one. When you become truly intelligent, that's just the way you think."

"It's not a matter of the right way or the wrong way," Alma Schooler added. "It's just a matter of how the universe is. Wishing it were otherwise doesn't work. Nor does it matter, because the universe is pretty nice the way it is. And it's getting better all the time. So are those who live within its confines and learn to think sensibly."

"This too much for me is," admitted the senior male Denkou.

"Not if you stop to think about it," said Lawson. "Like all great truths, it's really very simple. Cooperating is better than fighting. Thought and emotion can complement instead of clash with each other. If one respects one's surroundings, one is respected by them in return. The same goes for someone who doesn't quite look or act like yourself. All you have to have in common is intelligent thought."

"We will ponder on these things," the senior female Denkou decided, "but we are simple folk and there is little we can do about what you say, even if we were to agree with you."

"Don't underestimate yourselves," Nafasi deposed. "Thinking is just the first step. After thought comes action. You can tell those you know."

"They will think us mad," insisted one of the junior Denkou.

"All prophets are thought mad in their time," avowed Lawson. "It's only later that they ascend to prophethood. Time is the lens through which madness becomes prophecy."

"I just want to fish and work my garden," declared the senior male Denkou. "Why do you this burden on us lay?"

"Because you seem to be common folk, and this is too important a matter to trust to officials or professionals or specialists," Toyo informed him. "We're bound by our own rules not to intrude, but that doesn't mean you can't unsettle. A little common sense could break this cycle of misunderstanding and shape-prejudice.

"You're in a unique position. We've never before encountered a world shared by two distinctly different intelligent species. New discoveries call for new protocols. We can't meddle, but we can offer a little advice in the course of our passing through. Try it. Talk to your friends and associates. See if someone's willing to speak companionably with the next lot of B'eitara who come sailing your way. Their reaction might surprise you."

"I doubt it," contended another Denkou. Then, at a sudden thought, "Have you this message passed among the B'eitara as well?"

"We talked to a few of them. Less than you. Great endings often have small beginnings." She eased away from the mollusk, which by now was languid from her attentions. "That's all we can ask. We can't compel or force you to do anything. Not as long as you're restricted to this one world. You have no idea how special a place it is. I could spend a fair bit of leisure time here myself.

"All we can do is proffer a suggestion. Take it and seek applications. Maybe by the time we return you'll have surmounted your ingrained frivolities and will be ready for the next step." She shook seawater from her fingers. "Maybe by then you'll see the B'eitara as we see you, and they'll regard you similarly." Without a word between them the four visitors gathered among the rocks as if to depart. The juvenile had to be called away from Lawson by its parent.

"Wait!" squeaked one of the Denkou. The Solarians turned. "How can we this thing do without your help? As you say it will not be believed that such as you visited with us."

"Proof of our existence isn't important," Nafasi told him. "It's the thought that matters. Thought has no shape, no color, no alien origins to mark it. It's pure, like mathematics. It's an idea. Plant it, nurture it, and it will bloom by itself."

The Denkou family group was still dubious. "We might be able a few to convince that the B'eitara can be talked to, but who will the B'eitara persuade? You say you with some of them spoke. What if they abandon this notion?"

"Both of you have time on your side," Alma told them. "Your level of technology is so low and the seas separating you so extensive and storm-beset that by the time either of you has advanced enough to mount a serious assault against the other, you will have matured mentally. There's plenty of time for the idea to take hold on both sides of your common ocean. We think by the time that happens that both you and the B'eitara will have come around to see reason."

"Of course," Toyo added, "you could progress faster, but only if you cooperate."

One of the smaller Denkou couldn't resist adding, "What is to change the B'eitara's attitude toward our appearance?"

"Commerce and trade are wonderful equalizers," Lawson informed him. "They foster mutual dependence. When everyone is doing well out of cooperation it's hard to throw everything away in favor of a debilitating war." He raised a hand in farewell, as did his companions. The Denkou responded with a cheery, unified squeaking.

Lawson and his companions were reluctant to leave so pristine and untrammeled a world, but dozens of other systems beckoned. All had to be attended to, all had to be checked out, all deserved a little Solarian attention. The crew doubted they would find anything to compare with this planet of somnolent days and not one but two struggling, infant sentient species.

Back aboard he confronted Seguin. "Tell me, Nafasi, do you think they'll learn to cooperate?"

The senior Solarian considered. "Oh, I believe the odds are in their favor. Certainly it'll take a while for them to overcome their primitive shape-prejudice, but they're situated on opposite sides of the globe from one another. Even if commerce is interrupted by the occasional loud spat they're not likely to have the wherewithal to conduct a real fight over that distance for a century or two. By that time they'll be so accustomed to one another the fears and uncertainties will have become old hat."

Toyo was fiddling with a control panel. There were few controls on its surface but she knew the location of every one of them, visible or not.

"Can you really envision either species mounting an all-conquering invasion fleet against the other? By the time their ships crossed the ocean those aboard would be exhausted from the journey, if not seriously motion-sick. They'd be lucky to take a seacoast city or two. There's no way either of them could sustain a line of supply a tenth that long.

"No, they'll learn to tolerate one another and then to get along, because there's no practical alternative." She waved her hand at the board and a series of lights appeared just above its surface, hovering in the still air of the chamber.

Nafasi settled into the pilot's seat. "Pity we can't hang around to see how things work out. Our next system looks like an interesting place. Burgeoning intelligence emerging on a large habitable moon but not on its equally habitable primary planet.

"But not unprecedented." Lawson was thinking of the Callisians.

"Think these new prospects have what it takes upstairs to frame a dialogue?" Toyo asked aloud.

"Time to find out." Nafasi perturbed a control.

One of the oversized aerial gliders was brought up short by the wind that attempted to fill the cone of vacuum where the little ship had passed a nanosecond before. It struggled with its equilibrium, hooted disapprovingly at something it couldn't see, and then forgot all about the incident as it spotted something potentially tasty and filling crawling along the water's edge.

X

————————————————————■————————————————————

The details of his previous visit were as clear to Lawson as if they'd taken place yesterday. He was remembering as the little ship slowed, approaching the galactic lens from above. He had chosen this angle not out of necessity or the need to satisfy some special function, but purely for reasons of aesthetics. Having come so far, he felt that he and his crew deserved an overview of their destination.

There was something about being able to descry an entire galaxy with one's own eyes and without the aid of telescopes or other means of artificial enhancement, to take in millions of stars and their attendant systems at a glance. The colors were virtually unduplicatable, the effect on one's perceptions overwhelming. It required only the expenditure of a little time, which the Solarian crew had aplenty. Time, and the desire to do something with it.

The thought-form that interrupted his reminiscing preceded a deep, sonorous humming. A new shape entered the room and aimed oculars equally perceptive but different in design on the amazing panorama visible through the single port. Its tone was less than awed.

"A galaxy like any other."

Lawson turned to the Callisian hovering nearby. It kept a courteous distance. Had it chosen to hover next to Lawson's ear, or rest on his shoulder, the sound of its wings would have been deafening.

"Come now, Buzwuz. It's beautiful and you know it."

"Oh, I suppose the colors are nice, but frankly I prefer those of our own."

"It's not the look, it's what's there, what we're looking at. Millions upon millions of stars and five times as many worlds, uncountable moons and their attendant asteroid belts and comets and other assorted stellar objects."

The Callisian's buzzing rose an octave. "Doesn't mean much if they're all inhabited by quarrelsome dopes."

"I'll second that," came the thought-form of Lou from somewhere in back.

"You know," Lawson mused, "sometimes I can't figure out if you Callisians are naturally irreverent or if you just like to strike a pose."

"Definitely the latter." Buzwuz promptly pivoted in midair and hovered with his jacketed abdomen facing the ceiling and his head and antennae drooping floorward. "How's this?"

"Not atypical," Lawson assured him. The bee promptly reverted to his normal hovering position, once more focusing on the view.

"I don't mean to demean any galaxy," he projected, "but what's so special about this one? Besides the fact that we've a job to do here."

"He's been here before," came Freddy's thought-form from somewhere near Lou.

"I know that," Buzwuz responded. "But there's more to it than that." He hummed a little closer. "I've known you a long time, James. There's something on your mind you're not letting out for general discussion. Want to fill us in or should I keep guessing?"

Lawson sighed and looked away from the incredible view. "For a Callisian you're very perceptive, Buzwuz. It's nothing vital. It has to do with my previous journey here. I was part of a crew then, not the pilot. There were four of us."

Buzwuz caught the rest of the thought and recoiled. "All Terrans! Four of you! How did anyone get a word in edgewise?"

Lawson took no umbrage. "Much as it may startle you to know, we can take turns among ourselves."

"You hear that?" The Callisian projected his disbelief to his friends. "He says that four Terrans can talk without stepping on each other's thoughts. Me, I'll believe it when I hear it."

"Be that as it may," Lawson continued dryly, "it was a valuable learning experience for me. A study-and-record expedition. We covered a lot of territory."

"And now there's a problem," Lou thought toward him, "so they've cajoled us all into scooting out here to fix it."

"We and the other scouts recorded possibilities," Lawson continued. "It was hoped a visit like this wouldn't be required."

"Too bad," put in Freddy. "I'm not big on hops like this myself." His thought-form puffed itself up. "But somebody has to do it. Rules are being broken. The sanctity of emptiness is being violated."

"Don't get all gooey profound on us," Buzwuz chided him. He turned his attention back to Lawson. "So why the pause? To take pretty pictures? If that's what you want, check the files for M6482. Now *there's* a galaxy worth hanging around to have a look at!"

"I agree," affirmed Lawson, "but our job is here, not over in M6482. No matter where I'm sent I always like to take a moment to admire the scenery."

"Okay, so you've admired," said the thought-form of Tesz from well back in the ship. "Let's get on with it."

"You still haven't shared what you're concealing," Buzwuz reminded him.

Lawson bothered a tiny control. The vista forward smeared with sheer speed as he turned to regard his chitinous, humming companion.

"The expedition I was with visited and took notes on dozens of worlds and a respectable number of sentient species. But there was one particular place that was not only extraordinarily beautiful but unusual in the makeup of its population."

"Enlighten us," demanded all the bee-minds aboard in unison.

"It turned out to be home to two distinctly different species. One large, awkward, and hirsute. The other quite a bit like my type."

"Not another planet of verbose bipeds!" Lou screeched in mock outrage. "Even one per galaxy is too many."

"The similarities were largely superficial, as you can imagine. Both species were making progress technologically but had developed a shape enmity toward one another. Fortunately, they were separated by a vast ocean. They didn't possess the skills or means then to do each other any real harm and they won't now, but I'd like to check in on them."

"Why?" wondered Freddy. "Doesn't sound to me like there's anything much worth seeing there."

"It'll just take a moment," Lawson replied. "The group I was with talked to a very few individuals of each species. Before we left we tried to plant the notion of cooperation. Not on a scale large enough to blatantly affect their natural maturation: that would have constituted trespass. But I'm curious to see if any of our words took, or if we were simply ignored and both species are continuing down the same path."

"What about our work?" Tesz wanted to know.

"Yeah," added Freddy. "This sounds like strictly biped business to me."

"Except for that superficial similarity the other species wasn't like us at all," Lawson reminded them. "And the air is remarkably sweet. There are flowers in profusion. Don't you want out of this can?"

"When the situation demands, sure," admitted Buzwuz. "But I'd rather get on with the business at hand."

"If it'll just take a moment . . . , " another mind voiced.

"Thanks, Lou." Lawson broke away, reaching out with his mind, impossibly far back along the line they had traveled. A response was quickly forthcoming.

"The work is important, but if it'll only take a moment . . . , " a small portion of a vast mass-mind thought.

"Satisfy his curiosity," the rest of the mass-mind decided.

Lawson acknowledged the concurrence, as did his humming companions. It would be the briefest of detours, a quick flyby to ascertain the progress of those living on the surface of the specified world. From there it would be but a short jaunt compared to the distance they had already traveled to carry out the work they had been sent to perform. He was content.

The Solarian mass mind possessed a mass inquisitiveness of its own, but even it recognized that individual curiosity was an itch that sometimes had to be scratched.

xi

———————————————————————————•———————————————————————————

I t wasn't hard to locate the world in question. The records were quite clear and, excellent pilot that he was, Lawson had no difficulty understanding his ship's point of view. It was not intelligent in the same sense as its pilot and crew, but it bore an awareness that went far beyond the trappings of mere mechanism, to fall somewhere between the cognitive apotheosis of organic intellect and that of so-called artificial intelligences.

With Lawson's aid it had no difficulty in locating the indicated planet and slipping into a low orbit above it. Through the port he could see the billowing, swirling cloud cover, the vast oceans, the four continents. It looked as alluring as when he had first encountered it on that singular day some time ago.

"Well," he asked Buzwuz and Lou, who were hovering next to the smooth surface of the port, "what did I tell you?"

"Not bad," Buzwuz admitted.

"I've seen worse," Lou added with typical Callisian terseness. "Of course, if it's full of bipeds . . . "

Lawson didn't comment. It had been a running gag between them ever since he'd described the mixed population of the world below.

"Which species do you want to check in on first?" Tesz inquired from her position farther back in the ship.

"Please don't let it be either of the bipeds," Lou thought to no one in particular, quite aware that Lawson was picking her up.

"It doesn't matter," Lawson replied.

Buzwuz gestured with a hand. "How about the central plain on that northern continent? Looks like an active volcano there."

Lawson frowned to himself. "We didn't detect any evidence of active vulcanism on our earlier survey."

"Well, it's active now," Buzwuz told him.

Lou's thought-form intruded. "That's not a volcano. Even at this distance I can tell that the atmospheric pattern isn't right for a vented plume. It's something else."

"Just a minute." Lawson consulted with the ship's sensors. The answer he received to his query both surprised and disheartened him. "Lou's right. It's not a volcanic plume. There's an extensive area of atmospheric pollution. And according to the sensors it's not the only one. The planet's spotted with them."

Buzwuz framed a mental frown. "I thought you said that they wouldn't reach this level of development for another half millenium at least."

"They shouldn't have."

"Maybe they've been cooperating more than you could have hoped," Freddy suggested.

"It wouldn't make this much of a difference. Something else is responsible."

Tesz sighed mentally. "This means we're going to go in for a closer look, doesn't it?"

"I'd like to," Lawson thought at her.

"Better let him have his way," Buzwuz projected. "Otherwise we'll never have any peace. You know Terrans."

"I know," she said resignedly, as the ship delicately shifted its position surfaceward.

There were more surprises to come. This time casual inspection was possible only from altitude, as the presence of large numbers of heavier-than-air craft was detected. None could climb to the upper reaches of the atmosphere where Lawson's ship now drifted, but they were sophisticated in design and fleet of wing. And none of them were steam-powered.

"I don't understand," Lawson murmured as they tracked the path of a dozen massive, multi-engined aircraft. "Both species were clever and adaptable, but not brilliant. It should have taken them another four or five hundred years to learn how to build craft like this."

"I thought you said that their cities were modest in size and few in number." Lou was hovering near another sensor.

"They were," Lawson replied.

"Well that's not the case anymore." She relayed some coordinates and an increasingly glum Lawson pestered a few controls.

In an instant they were hovering above a central metropolis sited at the junction of two major rivers. It was at least five times the size of the seaport Lawson's survey team had visited previously, with smaller satellite cities and extensive residential and industrial suburbs spreading themselves in all directions. Instruments were necessary to ascertain its true size because they couldn't eye it: the entire conurbation was completely hidden from view by a thick layer of irritating brown pollutants.

Stumps of extensive forests now logged over ringed the city. The two rivers displayed streaks of color that indicated dumping of untreated chemical wastes. Lawson piloted a fast pass over the lower reaches of the smaller river, startling a lone fisherman out of his wits. It took the ship's sensors only a few moments to spit out a disgusted analysis of the water's contents: everything from arsenic compounds to heavy metals. The wonder of it was that the single fisherman expected to catch anything edible. Or maybe he was simply nostalgic for days long gone by.

There were many similarly massive urban concentrations and not much left in the way of native ground cover in their vicinities. Food production was restricted to less developed lands in the far north and south. Probably ringed by guards, Lawson thought.

There were also a few exceptional satellite towns, invariably located higher up in foothills or the mountains, or out on isolated peninsulas. These boasted relatively clean air and unpolluted streets. That suggested the presence of a privileged elite, something else not evident on his previous visit.

Lawson sent them speeding westward. "I want to visit the place where we were before." He did not have to explain himself because they could view the picture of the seaport and the memory in his mind as clearly as if it had originated in their own.

"Surely you're not expecting to find it unchanged?" Buzwuz challenged him. "Not after what we've seen so far."

"No," Lawson replied said grimly. "I don't."

"Nor encounter the local you talked with at length."

He glanced over at the humming insect. "She'd be long dead, Buzwuz. We were able to infer their life spans from the usual physiological analysis. Like most examples of a young, sentient species they don't last long." He paused a moment. "No, I don't expect to encounter her."

A moment later they arrived at the port. Lawson let the ship drift over the marvelous natural harbor, with its deep entrance and surrounding hills. Despite the periodic ocean breezes they could barely make out the towers and massive housing blocks of the city through the haze of pollutants. Several hundred vessels packed the bay, not a sail visible among them. Those maneuvering for docking or mooring position belched thick clouds of black smoke instead of white, relatively inoffensive steam. The bucolic little valley where he'd spent such a pleasant day on his earlier visit was covered with a thick irregular plaster of manufacturing plants, each belching its own patented flavor of industrial crud. The little stream he had strolled beside in the company of the curious native female was gone completely, diverted or channelized out of existence.

He thought nothing could shock him further, but the locals had a surprise in store. Automatic sensors sent the ship scooting skyward, punching a hole through smog and cloud. Far below, something long and cylindrical putt-putted at what the locals would have considered high speed through the lower atmosphere in search of a solid something that was no longer there.

Buzwuz eyed his friend sympathetically. "That was a missile. A pretty sophisticated one at that."

"It's impossible," Lawson avowed. "At most they should be exploring the possibilities of lighter-than-air travel. Heavy aircraft are unexpected enough. Now this . . . " His expression tight, he soothed a control. The ship vanished westward, leaving in its wake a spent seeker-missile that fell into the harbor as soon as its fuel was exhausted, and a group of highly agitated controllers.

It took no time at all to cross the great ocean. During the passage sensors recorded the presence on the surface of the

sea of hundreds of vessels, substantial in size and mostly metallic in construction. At first their presence served to salve
Lawson's concerns a little. At least there seemed to be a
great deal of commerce being conducted between the two
hemispheres and their respective dominant species.

It was only when they slowed several times to take a
closer look at the transoceanic traffic that the truth manifested itself.

"They're warships," Freddy announced on each occasion. "Somewhat crude in construction and design, but the
purpose is unmistakable. The projectile guns and missile
tubes are blatant."

"I'm sure if we dropped in alongside they'd start shooting," Tesz added.

"Enough of this," the other Callisians declared. "Time
to get on with the work."

"Yes," added Whizam from the back of the ship, speaking for those around him. "Indigenous disputations ain't
our concern."

"In a minute," Lawson requested. "There's one more
place I want to check out."

No one interfered with the ship as it settled down on the
deserted beach on the eastern shore of the other hemisphere. The waves still rolled in, noisy and brazen. Small
flowering plants still clung to rifts in the rocks and held
their own against the salt wind that howled in off the sea.
Crustaceans and their slower molluskan relatives hunted
along the shore.

But no hirsute, slit-eyed fisherfolk waded through the
shallow surf unrolling their nets in search of fat, soft-bodied
things to eat. None camped along the sand in search of soli-
tude or a chance to partake of family relationships. The
beach was empty.

There were fewer of the broken, water-logged tree

trunks he remembered from before. Their place was largely taken by the rusting hulks of two warships, their hulls scarred and battered. One had been nearly torn in half by the great explosion that had sent it steaming desperately for this shore. The other was pock-marked with hundreds of holes from smaller caliber weaponry. A few collapsed skeletons, now home to the efficient hard-shelled shore life, were all that remained of their vanished crews.

"What's happened here?" Lawson murmured, as much to himself as to his attentive companions.

"I think you know," Buzwuz pointed out, more gently than usual. "If you need further confirmation there seems to be a major battle going on a short hop to the south of here."

Lawson nodded once and vexed a device.

Two great fleets were battling for control of a cluster of offshore islands. These dots of land, formerly inhabited only by solitary fisherfolk and adventurous travelers, had been armed and fortified to the point where little of the original surface was visible. Nearly all of the trees were gone, and those few that had been left clung to the unforgiving boundary where the soil met the sea, as if waiting to cast themselves into the next large wave in a kind of mass xylemic suicide.

The fleets maneuvered anxiously around these islets, wheeling about them like the spokes of a battered wheel. They traded long-range gunfire and missiles with enthusiasm and regularity. Occasionally a ship on either side would take a hit, sending a plume of smoke and flame into the already soot-spattered sky while spilling sailors into an indifferent sea.

Tighter magnification revealed that one group of ships was crewed entirely by slim bipeds from the eastern hemisphere while the others were populated by representatives of the hairy locals. Farther out at sea an armada of troop transports held an invasion force that waited patiently for a chance to land.

"I've found the joker in the deck," announced Lou from her station. Her glistening compound eyes regarded him solemnly. "I think you've already guessed what that might be."

Lawson was too disappointed even to sigh. "We need to make a formal check. Coordinates?" The ship responded to his directions.

The formidable interstellar transport was just settling gently to earth much farther inland when the Solarian vessel appeared nearby. Extensive landing facilities had been gouged out of the earth close to a major river that flowed southward along the base of a high mountain range. A number of smaller cities had been established to service the crude spaceport. They in turn funneled their efforts and produce into a truly massive metropolis located still farther east.

As they looked on, a swarm of land transports rushed to the side of the transport like ants returning to their nest and began the frenetic task of unloading. Even the little ship's sensors couldn't determine exactly what was contained in the massive crates and packing containers, but everyone aboard could guess. As to the origin of the ship, there was no mystery.

"Nileans." Buzwuz pivoted in midair to gaze at Lawson. "What do you want to bet that if we made a fast scan of the other hemisphere we'd find a similar facility servicing visiting vessels of that praiseworthy benefactor of primitive species, the Great Lord Markhamwit?"

"What I don't understand," announced Freddy, "is why they bother. The Nileans and Markhamwit's kind are squabbling for control of a fair portion of this galaxy. Why divert even a smidgen of resources to a backwater world like this?

It's not like either of the indigenous species can help them against each other."

"Not yet. Despots like Markhamwit are always on the lookout for fresh cannon fodder," Lawson muttered. "A habitable world is a habitable world, an ally still an ally, and a planetary base is always useful from a military standpoint. Neither side can spare the warships to fight over this world, but they can drop off an occasional load of trinkets for the natives in hopes that one day they'll prove useful. Each side is betting its native proxies will dominate. They'll keep supplying them with more and more sophisticated weapons in the hope that by the time 'their' side wins, they'll have learned enough about contemporary weaponry to be of some use in the wider war beyond this one world." He sat back from the sensor projections and rubbed at his forehead.

"Of course, neither the Nileans nor Markhamwit's ilk care one whit about the future of the locals. As far as they're concerned the side they've picked can exterminate their opponents and take full control of the planet. Meanwhile and with very little effort on their part they've managed to exacerbate local differences, inspire further conflict, and give both sides the means to slaughter one another on a much more satisfying level. Instead of being allowed time to work out their interspecies dilemmas both sides have been dragged into a conflict not of their making. They probably don't even realize how far down the developmental ladder they are compared to their supposedly beneficent visitors."

"They will someday," Lou declared confidently, "but it'll be too late then for one species or the other."

"Maybe for both," added Freddy. "If they've been equivalently armed by the Nileans and Markhamwit's people they could weaken each other to the point where both civilizations collapse. Then they'd be of little use to either side."

"Which wouldn't cause Markhamwit or Glastrom and his ministers to lose a moment's sleep," Lou added. "Meanwhile it looks to me like they've done a pretty good job of trashing their planet. You can't blame all of that on outside influences."

"No," Lawson admitted. "They were headed that way when I was here before. But the Nileans and Markhamwit's advisors have given them a sizable push. Left to themselves they might have worked things out."

"Well, it's too late now." Lou hummed over to another cluster of projections. "We could do a few tricks here, but reversing time isn't one of them. Besides, it's not our mandate."

Lawson hesitated. "I hate to just leave them like this. The Nileans and Markhamwit have intruded. We could do the same."

"You couldn't the last time you were here and you can't now," Buzwuz reminded him sternly. "You know why."

Lawson was tight-lipped. "Normally internal planetary conflicts aren't our business, I know. And we've a much weightier predicament to attend to. But this is a special situation. This isn't the usual case of one species fighting among itself. If not for the interposition of outside influences the B'eitara and the Denkou might well have learned to cooperate. Both species are intelligent and basically sane. They deserve better."

"What about Markhamwit and the Nileans?" Tesz gestured skyward with a tiny hand. "Out there are dozens of sentient species whose lives are being interfered with and whose progress is being retarded because of this typically dim-witted interstellar punch-up. That's what we've been sent here to resolve. The internal difficulties of one world don't amount to much compared to that."

"I'm not disputing that, Tesz," Lawson replied quietly. "I'm just saying that this world is special."

"Special inherently, or special to you?" she asked.

Lawson would not have known how to lie had he wished to. Prevarication was an obsolete affliction among Solarians.

"A little of both. There's nothing wrong in that. My concern is for these people. I hate to see them throw away their collective racial futures because of the 'help' that's been thrust on them from outside. They've been shoved toward a future they don't deserve and aren't mature enough to handle. Nothing says we can't take a little time to try to preserve a couple of small civilizations along with the larger."

"First things first," thought Buzwuz softly.

"Mandates," insisted the rest of the crew.

"Priorities," reminded a collective mind from across the gulf.

Lawson recognized the wisdom of it even if emotionally he felt otherwise. "All right. Let's get on with it, then." He nudged a control and the little ship vanished in a surge of cloud, just as a pair of much more sophisticated missiles than they'd dodged on the other side of the world sped through the space they'd occupied a moment ago. They came from the Nilean transport, whose officers puzzled over the sudden disappearance of what they'd suspected to be one of the Great Lord's scouts.

Lawson did not look at the sensors that showed the once-beautiful planet receding rapidly behind them. Nor did they pause to pay any attention to the transport that was lumbering orbitward as they were heading outbound. This new vessel, which belonged to the Great Lord, never noticed the little ship, which crossed its course at a speed too fast to be detected.

Lawson encouraged the control a tad further, heading for a world neither of the local stellar combatants even suspected existed. It would take a little while to reach, which was fine with him. His thoughts were torn between the task ahead and the special place they'd just left behind.

There was work to be done, work on a vast and lofty scale. It was what he and the Callisians and many others had been sent here to do. But Solarians prided themselves on their thoroughness, and the work wouldn't be considered completed until not only the great but the small problems hereabouts had been resolved.

The least of those was receding behind him at an incredible rate, but he knew he would not leave, could not start on the long journey back home, without making an effort to fix it.

xii

—■—

Histories, he thought. History distant and recent. He put his reminiscences aside as they plunged toward their destination. The world was a wanderer, a planet torn loose from its parent sun by some catastrophe far back in the tremendous past. At an equally distant time in the future it would be captured by some other star and either join the new family or be destroyed. Meanwhile it curved aimlessly through space, orphan of a bygone storm.

It wasn't cold, it wasn't dark. Internal fires kept it warm. Eternal stars limned it in pale, ethereal light. It had tiny, pastel-shaded flowers and thin, delicate trees that pushed their feet toward the warmth and kept their faces to the stars. It also held sentient life, though not of its own creation.

There were fourteen ships on this uncharted sphere. Eleven were Solarian. They were there because they preferred to meet somewhere to exchange thoughts and greetings in person, because this was a pleasurable activity, and because the strange wayfaring vagrant of a world was fascinating in and of itself. It gave them something to think about besides the task at hand. After what they'd been dealing with, the amiable mental break was much appreciated by all concerned.

Of the remaining craft one was Nilean. Two belonged to the Great Lord Markhamwit. The Solarian vessels were grouped together in a gentle valley of one hemisphere. The other three were on the opposite side of the planet, the Nileans separated from their foes by a couple of hundred kilometers, each combatant unaware of the others' existence.

The situation of these last two groups was a curious one. Each of their three ships had detected the gypsy sphere at times a few days apart and had landed upon it in the hope of discovering talkative bipeds or, at least, gaining some clue to their whereabouts. Each crew had promptly suffered an attack of mental aberration verging upon craziness, exploded their munitions, otherwise destroyed every vestige of their respective vessels' weaponry, and thoroughly wrecked their ships, thereby marooning themselves.

Each crew now sat around stupefied by its own collective idiocy and thoroughly convinced that not another functioning starship existed within a billion distance-units. They shuffled about, gaping forlornly at the skeletal growths while trying to keep warm, and considering their situation. Now and then an individual overcome by circumstances would break down, to be comforted as much as possible by equally glum companions. They wandered aimlessly through the ruins of their vessels, trying to make sense of what had happened and failing miserably. Memories of the actual acts they had carried out with devastating efficiency were few and confused.

Yet sanity had taken firm hold along with resignation. No evidence of mental illness was manifest among any of them. The ships' medical teams had no answers, having turned temporarily psychotic along with the rest of the crews. In searching for explanations they found only more questions.

The secret of this state of affairs reposed with two of the eleven Solarian vessels. They had on board a number of homarachnids, spiderish sentients from a place unknown to this galaxy, a hot, moist world called Sunevv. It happened that this world circled around an equally unknown sun that slowly orbited a regional gravitational point not far from a companion star called Sol. Which meant that the homarachnids were Solarians along with the bipeds and bees and semivisible fuzzies.

From the purely military viewpoint there was nothing redoubtable about the homarachnids. They were even more unsoldierly than their companions, knew nothing of weapons contemporary or historical, and cared nothing about either. They were also singularly lacking in technical skills, viewing even a screwdriver as a cumbersome, patience-straining device.

Outwardly, their most noticeable feature was an incurable penchant for wearing the most incongruous feathered hats that the milliners of Sunevv could devise. In some respects they were the most childlike of the Solarian medley, but in one way they were the most deeply to be feared, for they had refractive minds.

With the absolute ease of those to whom it comes naturally, any homarachnid could concentrate the great Solarian mass mentality, projecting it and focusing it where required. The burning point of an immense magnifying glass was as nothing to the effect when a non-Solarian mind became the focal point of an attentive homarachnid's brain. The result was temporary but absolute mental mastery.

It *had* to be temporary. The Solarian ethic denied the right to bring any mind into permanent subjugation, for that would amount to slavery of the soul. But for this, any pair of homarachnids could have compelled antagonistic warlords to "see reason" in a mere couple of milliparts.

But mentally imposed agreement is worth nothing if it disappears the moment the cause is removed. The final aim must be to persuade Markhamwit and Glastrom to cooperate not out of fear or compulsion, but from motives of expediency and for keeps. The same ethic insisted that this goal be reached without spilling of life fluids if possible, or else at the cost of blood only to the high and mighty.

Nobody knew better than Solarians that modern wars are not caused, declared, or willingly fought by nations, planetary peoples, or shape-groups, for these consist in the main of plain, ordinary folk who crave nothing more than to be left alone. The culprits are power-drunken cliques of near-maniacs who by dint of one means or another have coerced the rest. These were the ones to provide the blood, if any was going to be shed at all.

Lawson and Reeder and the rest knew the operations of the Solarian mass-mind as well as they knew their own, for it was composed in part of their own. They were sharers in an intellectual common property. Therefore no issuing of detailed orders was necessary. Its decisions reached them as swiftly and directly as if thought out by their independent selves.

As others had found to their cost and would do so again and again, the Solarians had an immense advantage in being able to give highly organized battle without benefit of complicated signaling and communications systems. As far as the Solarians were concerned, lack of such antiquated technical adjuncts was lack of something susceptible to error, something to go wrong. There would be no mistaken charge of a light brigade in their history.

Lawson's ship was one of the assembled eleven. Reeder's was another. Seven more had come in from lonelier parts of the galaxy for the same purpose: to rendezvous with the remaining two and add a few homarachnids to their crews. Had the enemy been of different nature they might have been reinforced by a different kind. Perhaps elephantine creatures from Uro or dark dwarves from Sarim. The physical instruments were chosen to suit the particular task, and the hat-models of Sunevv would do fine for this one.

Two of them, gray-skinned and bristly-haired of body, eight-legged and with compound eyes, scuttled toward Lawson's vessel, sniffed suspiciously through organs that were not noses, and looked at one another.

"I smell bugs," announced the one adorned with a purple toque around which a fluffy plume was stylishly coiled. Compared with the outrageously garish chapeaus, the rest of the creature's attire, not to mention the rest of the creature, seemed decorous in the extreme.

"This can needs delousing," agreed the other, who wore a glaring red fez with a long, thin crimson ribbon protruding vertically from its top. Bright orange metallic braid swirled gracefully if not tastefully around the body of the fez.

"If you prefer," offered Lawson, "you can go on Reeder's ship."

"What, with that gang of spooks?" He cocked the toque sideways. "I'd sooner suffer the bugs. At least with them you can see where the smell is coming from."

"Me too," agreed Red Fez.

"That is most sociable of you," sneered the mind-form of Buzwuz, chipping in suddenly. He zoomed out of the navigation chamber and into the passage, an orange ball on flashing wings. "I think we can manage to . . . " He broke off as he caught sight of the new arrivals, let out a mental screech of agony, and began to whirl round and round in agitated circles. "Oh, look at them! Just *look!*"

"What's the matter?" aggressively demanded he of the purple toque, whose name this year was Nfam. Next year it would be Nfim. And the year after, Nfom. He looked behind, then beneath, concluding with a cursory inspection of his own self.

"The vile headgear," complained Buzwuz, shuddering visibly. When he did that it gave a peculiar resonance to his buzzing. "Especially that red thing. Talk about unsolicited assaults on the optic nerve . . . unless it can be shown that the combination already exists in nature, some minglings of shape and color should be banned from civilized company."

The owner of the fez, whose current name was Jlath, waxed indignant. "I'd have you know this is an original creation by the famous Oroni and . . ."

Frowning at all and sundry, Lawson interrupted, "When you mutual monstrosities have finished swapping compliments maybe you'll make ready for lift-off. The fact that we're inertialess doesn't mean you can clutter up the passageways." He cycled the lock, secured it, went to the pilot's chamber, and moved the contact.

Outside, trees of unsurpassed slimness bent forward with the force of the departure. Self-pollinating flowers quivered, then straightened and stilled.

That left ten ships. Reeder's departed soon afterward. Then the others, one by one. And that left nothing but three ruined warships and their three ruminative crews alone on the wanderer, unable to do anything but mourn their own inexplicable madness.

xiii

———————————————————————————▪———————————————————————————

F irst contact was with one of the Great Lord's heavy battle cruisers, a long, black vessel well-armed with heavy
particle beams, enhanced masers, and nuclear-tipped missiles. It was heading at a fast pace for Kalambar, a blue-white
sun with a small system of planets located on the rim of what
the Nileans regarded as their sphere of interest. Those
aboard it had in mind that while the Kalambar group was
believed to be habitable, little else was known about it.
Therefore it was a likely hiding-place of previously un-
recorded Nilean allies, two-legged or winged.

Lawson knew of the cruiser's existence and intent long
before it loomed large enough to obscure a noticeable portion of the starfield and even before sensitive detectors
came to life to mark the presence of something irregular in
outline, swift-moving, and emitting energy far outside the
parameters established for natural objects.

He knew of it simply because the exotically hatted duo
probing forth as twin channels of a far-away supermind had
no difficulty in picking up the foe's group-thoughts or de-

termining the direction, course, and distance of their source. All he had to do was take the ship where they indicated, knowing in precise detail what he'd find when he got there.

Even at the tremendous velocities commonplace only to another galaxy the catching-up took time. But they made it in due course, burst out of the plenum with such suddenness that they were bulleting along at equal pace and on parallel course before the other's alarm system had time to give warning. Though representing the apex of its species technological achievement, it was designed to detect and identify mass closing from interplanetary distances, not to alert its masters to objects that seemed to appear out of nowhere.

By the time the bells did set up their clamor on board the great warship it was too late. With remarkable unanimity of thought its crew had conceived several strange notions and were unable to sense their strangeness simply because all were thinking alike.

First, the alarm was sounding and that must be the signal for action. Second, it was sheer waste of precious lifetime to mess around in empty space when one could put in some real existence on good, solid earth. Third, there was a suitable haven shining through the dark four points to starboard of the ecliptic and much nearer than Kalambar. Fourth, to place the ship completely out of commission immediately upon landing would be the most certain way of insuring a long period of rest and relaxation, during which period time could be spent seeking higher ideals.

These ideas ran contrary to their military conditioning, were directly opposed to duty and discipline, and smacked of treason as well as mutiny, but they accorded with inward instincts and secret desires, and moreover were imposed with suggestive power too great to resist. Additionally, it seemed the most natural decision in the world to make when, without exception, every one of one's companions was expressing precisely the same sentiments, albeit with varying degrees of enthusiasm. There was great unanimity of opinion and no dissent.

So with its alarm system duly operating and detection screens flashing the alert, the battle cruiser at once turned four points on the navigational sphere. With the Solarian craft following unheeded it sped straight for the adjacent system, made its landing on a world owned by backward, neutral, and embarrassed Dirkins who were greatly relieved when a loud bang marked the vessel's disabling and its crew proceeded to lounge around like beachcombers.

The only thing the Dirkins could not understand was why this party of intended lotus-eaters suddenly became afflicted with vain regrets coincidentally with the disappearance from the sky of a much smaller second ship. Their initial zeal quickly gave way to sullenness and brooding, with much loud complaining and mutual accusation. Fortunately for the inoffensive Dirkins, this fresh burst of hostility among the crew of the disabled vessel was directed against each other. Officers in particular were singled out for much recrimination, though they were in truth as innocent of the self-inflicted disaster as the lesser ranks.

And over every one of these befuddled, angry, frustrated visitors hung a dense cloud of personal confusion.

In short order twenty-seven more vessels went the same way, turning off-route, abandoning their prescribed courses, dumping themselves on the nearest habitable sphere and sabotaging themselves clean out of the war. Seventeen of these belonged to the Great Lord Markhamwit; ten to the Nileans. Not one resisted. Not one fired an energy beam, released a missile, or so much as took evasive action. The crude products of physical science are pitifully ineffective when suddenly confronted with the superb end product, namely, the superiority of the mind over all material things.

Nevertheless, ancient ingenuity did try to strike an effective blow at the ultramodern when Lawson came across ship number twenty-nine. The manner in which this one was discovered told in advance of something abnormal about it. The detectors reported it while Jlath and Nfam were mentally feeling through the dark and getting no evidence of anything so near. The reason: the homarachnids were seeking enemy thought-forms and this ship held no thoughts, not one. Lawson promptly positioned his vessel to investigate this curious phenomenon more closely.

Orbiting around a lesser moon, the mystery craft's design and markings showed it to be an auxiliary warship or armed transport of Nilean origin. An old, battered, heavily utilized vessel long overdue for scrapping, it appeared to have been pressed into extended service for the duration of the war.

It had a smallish particle-beam projector in its bow, one set of missile launchers, and little visible in the way of advanced electronics. A sorry object fit for nothing but escort duty on short runs in a quiet sector, it hardly seemed worth the bother of putting down to ground.

But in addition to priding themselves on the thoroughness of their intended object lesson, Lawson and his crew were curious about it. An aged but quite intact starship totally devoid of evidence of thinking mentalities was somewhat of a phenomenon. It could mean several interesting things, all equally worth discovering. No matter how extremely remote the likelihood of anyone developing a screen that the homarachnids could not penetrate in their search for lurking mind-forms, the theoretical possibility could not be ruled out. Nothing is finally and completely impossible.

Alternately, there was the million-to-one chance that the vessel was crewed by a nonthinking, purely reactive and robotic life-form allied to the Nileans. Or, more plausibly, that one of Markhamwit's warships was employing a new weapon capable of slaughtering crews without so much as scratching their vessel and this particular ship was a victim. Or, last and likeliest, that it had been abandoned and left crewless, but despite the expense and difficulty, had been carefully parked in a stable orbit for some reason known only to the deserters.

The absence of complex electronic emissions likewise precluded the possibility that it was a robot itself, a craft designed to be operated and directed solely by mechanicals. There was nothing to indicate that anything half so sophisticated was present on board the vessel. Functional artificial-intelligence systems radiated their own peculiar and unmistakable signatures that the unbelievably advanced instrumentation on Lawson's craft could have easily picked up, had there been any to sense. But the venerable transport was as silent as a tomb, mentally as well as mechanically.

As the Solarian craft swooped toward the point marked by its detectors, Nfam and Jlath strove hurriedly to probe the nearby moon for any proximate minds that might hold the secret of the silent objective. Neither they nor the ship's mechanical sensors fixed on anything indicative of function or operation. Lawson was more and more convinced that it was deserted. At aphelion the homarachnids would be able to say for certain.

There wasn't time. They whirled high above the target, automatically recording its nature, type, and markings, and in the next breath had been carried far beyond it. The Solarian ship commenced to turn in a wide curve that would bring it back for another, final once-over. They did not get a second look.

Designed to cope with and react to objects moving considerably slower, the shielded instruments aboard the silent transport registered the presence of another vessel just a little too late. In barely a few nanoparts connections were established and the vessel exploded. It was a vivid and violent blast full of shredded atoms and intense heat, of boiling plasma and high energy particles that was more than sufficient to disable and possibly destroy any warship unlucky enough to be drifting within snooping distance.

It failed in its intent solely because the prospective recipient of the thump already was far outpacing the shock wave and accompanying flying fragments of which there were plenty.

"Booby trap," observed Lawson thoughtfully. "We'd have been handed a beautiful wallop if our maximum velocity was down to the crawl that local types regard as conventional. They're not entirely devoid of resourcefulness."

"Yes," responded a bee-mind from somewhere nearer the stern. "And did those two mad hatters warn you of it? Did you hear them screaming, 'Don't go near! Oh, please don't go near!' and feel them pawing at your arm?"

"It seems to me," remarked Nfam to Jlath, "that I detect the sharp, grating voice of jealousy, the bitter whine of a lesser life-form incapable of and unsuited to self-adornment."

"We don't need it," retorted the critic. "We don't have to resort to reliance on artificial devices as a means of lending false color to pale, insipid personalities. We have advanced beyond the need for such infantile affectations. We have . . . "

"No hands," put in Nfam, with great dexterity.

"And they fight with their rear ends," added Jlath for good measure.

"Now see here, frog-food, we . . . "

"Shut up!" roared Lawson with sudden violence.

Mental silence enveloped the little ship as it bulleted onward in search of target number thirty.

The next encounter provided an orgy that served to illustrate the superiority of mass-mind efficiency as compared with artificial methods of communication and coordination. Far off across the wheel of light that formed the galaxy a Solarian named El-Fann pursued a multitude of bellicose thought-forms traced by his homarachnids and discovered not a couple of ships but two entire fleets assembling for battle. The news flashed out to all and sundry even as he intercepted a monstrous warship lumbering toward the scene and planted it where it would stay put.

Lawson immediately altered course, boosted his vessel to detector-defeating velocity. There was a long way to go according to this galaxy's estimates of distances but a relative jaunt from the Solarian viewpoint. Unseen and unsuspected, the vessel scudded past a host of systems, most of them boasting worlds that were uninhabitable, sterile, deserted.

At one point Nfam's questioning mind found a convoy of ten ships huddled together and heading for the system of a stable binary, determined them to be neutral traders hoping to make port without interference by one or the other belligerents. Farther on, nearer the twin suns, a pair of Markhamwit's lighter warships hung in space ready to halt and search the convoy for whatever they saw fit to declare illegal transport of strategic war materials.

The Solarian vessel promptly cut its speed, herded these two wolves into a suitable cage, raced onward. The convoy continued to plug along innocent of the obstruction so arbitrarily removed from its path and utterly unaware that it had been chosen to be the recipient of extragalactic beneficence.

By the time Lawson arrived at the designated rendezvous the scene of intended conflict already had lost some of its orderliness and was dissolving toward eventual chaos. A Nilean force of many hundreds had disposed itself in a huge hemisphere protecting a close-packed group of seven solar systems that were not worth a hoot. Markhamwit's fleet commanders accordingly reasoned that such strength would be marshaled only to defend a sector vital to the enemy's war economy and that therefore these seven systems must be captured and scoured regardless of cost.

Which was what the Nileans wanted them to think, for, being slightly the weaker party, they knew the value of diverting attention from genuinely critical points by offering the foe a glittering but valueless prize elsewhere. So both sides beamed frantic orders to and fro, strove to get ready to rend the heavens for the sake of what neither could use. This was a course of action traditional to large-scale conflicts everywhere.

The trouble was that preparations refused to work out as they should have according to the book.

Established tactics of interstellar warfare seemed to have become disestablished. Orthodox methods of squaring up to the enemy and seeking points of weakness over vast distances were not producing orthodox results. The recognized moves of placing light forces *here* and heavy ones *there,* a spearhead *thus* and a defensive screen *so,* a powerful reserve in that place and a follow-up force in this one, were making a fine mess of the whole issue. Bewilderment among commanders on both sides resembled that of an expert who finds that a certain experiment produces the same results nine hundred ninety-nine times but not the thousandth, and continues to do so with maddening regularity.

Introduction of a new and as yet unidentified factor was the cause of all this. The time lag in their communications beam systems, with coded messages flashing from repeater station to repeater station, was so great that none in this sector knew what had happened to the impudent visitors on

their homeworlds or that visiting Solarians had turned from
argument to action.

True, some ships were overdue in this area and presumed lost, but that was inevitable. While it occasioned the
usual regrets, there was no especial alarm. Losses must be
expected in time of war and there was nothing to be gained
by investigating the fate of the missing or by trying to ascertain the cause of their disappearance. Other vessels could
carry out such routine follow-ups at the appropriate time
without draining strength from the sector of battle.

So deeply embedded were these notions that for quite
some time both sides remained blindly unaware of what was
happening right under their noses. And the emotions of opposing commanders remained those of extreme irritation
rather than real alarm. Inside their military minds conditioning masquerading as logic stated that a fight was trying
to get going, and that any fight is between two parties with
nobody else involved except maybe one or two accidental
and irrelevant lookers-on. Such pseudo-reasoning automatically prevented swift realization of intervention by a third
party. Who ever heard of a three-sided battle?

Mutually bedeviled, both belligerents postponed their
planned onslaughts while they continued to try to get ready,
meanwhile blundering around like a pair of once-eager
boxers temporarily diverted from their original purpose by
the sudden appearance of numerous ants in the pants.

And the ants kept them on the hop. Lawson's vessel
plummeted unseen and undetected right into the middle
of the Nilean hemisphere, picked up three craft thundering
along under orders to patrol off a certain planet, put them
down on said planet for keeps. As far as the Nilean Grand
Commander was concerned, three of his vessels had commenced to move in obedience to commands, had continuously signaled progress, and then cut off without warning or
indication of any difficulty as if snatched out of Creation.

They might as well have plunged into the gravity well of a black hole save that none was present in their vicinity.

In the absence of response to signals or communications of any kind, he sent a fast scout to try to discover physically what had occurred. That craft radiated messages until within sensor distance of the patrol's last recorded position and then went silent. He sent another. Same result. It was like dropping pebbles down a drain. He gave up, ordered a formal report filed with central battle headquarters on Nilea, sought under his backstrap for a persistent nibbler that had been pestering him all day.

The cause of all this cussedness would have been identified more quickly and easily had just one crew been able to beam a warning that they were about to come under the mental mastery of unidentifiable creatures traveling aboard a strange vessel of unknown origin. But none were ever aware that anything had happened until the cause had gone elsewhere, the influence had been removed, and they found themselves sitting on solid earth dumbfoundedly contemplating a vessel that they themselves had enthusiastically converted to so much scrap. And not just any ship but their very own, which until recently had served as home and refuge both for travel and for battle.

Nor did it matter if their deep-space communications systems remained intact. There were no lingering memories of what had occurred, no faint images of intellectual independence fading beneath some mysterious external influence. The thoughts that had motivated them seemed to be entirely their own, original of manufacture and subsequent execution. No one had told them to abruptly pull themselves from the field of combat. No one had ordered them to set down on the nearest habitable world and scuttle their ships. They had done this with energy and verve, destroying vital communications gear and pulling irreparable portions of their ships' drives to pieces.

Some went about the task of self-marooning with more zeal than others, going so far as to drag or otherwise transport critical components to the edge of deep canyons or restless seas and gleefully toss them in. These enthusiasts suffered consequently greater regret, since upon their subsequent changes of heart there was not a hope of somehow repairing the damage they had done.

If it had been up to the Sunevvians the most inventive of the marooners would have somehow been rewarded for their exceptional efforts, but they had no time for instructive sarcasm. There was still a great deal to be done.

It was like stealing lollipops from the inmates of a babies' home except that there always lurked an element of danger due to the lining up of unfortuitous circumstances that none could anticipate. The homarachnids could perceive mind-shapes and their fellow Solarians possessed other striking abilities, but not a one of them could predict the future.

El-Fann and his ship and crew went out of existence in a brilliant flash of light when they dived down upon what appeared to be a Nilean flotilla moving at sedate pace toward the hemisphere's rim and discovered one nanopart too late that it consisted of a large warship shepherding under remote control a group of uncrewed drones outfitted with object-coded and incredibly sensitive electronics.

Every Solarian in the tremendous area knew of this counter-blow the instant the stroke took place. Everyone sensed it as a sudden cessation of life that has been a small part of one's own. It was like the complete vanishing from one's mind of a long-held and favorite thought, or the memory of a specific place and time.

None brooded. None felt a pang of regret. They were not inclined to such sentiment because sorrow can never remove its own cause. A few hairs had fallen from an immense corporate whole, but the body remained.

Half a time-unit afterward, James Lawson and his crew exacted sweet revenge, not with that motive, but purely as a tactic. They did it by making opportune use of the enemy's own organizational setup, which, like many sources of great strength, was also a source of great weakness. Weld individuals and materials into a mighty machine and they are thereby converted into something capable of mighty collapse the moment the crucial fastener or seal is removed.

A formidable Nilean battle squadron of 140 assorted ships had flashed its drives and was running out of the hemisphere in a great curving course that eventually would position it slightly behind the extreme wing of Markhamwit's assembly. This was the strictly orthodox move of trying to place a flanking party strong enough to endanger any main thrust at the center. If Markhamwit's scouts and remote sensors detected this threat in time, his array would have to divert a force able to meet and beat it. It was all so easy for those who sat in opposing battle headquarters, planning and counter-planning, ordering vessels here and there, directing the great combat machines that were spread out over vast reaches of empty space.

And just because machines were machines, Lawson had no difficulty in pulling out an essential bolt. Disdaining to deal with the racing ships on an individual basis, he took over the entire squadron lock, stock, and barrel. All that was necessary was for Nfam and Jlath to gain mental mastery of those aboard the commanding officer's vessel directing the rest. One ship! The others did exactly as this enslaved vessel ordered, changing course like a flock of sheep that has been brought under the control of a good sheepdog.

These unorthodox maneuvers generated questions in the minds of subsidiary commanders, and one or two individual ship captains found themselves wondering if headquarters had lost its collective senses. None of this mattered because none dared disobey. The best they could do was file a formal protest of action or objection that, like any comparable communique, would take its own good time to work its way up the chain of command.

The extended squadron turned onto a new course, built up top velocity because the controllers on the commander's ship so ordered. They ignored the now-visible Solarian stranger in their midst because the commanding vessel unquestioningly accepted its proximate presence. They pushed for their faraway home system as fast as they could drive because the Boss so ordered.

Lawson stayed with them to the halfway point before disengaging to return to the main arena of almost-battle. Long after he'd left they continued on course, making no attempt to return. The Boss was not going to admit to an entire fleet that he was afflicted with mental confusion, nor were his immediate subordinates, nor his highly skilled combat programmers. None were about to confess that they could not remember receiving or transmitting an order to head for home. It helped that throughout the flagship everyone, at every level of command, was of the same assured, if inherently confounded, opinion.

As for the commander himself, obviously he must have received such instructions, or why were they *here*, making for *there* at top speed? Agitated mental contortions provided nothing in the way of elucidation. Best to keep straight on and hide the fact that he was subject to spasms of dopiness. So on they went, one hundred forty vessels bamboozled right out of the fray.

In short time Reeder's vessel performed a similar service for the Great Lord. A reserve force of eighty-eight ships, primed for heavy combat, pushed homeward with all communications channels closed in accordance with orders from their own commanding officer. Swiftly informed of this unauthorized departure, the top brass at battle headquarters foamed at the mouth, switched switches, levered

levers and stabbed buttons, filled the ether with counter-
mands, threats, and bloodthirsty promises while still the reserve continued to blunder through the starfield with all
receivers sealed and no mutinous ears burning.

Bombs and beams are of little avail without intelligence
to direct them. Take away the intelligence, if only for a little
while, and the entire warmaking appurtenance of a major
power is reduced to so much junk. The Solarian attack was
irresistibly formidable because it was concentrated on the
root cause of all the action, the very motivating force behind all the instruments of war great or small. Solarian logic
argued that gun-plus-mind is a weapon whereas gun-with-
out-mind is a mere artifact no matter how inherently efficient.

The Nilean booby traps were no exception, nor was any
other robotic armament, for in effect they were delayed-ac-
tion weapons from which minds had gone into hiding by
removing themselves in space and time. The minds wherein
each booby trap originated were difficult to trace, hence
the fate suffered by El-Fann and his crew. But in the long
run they were being dealt with as ship after ship became
grounded, squadrons and flotillas and convoys departed for
someplace else, and chaos threatened to become complete.
In proof of which the jumpy Nilean High Command twice
made serious errors by diverting ships that consequently
sprang their own carefully conceived traps and thus added a
pleasing note to the general confusion.

Irate communications criss-crossed the starfield, mixing
with furious denunciations and apologies that were countered with protestations of abject innocence. The harder
the respective battle headquarters strove to get a handle on
the confusion, the more their efforts came to naught. Uncertainty led to hesitancy, which led to disengagement. Attempts to remake or reform complex stratagems foundered
in a sea of total disarray.

The simplest maneuvers met with disaster. Even more maddening than the reports of crews scuttling their own vessels, which were at last starting to filter in, was the lack of response from whole squadrons detected speeding for their home systems. The great schematics of lights and indicators that marked worlds, systems, and ships were slowly blanking out as the last were automatically removed by the computators from the field of battle.

Meanwhile, ordinary merchant and transport vessels on both sides went blithely about their business, their progress uninterrupted by belligerent warships, their movements unchallenged by bellicose communications. In this they were joined by the neutrals and independents, who accepted their good fortune without question.

In fact, no one thought to investigate this interesting coincidence because the commanders on both sides were too preoccupied and too distraught to take note. It was only much, much later that anyone thought to organize the relevant statistics, which resulted in considerable chastening after the fact.

By the fiftieth time-unit the Solarians had an imposing array of statistics of their own to consider. Fourteen ships destroyed by accident or collision due to unavoidable circumstances, including one of their own. Eight hundred fifty-one vessels nailed down on various inhabitable planets and satellites. One thousand two hundred sixty-six shiploads of the mentally deceived hell-bent for other places, mostly home. Increasing evidence of severe demoralization in the battle headquarters of both belligerents.

Truly, the long-term chivvying of weaker neutrals was being paid for, heavily, with compound interest. Warships and the other starships involved in their support were among the most advanced representatives of both sides' skill at engineering and manufacturing. They took considerable time and effort to construct and equip, at burdensome expense to their respective populations. Those that had been severely damaged by their own exuberantly deluded crews and technical staffs would be difficult and costly to repair, while a goodly number had been so badly damaged that, due to the distance and situation involved, they would never lift beyond atmosphere again.

Taken in toto, the course and direction of events was sufficient to convince stubborn minds that a myth can be a very real thing when dragged out of the past and dumped unceremoniously into the present day.

Battle staffs, administrators, programmers, tacticians, and politicians conferred among themselves and across a galactic gap while their ships continued to rush aimlessly to and fro. If the opposition parties' battle headquarters were taken under mental control, the entire war parade could be scattered through the heavens at a few imposed words of command. Solarians were reluctant to take matters as far as that. It would come much too near a demonstration of near godlike dictatorship over all lesser creatures. The intent of the entire demonstration was to enlighten and educate, not to terrorize.

Besides, warmongers can always find an excuse for inappropriate orders issued by a few, countermand them, punish the presumed culprits, and issue new directives. It's far harder to assign blame when misaction is propounded simultaneously by hundreds of individuals holding positions of importance. Those who cannot themselves remain blameless are hardly in a position to ascribe blame to others.

The basic Solarian idea was to create respect for an essential law by creating respect for those behind it. To overdo the job by just a little too much would be to establish wholesale fear of themselves throughout the galaxy. Some dread here and there could not be avoided when dealing with less-developed minds inclined to superstition (an inevitable consequence of inadequate, merely verbal means of communication), but they were deeply concerned not to invoke ineradicable fear as a substitute for enlightened tolerance.

Since they were trying to cope with two dominant species of alien not quite the same either in physiology or thought processes, it was a touchy matter to judge exactly how far they must go in order to achieve the desired result while not triggering the other. How many times should a candidate for baptism be dunked to give him salvation without pneumonia?

The rather more superstitious, credulous Nileans required different handling than the Great Lord Markhamwit and his kind. Each species offered up different buttons for pushing, as did their closest allies. In such circumstances it was better to take a cautious approach, though not necessarily one that was less efficient. Their success thus far was testimony to careful preparation.

By mutual consent they carried on for another full time-unit, at the end of which the movements of vessels still controlled by the command headquarters showed that Nilean forces were striving to regroup in readiness for withdrawal. Their answer to that was to cease all blows at the Nileans and concentrate exclusively on Markhamwit's equally confused but more mulish armada.

Though slower to make up their minds, the Great Lord's commanders were swifter to act once they'd reached a consensus. In due time they decided with some conviction that this was an inauspicious date for victory and they'd do better to bide their time till next Friday week. Which meant that they started to pull out, fast.

"Enough!"

It flashed from mind to mind, the same exact conclusion instantly understood by creatures utterly different in appearance but identical in thought-set. Lawson punctuated the judgment with approval.

"Good work, boys." Though there was not a boy present on any of the several ships, the encomium was universally understood and appreciated.

"Our work is invariably first class." Removing his toque, Nfam blew imaginary dust from it, smoothed its feather, put it back on at a rakish angle. "Nor do I think formal assessment is required. I have earned myself a new bonnet."

"Treat yourself to a new head while you're at it," advised the thought-form of Buzwuz from his haunt nearer the stern.

"Petty spitefulness characteristic of the childlike." Jlath nodded his fez until its crimson ribbon waggled. "It puts me in mind of certain inescapable theories. Attend me a moment."

Nfam turned his toque front to back, studying the result in a mirror. "I eagerly await enlightenment."

The other continued decorously. "I have long been intrigued by a phenomenon that someday must be the subject of further investigation. It offers opportunity for significant exposition."

"Such as?" prompted Nfam.

"The more developed the sense of fashion and style, the higher the intelligence. The less so, the lower."

Buzwuz shrilled back. "Let me tell you, spider-shape, that any species with a modicum of color sense is infinitely more . . . "

"Shut up!" bellowed Lawson, thus staking a featherless-biped claim in this scramble for superiority.

They went quiet, not because they were overawed by him, not because they considered him any better or worse than themselves, but solely because it was notorious that his two-legged kind could argue the tail off an alligator and cast grave doubts upon its parentage while doing so. If the Solarian mass-mind had a special compartment reserved for flights of vocal fancy duly embellished with pointed witticisms it was without doubt located on a dump called Terra.

So they held their peace while he boosted the speed and headed for the gypsy planet on which two ships already were waiting to collect the various homarachnids and take them nearer home. Those worthies tended to become a bit more fidgety than most when extended space travel was required of them. Furthermore, they were understandably tired. All their reaching, probing, and mental controlling took a considerable amount of energy and no one disputed that the quasi-spiders had earned some time off.

It was to be hoped that after the demonstration they had just put on their services would no longer be required, but it was universally agreed that it was too soon to start them on their long journey home just yet. As the Solarians knew from much experience, when it came to common sense there was no underestimating the willful stubbornness of the rancorously inclined. Nfam and Jlath and their grandiosely chapeaued colleagues would be homeward bound soon enough, as would they all. But not quite yet.

For one thing, while the group might have accomplished all it had been sent to do, Lawson had not. Certain business had stayed firm in his mind while they had done their work, had not slipped away even while they were misdirecting entire fleets of heavily armed vessels. Buzwuz knew he hadn't forgotten about it, and so did the rest of his crew.

There was ample room for individuality of thought and action within the Solarian mass-mind, for good intentions and the doing of deeds that had more to do with personal desire than awesome necessity. Lawson had done what he'd been sent to do, had accomplished what was necessary. Now it was time to attend to something he could not shake free of.

But he couldn't do it alone, nor would he have thought of trying to act by himself. Solarians always functioned cooperatively even when pursuing individual ends. It was an inescapable component of their mental makeup. Consequently he addressed his thoughts to the two hat-wearers.

"I've formed something of a personal attachment to a world that lies between here and the designated rendezvous. The inhabitants are stuck in a mess of trouble not of their own making. While the Nileans and Markhamwit's people won't be troubling them anymore, the nastiness they've done will live on after them. Unless we do something about it." Nfam and Jlath exchanged a glance.

"It's not part of the mission," he went on. "Just sort of an adjunct to the whole business. Something I'd like to see benignly resolved. I'd leave here feeling a lot better about things if we could make an effort. For that I need your help. The Callisians are already familiar with the situation. How about it?"

"Another time-period mired in bug-blow." Jlath preened self-consciously. "I don't know if I'm ready for that."

"It shouldn't take long," Lawson assured him. "I'd appreciate it."

Nfam essayed a mental sigh. "You'd better. The things we do to engender empathetic understanding."

"Good." Lawson turned back to the controls.

A bee-mind intruded and there was a heavy buzzing in his left ear. "Hey," snapped Buzwuz, "how about us? We agreed to go back to the backwater with you, but you didn't say anything about being crammed in here with these flatulent flaunters for another few days."

Lawson smiled at the Callisian. "That's because I already know how understanding and tolerant you are, Buz-wuz. How ready to help those in need and to accommodate the personal request of a friend.''

"Harmless, hell!" the Callisian bawled. "If I have to look at those, those . . . "

"Regal chapeaus," Jlath finished for him, adjusting his own.

"Posh cerebral accouterments," Nfam added confidently. "Suitable only for those of inherently advanced taste and refinement and not for primitive, winged types incapable of appreciating the more sophisticated art forms."

" . . . Odious, brazen, offensive, adjuncts to empty heads one more day I won't even be able to retain the bacteria in my gut," Buzwuz finished. "I'll . . . ! "

xiv

———————————— ■ ————————————

As the little ship once more sat in orbit above the formerly tranquil world it was plain to see that war continued to rage on the sullied surface below. Whether either side had been apprised by its erstwhile allies of the change in reality beyond the immediate stellar boundaries Lawson and his companions had no way of knowing. There was no overt evidence that anything had changed.

At present no bloated interstellar transports reposed within the armed boundaries of the two nation-species, disgorging cargoes of advanced death-dealing technology. The hastily erected spaceports of both sides were deserted.

"Visitors," announced Lou from her position.

Lawson glanced at the two homarachnids. With a psychic sigh Nfam and Jlath went motionless, probing outward.

"Nilean transport," Jlath quickly declared, his mental voice oddly detached. "Bound to supply their vassals below. Where would you like us to park 'em?"

"Nowhere around here," Lawson thought. "I don't want them anywhere near the locals." He inspected several projections. "Nothing else suitable in this system. There's one six points back the way they've come." He thought the destination into the homarachnids' minds. "Let 'em ponder their sins there. Their load of armaments and munitions should make a nice bright cloud for them to contemplate when they've finished scuttling themselves."

Nfam and Jlath acknowledged the request and yet again sent the focused Solarian mass-mind questing outward. The captain of the transport, who was perpetually bemoaning his dead-end, no-promotion assignment, suddenly decided it would improve his prospects for advancement no end if he were to register his ongoing displeasure by toasting his ship and its cargo on a world located in a system other than the one he was just entering. The location of a suitable sphere providentially presenting itself to his thoughts, he promptly issued orders to proceed to this new destination, hardly able to restrain his sudden enthusiasm. He was delighted to discover that his fellow officers and the crew in general shared this epiphany and approved wholeheartedly.

Nfam scratched at an eye. "So much for casual troublemakers. What's left?"

"The locals," Lawson informed him. "Two different species distinct in appearance but equal in intelligence."

"As opposed to the situation on board this boat," Jlath pointed out.

"I won't argue with that," declared Buzwuz, "since we all know the truth of the situation."

"The truth of the situation," growled Lawson, "is that we have one more piece of work to do." He sent the ship plunging downward.

Oceangoing warships continued to intercept the commerce of their foes, while on land invasion parties sought to establish forward bases in their adversary's hemisphere.

Ship-based aircraft bombed industrial targets and ripped the atmosphere in plane-to-plane combat.

Meanwhile factories on both sides continued to churn out war material without their operators realizing that they were destroying their homeworld far faster and more efficiently than they were their presumed enemy.

Nfam and Jlath considered the millions of minds below.

"Simple thoughts driven by simple motivations," Jlath declared. "They make Markhamwit's kind look like mental giants."

"Yet for all that, there's little difference in what they're doing." Nfam's disappointment was plain in his mind. "The usual misdirected waste of life and energy."

"We'll redirect them," his counterpart announced. "What approach would you suggest?"

Lawson considered carefully. "We don't want to take control of their leaders for the same reason we don't do that sort of thing on a larger scale with Markhamwit and the Nileans. On the other hand we can't repeat the process we've just carried out on a smaller scale because they'll still be facing each other across a single ocean on one world. At least Markhamwit and the Nileans have been battling over a comprehensible abstract like power. Local aggressions haven't reached that level. They're still susceptible to delusions as primitive as shape-prejudice."

"As opposed to something comprehensible, like lack of taste," Nfam pointed out.

"Taste requires a modicum of original thought," declared Buzwuz, "as opposed to the ability simply to focus that of others."

"Quiet," snapped Lawson. "We could send all their ships back to port, ground all their aircraft, but it would still leave them despising one another simply on the basis of physical appearance. We have to change that somehow. We not only want to leave them living in peace, we want to show them why it's a better prospect than what they're engaged in now."

From Lawson's cerebral fabrications both homarachnids knew exactly what the two species who inhabited the world below looked like. "That should be manageable," Nfam remarked. "Thank goodness neither of them look like bugs. That'd be an impossible task."

"Insects are the fount of symmetry," Lou put in, "as opposed to goofy-looked stumblebums whose genes can't decide what phylum they sprang from."

"That's because our development, unlike that of lesser forms, has focused on our minds," Nfam shot back.

"And style," Jlath added. "A notion alien to hiveminds."

"Some sort of mass education," Lawson was murmuring reflectively as he ignored the sniping. "Something to educate them in a hurry, show them what they're doing to themselves and their surroundings."

"We can't do mass education," Nfam pointed out. "It won't last after we've gone."

"Hah!" said Buzwuz.

"Mass delusion, now, that's something we could handle." Jlath adjusted his stance. "Delusions aren't meant to linger."

Lawson made a face. "We want to show them the error of their ways, not frighten them to death. At the same time the more they believe that the change comes from within themselves rather than being imposed from without, the better it will take and the more lasting will be the results. This shouldn't be that complicated." He brightened, nodding mentally to himself, and of course his companions shared his thoughts.

XV

■

Commander V'seikin was feeling fine as he slipped into his boots and proceeded to fasten the rest of his uniform. Today would be a day of great victory for the B'eitara. His squadron had succeeded in slipping close to the enemy coast under cover of dense fog and cloud. It was a maneuver they would not have dared as recently as a year ago, but the most recent gift of equipment from their great friends from beyond the moon had included wondrous electronic devices that enabled one to see through bad weather.

The ugly savages operating the Denkou coastal defenses were in for a nasty surprise.

According to the best available intelligence the enemy's large naval base at Cape Chkhior was empty save for a few small patrol vessels. Aircraft would have a difficult time operating in this bad winter weather and while the squadron had heard several roar past overhead, there had been no subsequent response from the enemy's defenses. Either the squadron had truly managed to arrive undetected or else the pilots of the land-based craft thought the close-packed array of vessels some of their own.

Utilizing the new gear provided by their six-legged off-world friends, V'seikin's ships would be able to target their objective even if the weather failed to lift. He smiled to himself as he imagined the consequences. The Denkou on shore would suddenly find themselves the subject of an intense bombardment, the source of which they would neither be able to see nor locate. The base at Cape Chkhior was an important refueling and resupply port for the North Denkounan fleet. With its facilities destroyed, the ships of that force would have to travel southward to seek resupply.

That would leave the entire peninsula in the vicinity of the cape open to assault by seaborne troops. Such a force was even now steaming at full speed from home. If the attack on the cape facilities failed, they could put about safely out at sea and return to their port of origin.

If it proved to be the kind of success V'seikin anticipated, the convoy would move in under cover of the squadron and land soldiers on the wide beach just north of the port itself. If they could advance rapidly enough they could seal off the peninsula from the rest of the continent and hold it against the feverish Denkou counterattacks that would be certain to follow. With a successful beachhead established, troops could flow in from the entire Denkou theater of war, giving the B'eitara a real foothold on the northern continent to complement the one they had already gained in the south.

The Denkou were attempting a similar strategy in the central homelands and had in fact succeeded in establishing a more protected base there. But this would give the B'eitara two bases on enemy soil to the foe's one. They could then initiate pincer movements, attack from two different regions, while the Denkou could be kept pinned down in the lowland basins. Such a conquest would advance the cause of the war notably.

He glanced out an armored port. The fog was still holding. The squadron moved cautiously in these semi-familiar waters. Their otherworldly allies had promised them devices that would allow them to see the bottom of the ocean as clearly as they now could the surface. But that wasn't due to arrive until Nextmonth, too late to equip his ships. After much discussion the general staff had elected to go ahead with the assault anyway, relying on V'seikin's nautical skills and those of his fellow ship captains. He swelled with pride. If he and his colleagues managed to pull this off they would be regaled as heroes back home. Heroes to the cause of subduing the repulsive, loathsome Denkou.

He stepped in front of a mirror to adjust his cap and collar . . . and froze. The face that stared back at him was not his own. It was not even that of a friend or relation. It was utterly alien and yet utterly familiar, which made the horror of it all that much more immediate.

It was the face of a Denkou.

Duronid flipped the stub of the sense-stick over the old stone wall and contemplated what he could see of the sea. Given the thickness of the fog, that wasn't much. It had been hanging about for days now, bathing the coastline in its mournful shadow and making visual scans impossible. Not that there was anything to see anyways. All the action was on the shores of the southern continent, where home defense forces were battling with the B'eitara invaders for control of a strategic delta.

The outcome was inevitable, he knew. Eventually the hairless interlopers would be driven into the sea and all the way back across the great ocean. Instead of participating in the brave defense he was stuck here, far to the north, helping to guard an important repair and resupply base against nonexistent threats.

Still, everyone had their duty to do and complaining only damaged the war effort. So he kept his disappointment to himself and voiced it only when he was within a casual circle of friends or family.

Distancing horns tootled out on the islands that marked the entrance to the base. Heavy weapons were positioned there to defend against the assault that would probably never come. At least he wasn't required to suffer that kind of isolation. The islands' defenders lived by their guns; eating, sleeping, and working on tiny rocky projections that during a vigorous storm might for a time be completely under water. They were only allowed back on the mainland for short, rigorously regulated breaks. At least he could come and go into the nearby towns more or less as he pleased.

The parapet he was pacing on his meditation break was part of an ancient fort several hundred years old. It had been built to defend the snug harbor against the seagoing bandits of olden times. Now it served as an adjunct to the newer, much more solid fortress of poured black interface that loomed like a ziggurat on its southern flank. The intact old structures were still sound enough, however, to serve as storage chambers and living quarters for less critical components of the coastal defense. Many local families could trace work lineages back to the old port's ancient cut-stone construction.

Not his, though. He hailed from farther south. This was not his country.

Oceanic fliers skimmed uncaringly through the fog, their occasional harsh shrieks in sharp counterpoint to the bellow of the location sounders. Being as yet unmated Duronid missed his family more than many of his more sexually active colleagues. He had no leave accrued yet and would have to serve another quarter year before he would be allowed time off to visit them. There was a young female in one of the towns he had been courting in his free time, but of course the relationship could not progress any further until the two of them could meet with his parents. She insisted on it. Quite properly, too, and he agreed with her. But that did not make the waiting any easier.

His timer beeped, warning him that he was due back at his duty station. Blowing through his nasal cavity to express resignation, he turned from the mist-smothered overlook and headed back down the wide, ancient stone steps. There were vehicles to be attended to, and his superiors, while forgiving, could be harsh if delays grew lengthy.

Halfway down he met someone coming up. Eyes locked and for an instant he was paralyzed with fear and disbelief.

The B'eitara stared back at him, equally stunned by the unexpected confrontation. It was not armed, at least, not that he could see, but he took small comfort from that. The B'eitara were notoriously tricky and this one could have any manner of weapons or explosive devices hidden about its person. How it had slipped into the fortress he couldn't imagine. It had to be a member of some scouting party that had come ashore under cover of the fog, no doubt to map the layout of the harbor defenses or worse, to commit some dreadful sabotage.

Clearly he'd surprised it, for with a cry it whirled and vanished back the way it had come. He hesitated, wondering which alarm to sound first. Then determination overcame his initial surprise. If it was unarmed it was probably traveling with companions who were not. At all costs he needed to prevent it from rejoining its fellows and initiating either retreat or lethal mischief.

Plunging downward he took the stairs three at a time, his feet remembering the familiar layout. Fearful of falling at a crucial moment and thereby putting himself at the mercy of the weaker but more agile B'eitara, he took care to keep his attention focused on the stairway. In the course of this his glance naturally happened to encounter his pumping legs.

Despite this, he nearly tripped as he came to an abrupt halt.

His legs were bare. Naked and hairless. In place of his normal impenetrable coat of black curls was bare flesh, nauseatingly pale. Bringing up a hand he saw that it, too, was devoid of covering.

It was the B'eitara, he thought furiously. It had bathed him in some sort of invisible beam that had caused all his hair to fall out. But looking back the way he'd come he saw that the stone steps were clean and well maintained. No clumps of hair spotted their gray surfaces. What was going on? Could the B'eitara have developed a device that disintegrated only hair? And if they had, of what use was it to embarrass their enemies? It made no sense.

Neither did the feet he goggled at, nor the tiny, too many fingers that wiggled at the tips of narrow palms. A nearby movement made him look down.

It was the B'eitara. It had paused and was peering uneasily around a corner, watching him. This time a pistol hung from one hand, but it was not pointed in his direction. Still, he was unarmed, and the threat was implied.

"Who are you," the B'eitara demanded to know, "and how did you here get?"

Duronid blinked. Even his eyes didn't feel right. He stood on the step, not knowing now whether to advance and engage this enemy or to retreat, or simply to squat down and surrender to the mystery that had overtaken him.

"This my designated base is. My station in the vehicle sheds lies. How did *you* ashore slip without triggering the warning detectors?"

"Ashore slip?" the figure came back. "What are you talking about? I was going the same question to ask you."

Duronid noticed something familiar in the B'eitara's manner. That was impossible of course, but still . . . "Your voice familiar sounds."

"So does yours. That's crazy."

"This more than crazy is. You know, you're the first B'eitara I've seen in person. I've seen plenty on the visuals, of course, but to actually encounter one . . ."

"What are you babbling about? Are you insane? Who's a B'eitara?"

"Maybe we're both insane." *That voice.* "I swear by my grandparents' lines that I know you."

"I am Yeuorm, second apprentice in mechanical repair."

Duronid no longer wondered if he were going mad. Now he was certain of it. "You are not Yeuorm, though the way you hold yourself mindful of him is. You are B'eitara."

"Perdition says you. You are the B'eitara."

"What nonsense is this? Look at yourself!"

"Look to your own self, whoever you are."

Overcome by events, Duronid complied. Truly he was suffering from much more than missing hair. His entire body had been altered. It was not only bald but incredibly, unhealthily thin.

A reflective surface. He needed a reflective surface. Apparently the same thought occurred to the B'eitara that was calling itself Yeuorm because it fumbled at its duty belt until it found a small metal box. This it held up before its eyes, tilting it to reflect not only its face but the rest of its body.

Then the B'eitara did an extraordinary thing. Putting aside its sidearm it sat down at the base of the stone steps and began to cry.

Uncertain how to react, Duronid started downward. He

considered the weapon, apparently set aside mentally as well as physically now, and then picked up the metal stash box. When he got a look at himself he was stunned by his appearance but no longer surprised.

"How could this have happened? You have into one of you turned me!"

The sobbing seated figure looked up at him. "I do your voice know. You are Duronid!"

"Of course I am," he snapped. "What's to me happened?" He paused. What had happened to him could happen to others. "Are you truly Yeuorm?"

"Do you the senior transport we worked on two quarters ago remember, the one that Second Senior Triob took out and lost control of?"

"And went shooting off down the beach when the engine froze at speed and sent him, medals and all, into the ocean splashing? How could I forget that? Yet they never to us the trouble traced."

"Much less the intent," the Yeuorm figure finished. "You *are* Duronid." The B'eitara reached toward him. Duronid started to flinch back, then forced himself to meet the gesture. The other might look like a B'eitara, but clearly it was his good friend Yeuorm he was confronting. Their hands met and, surprisingly, managed the traditional greeting in spite of the absence of hair and a surfeit of digits. Despite their disquieting circumstances, it was good to have contact with a friend.

"Some kind of illusion being perpetrated is by the B'eitara," Yeuorm decided. "This must a prelude be to an attack, to off guard put us." He looked back the way he'd come. Distant yells and moans confirmed his suspicions. "From the noise I suspect everyone else suffering similarly is."

"If the B'eitara are this doing to confuse us they've certainly succeeded," Duronid decided.

"But it no sense makes." Yeuorm had forgotten all about his initial fears, grateful to have found a sympathetic (if unnatural-looking) ear to listen to his concerns. "If the B'eitara capable of a feat of science like this are, then why choose to make us look like them? Why not groveling *gespinners* or lowly *bilachs?* Wouldn't that be more mind damaging?"

"I agree. It doesn't any sense make."

"I wonder," said Yeuorm, "how long they can make the effect last." He was suddenly uncomfortable. "Surely it only a temporary affliction is. It could not be made permanent."

"Surely not," agreed Duronid, more out of desperation than assurance.

The landing party came ashore quietly, the crash of the small waves hiding the sounds of their movements as they hurriedly concealed their landing craft beneath some overhanging rocks. They adjusted their weapons and donned their packs, discarding most of their bulky sea gear. Camouflage suits covered all of their faces and bodies save their eyes, mouths, and breathing ridges.

"Up this way," the squad leader declared. He didn't have to talk much. His elite troops had rehearsed this mission on board ship for many days, poring over the maps and models of the harbor's defenses. Each one knew exactly what was expected of him and what he had to do.

Out there, the leader knew, out somewhere in the fog, was the invasion force, troop carriers preceded by the gunships. But before those powerful vessels opened fire it would be up to him and two similar squads to sow confusion and terror among the enemy by placing and setting off remote-controlled explosive charges. With luck they could destroy enough of the harbor's defenses to allow the landings to proceed relatively unopposed. It was a terribly risky assignment, but one that found no shortage of volunteers.

They moved quickly off the beach, guns held at the ready, loaded and set to go. They hoped their presence would not be detected and they would not have to fight until they'd been able to set at least some of their charges.

Their first target was a portion of the old fortress, a site of some historical importance. That was not a consideration to the leader. Of what significance was barbaric Denkou history? They would blow it to bits without a second thought. The old fort was home to the harbor's main vehicle depot. Destroying or badly damaging it would restrict the movements of the port's troops and prevent the enemy from moving reinforcements to the invasion beach.

Compressed-air boosters sent climbing ropes hissing silently over the top of the wall. While three of his soldiers kept a lookout, the rest went up the two ropes at great speed, using their strong hands and prehensile feet to ascend far faster than any Denkou could dream possible. Then it was the turn of the lookouts, and lastly of the team leader.

He reached the top of the old wall without incident. A quick glance showed the beach below still deserted. *The fog is a better ally than a dozen armored vehicles,* he mused as the lines were gathered up and reloaded for future use.

Silently they checked their diagrams. Not a great deal was known about the internal design of Denkou fortifications, but there were some records of older forts from earlier days, before the war for freedom had begun. And their allies, the minions of the Great Star Lord Markhamwit, had instructed them in more and more advanced techniques of military inference.

There should be a stairway nearby. Spreading out and keeping careful watch, they hustled along the wall, until the point trooper located the way down. Still there was no sign of any guards or patrols.

The Denkou are stupid and lazy, he mused. He began to

believe that he and all of his soldiers might be able to set their charges, do their damage, and get back to the beach alive. From there a small, swift pickup craft would be waiting offshore to meet them.

He waved his troopers on and took the lead down the stairs himself.

Duronid and Yeuorm heard the patter of approaching feet on stone. The approach echoed down the stairs as both soldiers rose and pressed themselves against the wall.

"No one's up there supposed to be but me," whispered Duronid tersely. "I didn't see anyone before I came down, either."

"The B'eitara," his companion whispered. "They must a lot of confidence in this deception of theirs have." Bending, he picked up his sidearm. "Go and sound the alarm. I'll try to hold them here."

"No," said Duronid. Looking around, he found the locker where he'd left his rifle and hurriedly recovered the weapon. Checking the magazine he saw that it was fully loaded. "If they've got heavy arms with them we can't let them inside. That's evening too much the odds. We'll both hold them here. The sound of weapons fire will around these old walls rattle as if in a recording chamber. That 'll help soon enough bring."

"Rightness!" agreed Yeuorm, clutching his pistol tightly. "And if we die here, it will for our families be to the justice of our actions enshrine!" He put a hand on his friend's shoulder. Despite the bizarre feel of the naked flesh Duronid did not pull back.

"Hold up here," declared the squad leader. "The air's liable to be bad inside. You know how the Denkou stink." Murmurs of agreement and knowing laughter came from his troopers. "Clear vision's vital," he reminded them as he tugged on the hood of his own camouflage suit. What had served to disguise them on approach would be of little use and awkward restraint in the confines of a Denkou warren.

Duronid's eyes widened as he peered around the corner. "Rightness saves," he muttered, and started forward. His companion clutched frantically at him and he smiled back. "It's all right, Yeuorm. Come and see." Turning, he raised his voice. "They've found a way to stop it, then? Maybe they can help us now."

The squad members tensed at the sound of Denkou voices. Several of them understood the words clearly, fluency in the debased Denkou language being a requirement for inclusion in the elite units. But the declaration made no sense to them.

At the same time they caught sight of themselves, hoodless and exposed now, and each soldier drew frantically away from his neighbor.

Duronid and a more hesitant but nonetheless relieved Yeuorm halted halfway up the stairs, their expressions puzzled, confused by the antics of their brethren. "Crestings Call, what's with you guys the matter?"

One of the squad members whirled to face the pair, gun at his side. When he saw them he relaxed and put it up. "Thank the spirits! What's happened to us?"

Duronid tensed. "He's speaking low B'eitara? To what purpose?"

"I don't know." Yeuorm was equally bemused. "But if I'm understanding him correctly he confused seems. They all do. Look at them."

Duronid frowned. "Why should they confused be? They look normal." He mounted another step. "Except that they're Denkou weapons carrying. I wonder what's going on?"

The squad leader managed to collect himself and approach the pair coming up the stairs. "I don't know how you got inside but I can't tell you what a relief it is to see a friendly face. I thought squad three was to assault the other side of this complex. You can stop speaking Denkou now." He glanced around. "The fog is our protector and the enemy remains unaware of our presence."

Duronid halted. "What are you talking about? And why the B'eitara babble? Are you under some kind of coded orders or something operating?" They were all so short, he thought. A requirement for some kind of special mission?

"The most disturbing thing has just happened to us." The squad leader stared hard at the trooper. "We have been overcome by some kind of sudden hypnosis. The Denkou, despite their primitive minds, have succeeded in convincing us that we look just like them. Our arrival must have triggered some kind of projection weapon previously unknown. You apparently have managed to avoid its effects."

"Your arrival?" Yeuorm made a face. "Where did you come from? I don't you from the vehicle pool recognize."

"Vehicle pool?" The rest of the squad members were crowding around their leader, hoping for an explanation or at least some degree of reassurance. "You are confused. We're here to destroy the vehicle pool. Aren't you part of the team designated to assault the communications complex?"

"Assault?" Duronid's mind was working furiously. "What," he asked slowly, "is your rank and family designation?"

"Family designation? What are you talking about? And until I know your rank, troopers, I order you to talk normally. I dislike speaking the debased Denkou tongue unless it is necessary to my survival."

Duronid reached a conclusion he very much disliked even as he was commencing a slow retreat. "You are not Denkou."

"What the Dust is that supposed to mean?" replied the squad leader. "Have you gone mad?"

"Maybe. Maybe the whole world's gone mad. You see, my friend here and I just bemoaning our own fate were. We look like B'eitara to you?"

"Of course you look like B'eitara, thank the Designate. What else should you look like?"

Duronid and Yeuorm exchanged a look before deciding not to bolt. "Like you," Duronid told the squad leader. "We should look like you. We're Denkou, but we have only our size retained. We fear we under the influence of some kind of mass illusion are. We thought it of your making was, but now it is clear you are invaders from the same kind of hallucination suffering."

"Nonsense!" snapped the squad leader. "This is the work of Denkou science, though I would not have thought it capable of such a thing."

"You're right: it's not," mumbled a disconsolate Yeuorm.

He sat down heavily and put his hairless head in his hands, bemoaning his condition.

"Something remarkable and disheartening happened has," declared Duronid. "The whole world, or at least this one part of it, seems to have been affected. We who are Denkou now look like B'eitara, while you, it seems, have into us been turned. Or at least that is the impression my eyes are given. You all B'eitara are?"

"Of course," replied the squad leader, only this time with much less force and conviction. "You . . . you're not?"

"I am called Duronid. This my friend Yeuorm is. We are stationed in this place. And evidently you are not."

"No . . . we're part of . . . we were landed here to disrupt your communications and resupply lines. Then this happened to us." He pulled at the thick curly hair that covered his face and entire body. It made him feel as if he was smothering in his own self.

"You look like us," Duronid told him. "We look like you. I could shoot you except that it would feel like shooting one of my own family. And if I'm about all this wrong, if something's even more amiss than it seems, then the illusion might run to thoughts as well as appearances, to what I'm thinking as much as to what I'm seeing. You might really be relations, in spite of your protests to the contrary. Therefore I don't see how I can take the chance of shooting you until I find some way to all this sort out."

"I would hardly shoot you," the squad leader replied. "You remind me of a clan cousin."

"We know who we are but we don't look like who we are, and unless something happens the situation to change we can't very well start shooting." How can we tell what is real and what merely a distortion in our minds?"

The squad leader considered. "This may only be a localized phenomenon, affecting only those of us here."

Duronid looked back down toward the corridor below. Yells and moans were still distantly audible. "I'd like to that believe, but from the sounds of things I don't think it the case is."

The squad leader was thinking hard. "Just a minute." Pulling a compact radio from his pack he flicked it to life. One of his troopers made as if to restrain him . . . they were not supposed to break radio silence while on shore . . . but the leader shook him off.

"We have to find out what's going on here," he muttered restlessly. "If it's some kind of incredibly clever Denkou trick we'll know soon enough. Meanwhile keep an eye on these two."

"Why?" said another trooper. "They look more like us

than we do. What if they're simply confused members of another landing squad?''

The leader hesitated, tried to think of a reply that would make sense, and gave up. ''Ignore them, then. Just leave me alone for a minute.''

It took the last of many, many calls to get a coherent response. Apprised of the chaotic situation that had overcome the invading force, which seemed to have become suddenly populated entirely by Denkou sailors, the squad leader sat down slowly.

''The whole fleet's affected,'' he muttered.

''Sir!'' exclaimed another trooper, shocked at this casual breach of security. The squad leader looked tiredly up at him.

''It doesn't matter anymore. Maybe nothing matters anymore. The fleet's been in touch with home port via relay. It's not just us. All the B'eitara have been affected. Everywhere. There has been panic in some of the major cities but it seems to be dying down now as people come to grips with the condition.'' He looked at the only two obvious B'eitara within view. Both looked distinctly unhappy. ''To all visible intents and purposes the B'eitara have turned into Denkou. Except they still speak B'eitara and act B'eitara and follow the B'eitara ways.''

Duronid nodded. ''I suspect that this fortress is now defended, to anyone who might care to look, entirely by very unhappy and confused B'eitara.'' Somehow, in the depths of his confusion and despair, he managed to summon up the rough Denkou sense of humor. ''Very tall B'eitara.''

The squad leader directed his troopers to put down their arms and relax as best they could. There was no point in trying to continue with the mission, no point in going on. How could they attack when everyone they saw looked like one of their own kind? It would be similarly difficult, he mused, for the Denkou to defend themselves against assaults by squads of their own relatives.

They had been defeated, not by force of arms or technological superiority, but by false images of themselves.

"What has happened to the world?" he murmured aloud. "Have we all gone insane?"

Duronid shook his hairless head. "It's an odd kind of insanity that afflicts one people with one delusion and another exactly with the reverse. This of design and intent smacks, not accident."

"But who?" the squad leader wondered dazedly. "Who would do such a thing to us? Who would have the capability, and why?"

"Not us," insisted Yeuorm, recovering a little from his bemusement. "We're not this clever."

"Or this insidious," his friend added. "Only our patrons, the glorious and beneficent Nileans, might the superior knowledge necessary have to something like this bring about."

"Or the science masters who serve the Great Lord Markhamwit," declared the squad leader. "But I ask again: Why?"

"I cannot imagine," replied Duronid. "They were helping us to defeat you, with eagerness. Why would they want to do something the fighting to stop? For such is the effect of this illusion. If they wanted to help us, they would have only made you look like us and not us like you."

"The same for the Nileans," said one of the squad members. "It goes against the intent of either side."

"A third party, then?" wondered the squad leader. "But who, and why?"

Duronid found himself looking up, past the squad leader's wonderfully hairy skull, toward the fog-shrouded

ramparts beyond the stairwell and beyond that, the sky itself.

"You know, whoever you are, I only a common soldier
am. I watch over and repair broken or damaged vehicles.
You don't much imagination for that need, only how to
study manuals and handle tools. But ever since the Nileans
came among us all the Denkou have of other things been
made aware. Of the fact that there are other intelligent
creatures on other worlds, who fight and trade among
themselves. Of these the Nileans are by far the greatest . . . "

"Save for those who take direction from the Great
Lord," put in one of the squad members with admirable
but misplaced assurance.

" . . . Along with the servants of the Great Lord," Duronid magnanimously finished. "But we know, because we
told have been, that there are many, many other races out
there. Races with abilities to themselves peculiar, with tal-
ents we cannot imagine because we not developed enough
are.

"Why should the Nileans or the servants of the Great
Lord be the most advanced, the most powerful? Because
they say this is so? We can only what they tell us believe because we cannot beyond the bounds of our own world
travel. If we could, might we not discover that they are not
being entirely truthful with us? Might there not be some
other kind out there more powerful than either of our respective patrons?"

"Powerful enough to do this?" the squad leader wondered. "To fool an entire population into believing they
look like their enemies?"

"Who says we enemies must be?" Duronid came back.
"Right now you don't like an enemy to me look. You
look . . . like me."

"And you like a proper person," the squad leader informed him.

"Proper?" said Duronid. "Naked like this, with round pupils and all these digits?"

"It beats being smothered by all this damnable hair," the squad leader swore. "I can hardly breathe!" He looked up and his eyes met those of the guard. There was a startled pause. Then, to the surprise of the rest of the squad and to Yeuorm, both soldiers began to laugh, the Denkou uttering gruff, short squeaks from its tiny B'eitara mouth, the squad leader barking uncontrollably through thick, heavy lips.

The others watched in astonishment as unnatural sounds emerged from familiar mouths. Then Yeuorm, wiping water from the corners of his eyes, joined in, and one by one, so did the rest of the squad. Soon the stairwell was filled with uncontrollable, unrestrainable laughter.

After a while, so was the rest of the planet.

XVI

·

It's been four days," said Nfam. "I think they've had enough time to get the point."

"Laughter," agreed Jlath, "can smooth the path for even the most difficult decisions. For example, only my amusement at the sight of overweight, underdressed insects crashing into walls and ceilings enabled me to repress my natural disgust against coming on this ship."

"You can imagine what I've been going through," put in the thought-form of Buzwuz. "If we've had the occasional collision or two it's only because our optics are temporarily overwhelmed by a clash of shape and color that verges on the physically painful."

"Shut up," said Lawson softly. He was studying the projections that gave a complete picture of what was taking place on the surface below.

Initial, brief chaos had given way to horror, then outrage, and lastly enforced contemplation. Tentative communications on less than the historically contentious level were being swapped between B'eitara and Denkou. Governments were talking to one another. Meanwhile there was a continuing lull in the fighting not because of a weakening of resolve by either side but because it was impossible to order troops to shoot at groups of soldiers who looked just like the folks back home. Especially when you yourself looked just like the horrid foe you were supposed to be annihilating.

It was an impossible situation in which to try to conduct a war, with the result that the war stopped.

"I think they've had time enough to see the other guy's point of view," Lawson decided. "In spades." He thought at the homarachnids. "You've done quite a job."

"Our work is unmatched," announced Jlath. With that he and Nfam simply stopped concentrating. The Solarian mass-mind no longer flowed through them, or through the little ship drifting in orbit above the planetary equator equidistant between the two hemispheres.

Commander V'seikin's personal valet looked up from where he was arranging the commander's uniforms in his storage locker and let out a startled cry.

"Sir! You . . . you are yourself again!"

V'seikin frowned as he turned to his servant. "What nonsense are you talking now, C'c'rir? No one is . . . "

"Look at yourself, sir, look!"

A cautious V'seikin wandered over to the damned mirror. What he saw there made his eyes widen as they hadn't since he'd consummated clan relationship with his present mate. Reaching up with both hands, he felt of his face. There was no unnatural, prickly sensation of impenetrable hair, no massive, uncouth skull.

Or was it really so uncouth? In the past days he'd managed, because he'd had no choice, to grow used to it.

C'c'rir, too, was himself once more. It was an occasion for celebration unrestrained. Sternly he suppressed the immense, indescribable relief he felt. He was commander of the battle squadron and it was his responsibility to remain in control of himself.

He didn't have to ask if the same restoration had occurred elsewhere on the flagship: he could hear the shouts and screams and weepings of joy even within the cabin. But he took the time to communicate, one by one, with every other ship in the fleet, until he was certain the restoration was universal.

Communications soon was able to inform him that the general population back home had likewise undergone an identical transformation. All the B'eitara had their smooth features and proper number of digits back, in addition to other, less mentionable characteristics. What then of the Denkou? How were they faring?

He had been in close communication with one Darpidiwe, commander of the target port, ever since the delusion had taken control. They had grown easy with one another, if not completely comfortable. Now as he started to give the order to re-establish communications with shore, he hesitated.

Physically, the fleet was unharmed. Morale would return, indeed would surge, with the reinstatement of natural appearance. They had lost the element of surprise but still retained their full store of munitions and supplies. They might not now be able to completely destroy the enemy and take the peninsula, but they could still try, and if naught else cause a great deal of damage in the process.

He saw the chief communications officer looking up at him, obviously waiting for instructions. Around him his staff likewise waited on his decision. He thought of the crudely mannered but nonetheless admirable in his own fashion enemy commander. They had talked, and when he thought of the image of Darpidiwe it was the face of a concerned, troubled B'eitara he was seeing. Because that was what he had seen, these past troubled days.

Could he now send ship-to-shore missiles and heavy explosives flying in that direction?

"Commander?" his senior staff officer prompted.
"Your orders, Commander?"

V'seikin thought a moment longer, then, "All ships to
stand on ready, with defenses on full alert. We've lost surprise and the fog bank both. Let's see what the Denkou do,
how they react now that they know we're out here."

Had he made the right decision, he wondered? Should
he, in spite of what he was thinking, what he was feeling,
have ordered the attack to proceed forthwith? A knowing
glance around his circle showed that the sense of relief on
the faces of his officers was palpable. Whether they were experiencing the same conflicting sensations he had no way of
knowing, but clearly the martial spirit that had accompanied them across the great ocean had absented itself. They
had no more desire to attack the mainland at that moment
than did he.

They would wait to see how events developed. Perhaps
uppermost in all their minds was the unspoken fear that,
somehow, for some undefinable, inexplicable reason, if
they did attack, if they made so much as a single hostile gesture, the delusion might return to take hold of their minds
again.

Permanently this time?

They could not know, might not ever know. Because
they didn't know what had caused it in the first place, or
why, and they weren't about to chance it again. Least of all
V'seikin, who had everyone else's welfare on his mind.

"Commander, communication from shore. The Denkou fortress is hailing us."

He took a deep breath. That would most likely be Darpidiwe. Maybe he would have some answers.

The two old soldiers talked. Meanwhile the fleet's missiles and the shore batteries' guns remained silent, neither

commanding officer realizing that the answers to their questions could be found in the simple fact that they *were* talking.

"I think the lesson'll hold," Lawson announced with satisfaction. "Neither side is willing to risk taking the first shot at the other out of fear that they'll snap back to looking like the guys they're shooting at again."

"They're burning up their low-band airwaves," Lou announced from her position. "Now that they've spent time looking like the traditional bad guys they've decided that maybe their old opponents aren't so ugly after all. Certainly not to the point of risking their collective sanity in hopes of exterminating them."

Lawson nodded. "And without the Nileans or Markhamwit's minions to keep them stirred up, they can get on about the business of talking sense without outside interference."

"An unscheduled detour, a stop along a back road," Buzwuz mused poetically. "It's always nice to be able to dispense a universal truth when the occasion presents itself. Namely, that talk-talk is lots better than bang-bang."

"I wouldn't have expected you to know-know that much common sense-sense," thought Nfam.

"Now listen here," the bee-mind shot back, "I've had just about enough of . . . ! "

"Heading out," Lawson said curtly, unwilling to become involved this time. He harangued a control. There was no need to consult star charts and plot the highly erratic course of the wandering sphere. Lawson could have chased it across half the galaxy and hit it dead center with his eyes shut. All that was needed was to steer straight along the thought-stream emanating from the pair of Solarian vessels already waiting there.

It was as easy as that.

xvii

The follow-up process was delayed. As always. Held back deliberately and of malice aforethought. The sluggish communications systems of both warring life-forms had been greatly to the advantage of Solarians, but now time must be allowed for those same primitive systems to deliver applicable data to Markhamwit and Glastrom. There was no use in Lawson and Reeder taking them the news in person. They would not be believed until confirmation arrived in large dollops.

And after the warlords had gained a clear picture of recent events, additional time must be given for the complete digestion thereof. Since the Nileans were by nature a little more impulsive and a little less stubborn than their opponents it was likely that they would be the first to agree that it is unprofitable to play hob with common property (or rather, common non-property) such as the empty space between worlds.

Markhamwit would be the last to give in. Unlike Glastrom, who was simply the currently elected head of a board of equals, the Great Lord stood alone at the pinnacle of his kind's government. It's always harder to vote on a decision when the entire committee consists of yourself. While a correct decision can bring you all the glory and honor, if it's a flop it leaves you with no one else to share in the blame. Compared to Glastrom, Markhamwit would tend to be overly cautious.

He would suffer a soul-searching period balancing loss of face against the growing pile of awkward facts. Consequently he must be allowed time to work out for himself that it is better to drop an autocratic obsession than ultimately drop at the end of a rope. Being what he was, a prominent member of his own contentious species, he'd have no illusions about the fate of one who insists on leading his people to total defeat, especially since it would quickly become common knowledge that far more benign and relatively painless alternatives had been made available.

A couple of days before the Nileans were due to become mentally ripe, Reeder burst through the defense screen of their homeworld, dropped a packet in Glastrom's palace yard by way of demonstrating that he and his kind were indifferent to far safer means of communication such as long-range reciprocating subspace beams, and whipped back into the eternal starfield before guards or atmospheric patrols fully realized what had taken place.

Ten time-units later, making carefully estimated allowance for Markhamwit's more truculent character, Lawson obliged with a similar bundle that crowned the fat Kasine as he waddled across the landscaped open area outside the central interrogation center. The thump on that worthy's dome was not intentional. Nobody could go by at such velocity and achieve such perfection of aim, not even the Solarians, much less prepare such an impossibly well-orchestrated delivery. It was wholly coincidental, but to the end of his days Kasine would never believe it.

Struggling to his feet, the chief interrogator addressed a few well-chosen words to the sky, in which nothing save a few migrating *tepawts* was visible, and took the bundle indoors. After a quick check ascertained its origin he hastened to give it to the captain of the guard who gave it to the garrison commander who gave it to the chief of intelligence. That official immediately recalled the fate of a predecessor who had hurriedly burst open the inner contents of a parcel from someone who was not a friend. So with the minimum of delay and an admirable dedication to duty he passed it to Minister Teruon who turned it over to First Minister Ganne who with equal alacrity handed it personally to the addressee, the Great Lord Markhamwit, and found an excuse to get out of the room.

Viewing the unsolicited gift with much disfavor, Markhamwit found an earpiece and cylinder, called the chief of intelligence, ordered him to provide an expendable warrior to come lean out the window and open the thing. The chief of intelligence told the garrison commander who told the captain of the guard who duly pushed along a loyal thick-head of low rank and no importance.

The task performed without dire result, Markhamwit found himself with a thick wad of starmap printouts. The originators of the package had disdained the use of more compact but incompatible information storage systems in favor of a method that was primitive but easy to understand. There is something about a simple pictorial representation on a flat sheet of solid material that enables it to overcome the most tangled linguistic barriers. There are no semantic convulsions inherent in a straight line and accompanying number.

Spreading the charts of stellar topography over his desk, the Great Lord stared at them irefully. All bore copious markings with appropriate footnotes in the master tongue.

Certain worlds and satellites within systems that had been singled out were marked in greater detail.

Overlaid on each map by a transparency fixation process Markhamwit neither recognized nor understood was a list of ships stalled on the appropriate spheres, plus roughly estimated strength of crews thus marooned and a further estimate, depending on the hospitableness of each respective globe, of how long each group could survive unaided.

The longer he studied this collection the more riled he became. If the figures were to be believed, approximately one-fifth of his total forces had been put out of action. One-fifth of his warships, representing the apex of modern technology and the greatest technical achievements of his kind, were so much scrap metal scattered across the light-years. Assuming that it would be asking for further trouble to employ armed vessels, it would require the full mobilization of his weaponless transport fleet to rescue and bring home the crews presently languishing on a couple of hundred worlds. And if he made no attempt to save them, regardless of their inexplicably traitorous behavior, there would be trouble aplenty on this world.

He did not know it, but he had another twenty time-units in which to think things over.

At the end of that period Lawson returned.

The second arrival was exactly like the first. At one moment the plain stood empty, with the city gray and grim in the north, the bluish sun burning above and the smallest of the three moons going down in the east. A light breeze ruffled the scrub growth that collected in hollows in the polished granite boulders. Next moment the ship was there, a thin streak of dust settling around its edges as if to show that there had been motion even though unseen. It appeared so suddenly and silently that even the wary high plains animals were not startled. As far as they were concerned there was another large, somewhat shinier-than-normal rock where none had existed a moment ago; and a brief, warm wind pungent with an odd, otherworldly smell had swept up out of nowhere and drifted off on its way.

Overhead the atmospheric patrol circled and swirled as before. This time there was some risk that they might attack without waiting for orders. A slick trick creates greater fury when repeated and sometimes becomes too much to bear: "If a man does thee once it's his fault; if he does thee twice it's thy fault!"

But again the Solarian visitor's behavior was that of one completely unconscious of such dangers, or completely indifferent to them. It lay on the plain, unmoving and to all intents and purposes unshielded, a clear target. The patrol leaders caucused electronically. Puzzling rumors had begun to reach the homeworld, of multiple disasters out among the grand fleet that weren't quite disasters, of disorder and disarray and resignation. There were whispers that this colossal confusion might, just might, have something to do with the peculiar entities called Solarians.

Therefore, if the small ship sitting openly on the plain below was a Solarian vessel, intelligent individuals might do well to restrain their natural impulse to blast it out of existence and instead pass the decision along to higher-ups. So the patrol dropped nothing save some choice invective while screaming the news to the city's central communications.

The immediate result of all this agitated aerial braying took the form of a couple of aircar loads of troops that raced out onto the plain even as Lawson emerged from the ship's lock. He came out breathing deeply, enjoying the fresh air, the feel of solid earth underfoot. The pollution that afflicted the manufacturing sections of the great city was being carried away from his position by prevailing winds, while the temperature verged on the balmy. As did, no doubt, the local military command's state of mind. That, if not the weather, was a condition that hopefully could be improved.

Several winged shapes buzzed ecstatically out of the lock, zoomed into the sky, chased after each other, and put over a plausible bee-version of sailors in port. Several projected their happiness for general distribution and Lawson was able to share in their pleasure. For their part they partook of his delight in the unrecycled atmosphere while viewing his satisfaction at the feel of solid ground underfoot with considerable sympathy.

"Pity," thought the mind-shape of Buzwuz. "Even with artificial wings you'll never be able to experience the same feeling of freedom."

"That's all right," Lawson thought back. "Nature is fair. You'll never be able to do more than conceptualize what it's like to enjoy solid food."

"Why would I want to?" Buzwuz responded with a mental shudder. "Company's coming. Want us to go say hello?"

"I don't think that'll be necessary this time, but keep a lens peeled in case I'm wrong and there's a joker in the deck."

"They're all jokers," thought Lou in a rather lame attempt at humor.

"Now, now," Lawson chided her. "It is to be hoped they have seen the light."

"Illuminating statistics," said Buzwuz, dropping to investigate a native flower.

Disregarding the oncomers from the city, the bee-minds continued to swap thoughts mainly for the benefit of the biped. They continued to deplore his lack of wings and bemoaned the weight of skeleton he was forced to carry about. They questioned the wisdom of Nature in putting sentient life upon two inadequate feet. Ah, the pity of it all!

So far as Lawson and his crew were concerned, the air-car-loads making toward them contained an armed company of mental moppets of no particular shape or form. And Markhamwit himself would have been appalled to learn that his own status was that of the muscular bully of grade one.

The vehicles pulled up and the troops tumbled out. Though Lawson did not know it, his attitude and expression had been perfectly duplicated in the dawn of history by a gentleman named Casey who wore a cap and badge: the corner cop, watching the kids come out of school. The lesson learned was the same now as then, produced the same results. The unruly members of this crowd had to be taught respect for Casey.

They'd learned it, all right; it was evident from what they did next. This time there was no hostile surrounding of the ship, weapons activated and held ready. No heavy artillery pieces were wrestled into position, their muzzles aimed at the open lock. Instead the panting arrivals formed up in two ranks, wide apart like a guard of honor. Some distinctly grating, atonal music blared from an unseen speaker and Lawson winced. Fortunately for them, the Callisians were relatively immune to this aspect of the formal welcome.

A three-comet officer marched forward and saluted ceremoniously. It was an interesting procedure performed with two arms on the same side and Lawson quietly admired the physical dexterity necessary to execute the limited gymnastics.

"Sire, you have returned to see the Great Lord?"

"I have." Lawson blinked, looked him over. Despite the haste with which he and his fellow soldiers had obviously been dispatched, his harness gleamed and his fur all but sparkled. "Why the 'sire'? I do not have any military rank."

"You are the ship's commander." The other signed toward the vessel.

"I am its pilot," Lawson corrected. "Nobody commands it."

With a touch of desperation the officer terminated the disconcerting talk by motioning toward the nearest of the two large aircars. "This way, sire."

Grinning to himself, Lawson climbed into the vehicle. A trio of immaculately dressed-out soldiers remained seated in back, their eyes fixed resolutely forward. He offered them a smile, shrugged when no response was forthcoming, and turned to face the bow.

The vehicle lifted, turned, and headed cityward. Lawson kept silence during the journey. The officer did likewise, inwardly feeling that this was one of those days when one can be tempted to say too much.

There was another well-turned-out guard waiting at the entrance to the tower complex. The corridors and hallways inside had been cleared and Lawson saw none of the indifferent bustle that had been evident on his previous visit. For the second time he was escorted to the antechamber with its grandiose doorway. The room had been completely cleared of minor functionaries, adding to the air of expectation his escort was giving off like stale perfume. He gave the door a gentle shove. His features poised and composed, the Great Lord Markhamwit was sitting in his ever-elegant chair with his four arms lying negligently on their respective rests. Many days ago he had been in a choleric frenzy of activity as he strove to organize a war that refused to jell. More recently he'd been in a blind fury, pacing the room, hammering tables and destroying equipment, volleying oaths and threats as he contemplated an enormous mass of frustrating data topped by the star maps that had ricocheted off Kasine.

Now he was resigned, fatalistic. It was the calm after the storm. He was nearly ripe for reason.

This was to be expected. Solarian tactics did not accord paramount importance to the question of *what* must be done to achieve a given end. It was of equal and occasionally of greater importance to determine precisely *when* it must be begun, how long it must be maintained, and when it should be ended. Concepts like *how* or *what* did not dominate a word like *when* in Solarian thinking.

Circumstances were radically altered when Lawson ambled into the audience chamber for this third interview. His manner was the same as before, but now Markhamwit and Ganne studied him with wary curiosity rather than spiteful irritation. There was no sign of the open hostility that had characterized their previous encounters, and certainly no evidence of overbearing contempt. Their attitude was that of people trapped in a room with an especially large, powerful, but not unattractive carnivore. In other words, they had hopes of establishing a certain rapport that would not involve their becoming a part of the evening meal.

Seating himself, Lawson crossed his legs, smiling at the Great Lord rather as one would at an obstreperous child after a domestic scene.

"Well?"

Markhamwit said slowly and evenly, "I have been in direct touch with Glastrom. We are recalling all ships."

"That's being sensible. More's the pity that it's had to be paid for by many of your crews languishing on isolated and often lonely worlds."

"We have agreed to cooperate in bringing them home. The Nileans pick up and deliver any of our people they find. We do the same for them. There are some minor protocols that need to be resolved but they can be finalized later."

"Much nicer than cutting each other's throats, isn't it?"

Markhamwit countered. "You told me you didn't care."

"Neither do we. It's when innocent bystanders get pushed around that we see fit to chip in."

Lawson made to get up as if at this stage his task was finished because Solarian aims had been gained. Nothing daunted, the Great Lord spoke hurriedly.

"Before you go I'd like answers to three questions."

"I'd love to stay and chat," Lawson smiled, "but duty calls. It's time we were on our way."

"Three questions. You owe me that."

"The question of owing doesn't enter into it." Lawson paused. "But I acknowledge your self-imposed limitation. It smacks of comprehension, and that's to be encouraged. What are they?"

"In honest fact do you come from a galaxy other than this one?"

"Most certainly."

Frowning at a secret thought, Markhamwit went on. "Have you sterilized any world belonging to us or the Nileans?"

"Sterilized?" Lawson registered puzzlement.

"As you are said to have done to the Elmones."

"Oh, that!" He dismissed it in the manner of something never contemplated even for a moment. "You're referring to an incident of long, long ago. Took me a moment to remember. Hard to believe, looking back on it, but then every ending must have its beginning, mustn't it?" The Great Lord made no comment.

"We used weapons in those days," Lawson continued. "We have outgrown them now. There are better ways to educate people than to make them dead. We harm nobody."

"I beg to differ." Markhamwit pointed to the star maps carefully arrayed on a large platform off to one side. "On your own admission eight of my ships have been destroyed, crews and all."

"Plus five Nilean vessels and one of our own," Lawson informed him. "All the result of accidents over which we had no control. For example, two of your cruisers collided head-on while trying a too hasty docking maneuver near a large orbital supply station. Someone or several someones panicked. Another instance involved, I believe, a fielddisruptor unit going berserk on one of your smaller ships. In every one of the instances to which you refer our presence had nothing to do with the unfortunate results."

Accepting this without dispute, Markhamwit leaned forward, put his last question. "You have gone to some trouble to establish a law that interstellar space beyond the boundaries of individual systems shall be completely free to all, and that movement therein shall not be in any way questioned or challenged. We have recognized it. We have given in. I think that entitles us to know why you are so interested in the ethics of species, not to mention another galaxy, not your own."

Standing up, Lawson met him eye for eye. "Behind that query lurks the agreement you have just made with Glastrom, namely, that you drop all your differences in the face of common peril from outside. You have secretly agreed to conform to the common law until such time as you have developed ships as good as or better than our own. Then, when you feel strong enough, you will join together and shave us down to whatever you regard as proper size."

"That does not answer my question," Markhamwit pointed out, not bothering to confirm or deny this accusation.

"The answer is one you'll fail to see."

"Let me be the judge of that."

"Well, it's like this," Lawson explained. "While I am a Solarian, I'm not *the* Solarian. Neither are my winged companions or any other of a number of varied physical types. Solarians are not a shape or form. They're a multikind destined ultimately to lose its identity in a combine still greater and wider. They are the beginning of a growth of associated minds designed to conquer universal matter. The free, unhampered utilization of space is one basic essential of such growth."

"Why?"

"Because the next contributions to a cosmos-wide supermind will come from this galaxy. That's where the laugh is on you."

"On me?" The Great Lord was baffled.

"On your particular life-form. In all your petty machinations and maneuverings you overlook the question of time. And time is all important."

"What do you mean?" With some difficulty Markhamwit strove to follow the other's reasoning.

"By the time either you or the Nileans have developed techniques advanced enough to challenge us even remotely, both you and they will be more than ready for assimilation."

"I don't understand."

Lawson was at the doorway. "Someday both you and the Nileans will be inseparable parts of each other and, like us, components of a mightier whole. You will come to it rather late but you'll get there just the same. Meanwhile we will not allow those in front to be held back by those behind. Each comes in his own natural turn, delayed by no persnickety neighbors."

He smiled. Then he departed.

"My lord, did you understand what he meant?" a somewhat plaintive First Minister Ganne asked.

"I have a glimmering." Markhamwit was thoughtful. "He was talking about events not due until five, ten, or twenty thousand years after we two are dead."

"How did he get to know our arrangement with Glastrom?"

"He doesn't know, since nobody could have told him. As you are aware, the arrangement was only just concluded, so even with abilities we cannot imagine there is no way he could have detected it. He made a shrewd guess, and he was absolutely correct as we are aware." Markhamwit brooded a bit, added, "It makes me wonder how close he'll get with his longer shot."

"Which one, my lord?"

"That by the time we're big enough to dare to try to beat up what he calls his multikind it will be too late, for we shall then be part of that multikind."

"I can't imagine it," admitted Ganne.

"I can't imagine living beings crossing an intergalactic chasm. Neither can Yielm or any of our experts," Markhamwit said. "I can't imagine anyone successfully waging a major war without any weapons whatsoever." His tone became slightly peevish as he finished. "And that supports the very one of his points that I dislike the most: that our brains are not yet adequate. We suffer from limited imaginations."

"Yes, my lord," agreed Ganne.

"Speak for yourself," snapped Markhamwit. "I can stir up mine a bit even if others can't. I'm going to see Glastrom in person. We'll set our best technical teams to working side by side. Now that we know that intergalactic travel is possible we know there's an understandable, duplicatable method of accomplishing it. It's only a matter of reducing possibilities to one that works.

"There are other steps we can take. Maybe we can get together and, by persuasion rather than force, so reorganize not only our own systems and that of the Nileans but those of our allies and every other semi-sentient race so that the galaxy becomes too big and strong and united to be absorbed in any way, shape, or form by some wild menagerie from elsewhere. It's well worth a try." He stopped, stared at Ganne, demanded, "Why do you look like a bilious *skouniss?*"

"You have reminded me of something he said," explained Ganne unhappily. "He said, 'Someday both you and the Nileans will be inseparable parts of each other and, like us, components of a mightier whole.' If you go to see Glastrom to talk close cooperation it means we're heading exactly that way . . . already!"

Markhamwit flopped back in his seat, gnawed the nails on four hands in turn. The familiar chair, the Spartan but comfortable surroundings, the knowledge that the destiny of whole worlds lay at his fingertips: none of this any longer gave him comfort.

He hated to admit it, but Ganne was right. The only satisfactory method of trying to catch up on Solarian competition was to toil along the same cooperative path to the same communal end that could not and would not remain compartmented in one galaxy. Not to try was to accept defeat and sink into dark obscurity that ultimately would cover them for all time, making them like the Elmones: a name, a memory, a rumor.

There were only two ways to go: forward or backward. Forward to the inevitable. Or backward to the inevitable. And it had to be forward.

When Lawson returned to the ship he knew that his crew already were aboard and eager to go. Getting out of the aircar, he thanked the driver, walked toward the lock, stopped when nearby to carefully examine the last sentry posted outside it.

"I think we have met before," he offered pleasantly.

Yadiz refused the bait. He kept a tight hold on his gun, ignored the voice, ignored a couple of persistent itches. One learns by experience, he had decided, that when in the presence of a Solarian the safest thing is to play statues.

"Oh, well, if that's the way you feel about it." Lawson shrugged, climbed into the lock, looked down from the rim, and advised, "We're taking off. There'll be some suction. If you don't want a sudden rise in the world you'd better take shelter behind that rock." The lock silently cycled shut, removing the biped from view.

Thinking it over, Yadiz decided to take the suggestion. He marched stiffly toward the indicated point, joined his colleagues, still saying nothing.

Lawson sat in the pilot's seat, fingered the composite alongside the contact switch. Presently the control was set to his exclusive body signature and would operate for no other living creature. It was an extension of him, though in a way different from the Callisians and Rheians and the others.

Far out at the edge of this galaxy, lost to view in the great spray of stardust, were a pair of life-forms developing a kindred spirit. Near to them was a third form, more numerous, arrogant, and ready to fill the power vacuum left by Glastrom and Markhamwit. Far out there among the stars the stage was set for interference. Something must be done about it. A few knuckles must be rapped. He nudged the switch.